Warlord's War

Book 11 in the Anarchy Series

By

Griff Hosker

Rouen
Evreux
Paris
Dreux
Alençon
La Ferté-Bernard
Le Mans
Chateaudun
La Flèche
Tours
Chouzé-sur-Loire
La Roche sur Yon
Chinon
La Rochelle
Chateauroux
Châteauponsac
Limoges
Bordeaux

N

30 Miles

Griff 2021

Anjou and the Winter of Despair

Prologue

The English Channel - June 1141

As the cog headed towards Anjou I stared not ahead but behind. I had been ordered from England by Empress Maud. I had not wanted to leave England for the work of establishing her on the throne was far from finished. Having secured the support of the church we had been within hours of placing the crown upon her head when the fickle populace of London had risen against her and we had been forced to flee to Oxford Castle. Although we had made it safely and the Empress was secure in one of the strongest castles in England, we had paid a price. Sir Harold and I had both been wounded. A sword had hacked into my side. It had broken ribs and almost killed me. Had not Father Abelard been a good healer then my son would now be Earl of Cleveland. It had taken time for me to heal and, indeed, I was not yet fully healed. I suspect that was one reason why the Empress had sent me to Anjou. She had wanted me healed. That was not the reason she and her half brother, Robert, Earl of Gloucester had given.

"The war here is almost over, my brave champion. Henry of Blois will summon the prelates and clergy again and we will take an army to London to ensure that I am crowned. Stephen is safe in Bristol Castle. The opposition is broken."

The Earl had agreed with his sister. "She is right, Alfraed, and we need Henry Fitz Empress back here. If London will not accept my sister as ruler perhaps they will accept her son. Bring him back to England and we can end this war."

It had been this last argument that had persuaded me. Henry was my son. He was the son I could never acknowledge but he was my son. However, I was not convinced that the opposition was broken. Stephen's wife, Queen Matilda, was a resourceful and ruthless woman. She had an able commander in William of Ypres. He commanded Flemish soldiers who would not change sides. At the battle of Lincoln, we had hurt the enemy but we had not ended the anarchy.

Although the war in Normandy was going well I wondered how I would persuade Count Geoffrey of Anjou to allow me to bring Henry back. To all the world he was Henry's father. I was fortunate that Count Geoffrey held me in high esteem. Indeed William, my son, was so highly thought of that he was one of Geoffrey's key leaders. It was the two of them who had brought most of Normandy to heel. It was just the Cotentin Peninsula and the capital, Rouen, which held out. One hard push might just rid Normandy of opposition to the rightful rule of the Empress. Then she could add Duchess of Normandy to her title of Lady of England. One day, I prayed, she would be crowned Queen and, if that did not happen, then Regent for her son.

As I turned to look ahead to the coast of France I saw my two squires, Richard and Gilles. Gilles was going home for he had been born in Normandy but this would be Richard's first visit. I had sent the rest of my knight's, archers and men at arms home to my valley. The Tees needed protection and I was loath to allow their lives to be wasted by Robert Earl of Gloucester. He could be a reckless commander. He had also realised, of late, the position of power he held. Perhaps that was why he had encouraged the Empress to send me to Normandy. He could be the centre of attention and control all the armies of the Empress. I was just grateful that the Empress had knights like Sir Miles and Sir Brian with her. In my absence, they would give her the sage advice she needed. I had only left because we had destroyed all but the men of Flanders. We had undermined the walls and one more push could bring the whole edifice down. The war was drawing to a close. My journey might be the last act of a brutal civil war.

Time alone would tell if this voyage was a wise thing which I did but I obeyed Maud. She was not only my Empress she held my heart in her hands. My destiny and that of her and her son were entwined like the Gordian knot.

Chapter 1

Although the count was still in Angers I intended to go to my manor at La Flèche first. My castellan, Sir Leofric, had fine men at arms and archers. I had too many enemies to risk riding a strange land with just two young squires. Besides, I hoped that Leofric might give me more news about my son. He was never a good writer of letters. I knew little of his wife nor his son. He appeared to love Eliane but I had never even met her and I had a two-year-old grandson on whom I had never laid eyes.

The cog in which we travelled was commissioned by the Earl of Gloucester. It was a sturdy vessel but I wished that I was aboard my own ship, '*Adela*', captained by William of Kingston. I would make sure that when I returned to England with Henry, we would travel on my cog. I would feel safer.

The Loire was a torture to negotiate. There were many islands and, although wide, the river twisted and turned. In the days of oars, it would have been simpler. I now understood why some of William's journeys took far longer than I anticipated. We had to tack so often that the crew were exhausted furling and unfurling the sails. Even when we reached the Maine it was a tortuous journey to La Flèche. We had to travel on the Sarthe river before joining the Loir which looped towards La Flèche. The journey did give me time to speak with William of Kingston. The captain and I had words about my final destination. He had messages for the Count from the Empress. I had told him, in no uncertain terms, that he could deliver them on his way downstream. I did not wish to arrive at the court of Count Geoffrey like a beggar. I would arrive with squires, men at arms and horses furnished by my Angevin estate.

La Flèche was a beautiful little place. I often wondered if it had given it to me because it was so pretty or perhaps because it was close to the centre of power in Angers. Either way, I was grateful. Sir Leofric had not had the chance to be warned of our arrival and I expected no ceremony. However, someone must have spied us as we travelled along the Maine for I saw Leofric and his men at arms as they awaited me on the quay.

In my mind, I still saw Leofric, as I did John, as the two orphans who had come to serve me as squires. I saw John most days but I had not seen Leofric for four years or more. I had appointed a youth and now he was a man. He had aged. Then again we all did. He had filled out and looked comfortable. Brian and Padraig who flanked him had both been my first men at arms and, along with Sir Wulfric and Sir Edward had served me the longest. Both were now grey. Their waistlines showed the good, prosperous and peaceful life they now led.

The smiles of all three had, however, not diminished. I was gratified that they were so pleased to see me. "An unexpected visit, lord." Sir Leofric grasped my arm firmly.

I nodded as I stepped from the cog and clasped his arm. "I come on the Empress' business." I turned and pointed to Gilles and Richard. "You know Gilles and the other is Richard. Padraig and Brian help them with our chests. We are here for some time."

They nodded and Brian said, "Good to see you, lord! Perhaps now we can have a little action and I can rid myself of this paunch eh?"

"It is deserved, Brian, you have given me a lifetime of service. Enjoy your time of peace now." I walked with Sir Leofric. After being at sea so long I was a little unsteady on my feet. I wondered if people would think me drunk.

Leofric was anxious to know the events in England. His keep was in the heart of the town. I told him most by the time we reached his enormous gates.

"So we have the Usurper but the Empress is not yet crowned."

"That is our dilemma, Leofric. The Earl is convinced that he can bring Stephen's Queen to heel and the Empress that she can persuade the clergy to back her once more."

"But you are not so sure." Leofric was shrewd and thoughtful.

"No, but we are in a better position now than we were last year so there is hope." The words I spoke were to reassure myself as much as Leofric. I did not trust the clergy.

Just then two boys and a girl appeared with his wife. I suddenly felt embarrassed. I could not for the life of me remember Leofric's wife's name. It was at times like this that I missed my own dead wife, Adela, the most. She would have reminded me. I covered my embarrassment by complimenting the children. "What fine children."

Leofric's wife curtsied. I remembered that she had been the daughter of a local merchant. "Thank you, lord. This is our eldest, Henry, my daughter, Marie, and my youngest, Geoffrey."

"I am pleased to meet you. And will you two boys be serving with your father and me?"

They both nodded. "Yes, my lord. We both have a sword!" Henry drew his short sword. It took two hands to hold it firmly. Leofric was doing the right thing and preparing them early for a life as a knight.

"And what a fine sword it is." I turned to Marie, Leofric's wife; I had remembered her name and felt relief, "I know not how long I shall be here, my lady. I hope we do not inconvenience you too much."

She looked shocked, "My lord, this is your castle! We just keep it for you."

"True but it is your home and that is far more important."

We turned as our chests were brought in. Leofric said, "Take them to his lordship's quarters. Come, my lord, let us enjoy some wine and I shall tell you of events here."

The castle had a pleasant aspect and the wine was amongst the best I had ever tasted. After the sea voyage, it was to be savoured.

"I know, lord, that the war is not going as well in England as it is here but we have yet to conquer Normandy. The situation is improving. Theobald of Blois finds himself beset by the King of France. It means he cannot raid into Anjou. Flanders still waits like some crouching fox to take any tasty morsels which fall from the table but their Count, William, is fighting the war in England with Queen Matilda. Count Geoffrey is prosecuting the war well. He and your son make forays each year and add a little more to the Empress' domain."

"Where is my son now?"

"The Count has yet to set forth on his campaigns. Your son is at his manor of Ouistreham. It is an enclave within the manors that support Stephen of Blois. He has a castellan who holds it for him but when he can, he likes to return there. He fights any foes foolish enough to face him. When the Count needs his services then he returns to Angers."

I was proud of my son. He had been a knight for a long time and he had earned the respect of his liege lord. That was a mighty achievement. He had done so without me. It was a reputation he had earned. He had once told me that he did not wish to be known as the cub to my wolf. He was not.

"I will need men at arms and archers as well as horses. Are we well supplied?"

"Aye lord. Brian and Griff of Gwent had trained up some to send to you in England on the *'Adela'*."

"When is she due here?"

"By the beginning of July."

"Then I want her to stay here until I have spoken with William of Kingston."

"Aye lord. When do you go to Angers?"

"On the morrow. The Count may not be happy that I came here first. Besides the sooner, I see him then the sooner I can persuade him to allow his son to return with me to England."

The war in England meant that many things we wanted were in short supply. Here there was no such restriction. Aquitaine, to the south, was both rich and prosperous. Ships plied their trade along its rivers. Count Geoffrey's father was

King Fulk of Jerusalem. Trade with the east was brisk and the markets of the Angevin had exotic items for sale. I gave Philippe, the steward of the manor, a list of items I wished. Their cost would be taken from the tithes we collected from the manor. La Flèche was a rich manor and I rarely took money out of it. Leofric and Philippe husbanded my coin well. If I had chosen to live in Anjou then I would have had a life of luxury. My home, however, was in the cold North of England where life would ever be hard.

As I headed, with my squires and Padraig and Brian, I thought of the circle that was life. I had had a rich and pampered life in Miklagård. My father had chosen to tear us away from that and fate had thrown us into a dangerous melting pot of border raids, intrigue and poverty along the Tees. Now I could, if I chose, complete the circle and return to a life of luxury. My father's blood coursed through my veins and I was an honourable man. I would do my duty in England.

I knew that I was lucky that Geoffrey was in Angers. Frequently, these days, he lived in the castle at Le Mans. It was closer to the disputed region of Normandy. The journey by horse was but thirty miles to Angers. It was a more direct journey than by river. We made good time. The roads were clear and there were few bandits in this part of the world. Count Geoffrey, like his father before him, ruled with an iron fist. My surcoat and standard were well known in Anjou. I had helped Count Geoffrey on the campaigns against the French, the Flemish and the forces of Stephen of Blois. I had trained many of his knights. When we were seen on the road we were greeted with both warmth and affection. It was in contrast to the reception I received in many places in England where I was the Warlord or the Wolf of the North.

We crossed the bridge over the Maine and clattered on the cobbled road towards the castle. In the time of the Vikings, this town had been raided many times and the well-built castle had been made even stronger to withstand them. Now it was attacked from the land which was the danger but the castle still used the river for defence. Although the sentries recognised my surcoat I was still asked my business.

Before I could answer a young shrill voice said, "Let him in! That is my Uncle Alfraed!"

My son had grown. He was still to see ten summers but he looked older. Partly that was his dress. He was dressed as a young noble. I dismounted. He ran up to me and threw his arms around me to embrace me.

I shook my head. "You will be a king one day! You will not be able to greet me thus then!"

He laughed and took my hand, "You will always be my mother's champion and that means you have special treatment! I am pleased you came. Did not my mother come with you?"

"No, she had business in England but I have messages for you."

He looked around, "Did you not bring Wulfric?"

"No, he guards my lands in the north."

He looked disappointed, "A pity." He laughed. "He frightens my brothers Geoffrey and William. They think he is a bear!"

"He has that effect on my enemies too. But you are not afraid of him?"

"No, for he is one of your men. They are the most loyal of all my mother's followers. When I am old enough to lead men I will have such warriors around me. Loyalty is all!"

"You are right, young Henry Fitz Empress."

We had reached the inner bailey and grooms came to take our horses. Brian said, "Padraig and I have items to buy in the city, my lord. When shall we return?"

I smiled. I knew them of old. That meant there was a tavern they wished to visit. I had no doubt that there would be women whose company they sought. "I think we shall be staying the night." They smiled and nodded, "Just make sure that you return in a fit state."

Brian assumed a look of outraged innocence. "My lord, you know us!"

"Exactly, so heed my words."

"We will, lord."

"Gilles and Richard, go with the horses and make sure they are cared for. Wait for me here and I will send it to you."

As Henry led me indoors he asked, "Why do you not just leave the horses to our grooms? They are good grooms."

"I have no doubt but these are our mounts. I have only ridden this horse today but while here in Anjou, he is my mount and a knight always ensures that his horse is cared for. Along with his mail and his weapons, they are vital to him. Your great grandfather conquered England using horses with mailed men. Your grandfather has conquered the Holy Land with good horses and mailed men. You should not forget your heritage."

He nodded, "That is why I like being around you, you do not talk to me as though I am a child. I learn much."

I smiled at the words from this child. He was serious. My other son, William, had never been as serious. He had always wanted to go off on some adventure with John and Leofric. It was a shame that Henry would not enjoy that sort of rough and tumble life.

The Count appeared. He was no longer the callow youth I had trained in the tourney. He was now a powerful leader. "Alfraed! How good to see you. The captain of the cog told me you would be coming." He wagged an admonishing finger at me, "You should have stopped on your way to La Flèche!"

"I am sorry, Count, but I did not wish to appear ill-dressed. When I left the Empress I did not have any clothes fit to meet the Count of Anjou. I am now dressed appropriately."

"You need no fine clothes to impress me. I see beyond the silks." He nodded and put his arm around me. "In her letter, Maud tells me that she barely escaped London with her life and you were wounded rescuing her."

I nodded, "Aye the people of London are treacherous." I noticed that Henry was with us and was taking a keen interest in all that I said. He was learning. He would rule one day as King of England. I would see to that. He had to learn

11

about the land he barely knew. "As for the wound... I live and it will heal."

"She said that she and her brother plan on using the clergy a second time."

"Aye, with Stephen incarcerated our forces have the upper hand. They can go to Winchester and put pressure on Henry of Blois. He is the effective leader of the church in England."

"And that is why she could afford to allow her best general to travel to Anjou."

"I am a wounded warhorse. There are others who can lead your wife's armies." We had reached his Great Hall. Servants hovered close by with wine and food.

Henry said, "Are you here to fight the rebels?"

Before I could answer Count Geoffrey said, "Little mice have big ears! Go and play with your brothers."

"But father...!"

"Go!"

He went reluctantly from the hall. The servants placed the wine and food on the table and then the Count dismissed them too. I was disappointed that Henry had been dismissed. He needed to hear our words. However here I had no rights and so I held my tongue.

Count Geoffrey poured the wine, "Help yourself to the ham and the cheese. We have better hams and cheese here than you do in England."

I did not agree but I smiled, "I like the fact that we have different foods. It makes for a more varied diet, Count."

"Ever the gentleman. I sent Henry hence for his mother spoke of him in her letters. She wishes you to take him back to England?"

"Aye, Count. The problem in England is that many people want a man as a ruler. They have nothing against Empress Matilda but they are a conservative people."

"It would be the same here. I understand that King Louis of France is finding his wife to be hard to control. She should be a ruler."

"You are right. I have met Eleanor. She reminds me of a younger version of the Empress. She knows her own mind."

"And taking Henry to England would persuade them?"

"We have almost won the war, lord. It has been six years since King Henry was killed. We are as close now, to the crown, as we have ever been. It is like a mighty oak which you hew. It may not need the blow from a mighty axe to finally fell it but a hatchet. The Empress believes that Henry may be the crucial piece on this chessboard."

"I am not certain." He sipped his wine and changed the subject to give himself time to weigh our words. "It was a good harvest last year. This wine is amongst the best we have had."

I knew why he had changed the subject so abruptly. I had known him since he had married the Empress as a callow youth of fifteen. "It is a fine wine. The wine produced on my manor was also good last year."

He nodded, absentmindedly. "I need time to deliberate on this and I would use you while you are here."

"Use me, Count?"

"I was about to head north and begin a campaign towards Vire. I already have your son at my side with you as well then I am certain we would have great success. Perhaps if we can defeat Stephen's allies here then it might be easier to persuade Queen Matilda to sue for peace."

"I cannot be away too long, Count. As much as I am flattered by your request I am needed by the Empress and by my country."

"It is now May. Give me until September and then you have my word that you can return to England."

"With Henry?"

He smiled, "You drive a hard bargain, Earl." He nodded his agreement and raised his goblet. "With Henry."

"Good."

"Although we will not tell him until closer to September. He becomes over-excited. I would not have him distracted."

I thought it was sad that the Count did not want Henry to be excited. When I had been young I had enjoyed the company of the Varangian Guard. My life had been filled with excitement.

"When would you have us leave for this campaign?"

"I am meeting your son at Le Mans on Midsummer Day. It will take us a week to reach there."

"I will go directly to Le Mans then, Count. I have not seen my son for some time. We have much of which to speak."

"Stay this one night then. I am certain my household knights would like to hear an account of the Battle of the Standard and the Battle of Lincoln. All of the reports they have had have been second hand."

I would have hated the attention save that Henry was allowed to attend and drink watered wine. It made the evening easier. I did not like speaking about myself and my actions. It always struck me that it was a form of self-aggrandisement. I tried to keep the accounts as factual as possible. Henry Fitz Empress was seated on the other side of the Count and he hung on to every word. The men to whom I spoke would soon be in battle; although some had fought before I could see from the young faces before me that some had not. I did not spare them nor Henry as I told them the realities of battle. Even though I had been realistic I saw that their faces showed that they wished to emulate me and my household knights.

Gilles and Richard attended and were seated to my left. Henry leaned across and asked them, "Were you two at the battle?"

They nodded. Gilles said, "I was at both and Richard was at Lincoln."

"Did you get to fight?"

Gilles smiled, he had known Henry for some time, "There is no place to hide on the field of battle, lord. At the battle of the Standard, Prince Henry brought his horsemen around to try to flank us and it was the squires in the rear who had to fight them off. I lost friends that day for it was boys fighting men. If you go to war then you must be ready to shed blood."

I nodded my approval. Gilles had said the right thing to a future king. His grandfather and great grandfather had fought in hard-fought battles with quarter neither offered nor taken.

"And have you shed blood?"

14

They both nodded.

He leaned back and the Count said, "So, my son, now do see why we keep you away from danger. You will be the King of England one day. We cannot have you hurt or killed in a minor skirmish."

He shook his head, "Then it is right that I risk what others do. These squires fight not for themselves but for England."

I shook my head, "Actually they fight for me and I fight for you, your mother and England. It is how our system works. These two swore an oath to me, did you not?"

They nodded and Richard said, "I should have been imprisoned for my lord was slain by the Earl and there was no one to ransom me. He offered to take my sword. I owe my life to him and I would die for him."

I laughed, "And hopefully it will not come to that for if you do then it means my standard has fallen."

"Did you bring the standard with you?"

"Yes Count."

"Then when we fight that will mean much. They say your presence and your standard is worth a hundred men on the field."

"As I do not have my men with me, Count, then we will have to hope that it is true."

"And we have your son too. You have not seen him fight for some time but take my word for it he is a copy of you."

I nodded, "Perhaps we get it from my father for he was the greatest warrior that I ever knew."

The next day we headed back to La Flèche. I had not asked Brian and Padraig to find information but I knew that they would. As we crossed the bridge over the Maine and headed along the old Roman Road I asked, "Tell me, what is the mood in the town and of the men at arms?"

They looked at each other.

"Come you know me well enough to know that whatever you say I shall neither be offended or angry."

Brian said, "They are confident, my lord. They have defeated all of the lords against whom they have fought."

There was a pause, "But..."

Brian shrugged, "But there is a feeling that Count Geoffrey has every right to be Duke of Normandy. They say he has fought for the land and the Empress can have England."

"And Henry?"

"He is popular lord and they think that he will have both titles one day."

"Thank you." I turned to Gilles and Richard. "You did not hear that."

"Heard what, my lord?" They had both learned to be discreet.

I now wondered about the Count's motives. He and his wife lived apart. He was far younger than she was. I had no doubt that he had fathered children other than with the Empress. Was he using me to become Duke of Normandy? Would he abandon the support of his wife then?

The road north was pleasant and it was warm, far warmer than in England. I was able to reflect on my position. I had to stay until September. I had given him my word and besides I had come to fetch Henry. That decided me. I wanted Henry to love England. He had to come back with me and see that it was worth fighting for. Apart from one short visit to England he had spent all of his time in Anjou. I was convinced I could make him see that being King of England was worth more than Duke of Normandy. I would help Count Geoffrey to get his title. It was all a game anyway. The important title would be Henry's and his father would help him to get it.

Chapter 2

Once back in my manor I sat with Leofric to plan for the campaign. I had changed from the heavy woollen clothes we needed in England to lighter materials. I had forgotten how warm and pleasant it could be. The wine, brought from the cooled cellar, was refreshing. We sat overlooking the river and it was pleasant. "We have a short time to equip a conroi for me to lead into battle."

"We have everything ready that you would need. There are horses, mail and weapons aplenty. Alf the Smith keeps us well supplied." Sir Leofric pointed towards the north, "Would you wish me to accompany you, lord, when you go to war?" His face remained neutral but I knew that he would be having conflicting emotions.

"If you mean would I be happier with you fighting alongside me then the answer is yes but I do not wish you to come with me as I need this manor protecting? You are the castellan and difficult times may lie ahead." Brian's words about Count Geoffrey's people's ambition made me realise that one day, there might be a conflict here in this peaceful valley.

Leofric had always been clever and he asked, "Lord, is there something I should know?"

We were alone and I spoke quietly. "I fear that the Count of Anjou plans to be the Duke of Normandy."

Leofric sipped his wine. He nodded and said, "I had heard rumours but nothing more. It would not surprise me, lord, for many of my neighbours see him as the rightful lord.

They think King Henry deceived Count Fulk. I know not the truth in that." He shrugged, "And this manor is in the fiefdom of Anjou."

"There is no simple solution to this. It is why I wish you to stay here. You are already considered a beneficent lord who is thoughtful and fair. I wish you to continue to do so while making sure we recruit as many warriors as we can."

"Is that not something which might offend the Count, lord?"

"No for the men are for the defence of the manor. It is right that the castle is garrisoned and the town well protected. Besides, it is my decision and no blame will attach itself to you. I will take the experienced archers and men at arms with me. I need a conroi of ten men at arms and ten archers. Will that constitute a problem?"

"No lord. You have twice that number already here and more are already being trained."

"Do not forget that I will be taking those who train them with me."

"I know, lord. We will manage." There was a lull in the conversation. He smiled, "I never thought the war would last this long. My son may soon be old enough to fight in it."

"True and I thought we had ended it in February at Lincoln. I was wrong."

We sipped our wine and I saw, in Leofric's eyes, memories as he thought of his former home, England. "So John is married now?"

"He is, to Alf's daughter. He has done as you did and tied himself to the manor. It seems it is meant to be."

"Your father's word, *wyrd* comes to mind."

"Aye, *wyrd* indeed." The two boys had been from poor backgrounds and yet now they were both powerful knights with manors of their own.

The *'Adela'* docked two days before we were to leave for Le Mans. William of Kingston brought bad news. "My lord the clergy have refused to back the Empress' renewed claim to be crowned. Bishop Henry and she have had words. He returned to his cathedral. It is said that she and her brother are heading to Winchester to force the matter with their armies."

I was not saying it for William and Leofric's benefit but my own when I said, "A foolish move which will just antagonise the clergy and the people. Why could they not be patient? All that we have done is undone!" I could see the Earl's reckless hand in all of this. He would see his chance for glory on his own without the Warlord of the North there to take credit. He could be bullish and bullying when he wanted to be. He still resented that I had been present at our victory against the Scots and he had not.

"And there is more, lord. Queen Matilda has another army and is said to be leaving for Winchester to go to the aid of her brother in law."

I had heard the phrase horns of a dilemma and now I truly understood it. I had given my word to Geoffrey Count of Anjou to stay until September but my absence might result in disaster. The Earl sometimes made rash battlefield decisions. On the other hand, even if I set sail now there was no guarantee that I would reach England before the matter was resolved one way or another.

"My lord?"

"I am sorry, William! I must be getting old and rude. I have messages for you. I would have you go first to Stockton and thence to Gloucester. It will be a long voyage but I need to know that my land is aware of the problems we might face. Then I wish you to return to Ouistreham. I know it is surrounded by enemies and rebels but it is a shorter voyage than coming here and I can get there. I need to know the outcome of this confrontation."

"Very well, lord."

"And we need both manors to keep in touch with each other. I want your holds full when you return home and then when you return here, after leaving me word in Ouistreham. I want my castle well provisioned and Sir Leofric needs all the weapons which Alf can produce. I will write your letters now."

This was where I missed John, my steward. He would have penned the letters far quicker than I could have managed. I wrote one to Sir Harold and one to the Empress. William was at his ship loading it when I had finished. Both letters had my wolf seal upon them.

"These must be delivered personally by you. If you show the Empress' guards my seal then you will be admitted but, just in case use this to gain you admittance." I handed him my seal of Liedeberge. It was the manor the Empress had given me. Sir William of Liedeberge was my castellan there. I could trust him too. "If you are attacked then throw the letters into the sea. No one other than Sir Harold and the Empress must read them."

"You can trust me, my lord."

"I know but the number I can trust is getting fewer by the day."

As the ship sailed, later in the day, I hoped that my messages would reach Sir Harold and the Empress in time. I wanted Sir Harold to be prepared for treachery and I wanted the Empress to know of her husband's plans and to advise caution with the clergy.

As we headed for Le Mans with my small conroi we used caution ourselves. Griff of Gwent and James the Short had lived in this land long enough to be able to scout out the safest route. This was supposed to be Angevin territory but as I had learned to my cost, there could be traitors and enemies anywhere.

It was just over thirty miles to Le Mans. It was a key stronghold and the walls and towers were formidable. I was glad when we reached it. It meant I would soon see my son. The castellan recognised me as we rode into the outer bailey. "Your son is hunting, lord. He will be back before dark."

"We will be here for some days. The Count comes with an army."

"We had word, lord. It may be crowded."

"We are warriors, Sir Raymond. We do not mind a little hardship."

Our quarters were well apportioned. My squires had wool stuffed mattresses and would sleep across my door. I went to the gatehouse to watch for his return. I spied them coming from the east. There were six of them. I guessed his squire

20

would be with him but I did not know the other four. Three of them led sumpters with deer upon them. I deduced that they would be archers or men at arms.

I descended to greet them. My son had been a mere stripling the last time I had seen him. Now he had filled out and was as tall and as broad as I was. He was clean-shaven and the hot sun of this region had made his face a nutty brown. His mother would have been proud of the way he had turned out. He was always her favourite. As soon as he saw me he leapt from his horse in one bound and rushed up to me to embrace me. "I did not know you were with the Count! This is great news. Our enemies will be shaking with fear when they hear the two of us come!"

I laughed, "You, perhaps, but these are grey hairs in my beard."

He put his arm around my shoulder and led me to the hall. "You could be a white beard and still be the greatest knight in England or the Empire for that matter! It is a pity I did not know you were coming. We could have visited my wife and children. You will like her, father!"

"I know but is it not dangerous between here and Ouistreham?"

He nodded, "Certainly the barons who support Stephen keep a close watch but since Theobald decided to pull back and guard his lands against Louis the Younger if you have enough men you are safe on the roads. I have enough men and my banner is well known. Men take us on at their peril."

I looked at his squire who followed us. The archers had disappeared with the deer. "Is your squire to be trusted?"

He stopped and stared at me, "I could be offended at such a remark. Do you know me so little that you do not remember it was you who trained me? Robert may be young but I trust him with my life and that of my family."

"You are right and I apologise. It happens each time I reach this land. I see conspiracies and plots behind every smile. I fought the Count's father here as well as Stephen of Blois."

"And you would be right to do so but my men are like yours. You can trust them."

"In that case, I have some disturbing news," I told him of the Empress' dilemma in England. When I had finished he nodded as he considered the information. We had reached the hall and servants fetched us wine.

William said, "Robert, guard the door and make sure that we are not disturbed." When the huge doors slammed shut he said, "And there is something else. Is there something you are afraid to bring up?"

He was my son and he had grown up watching me talk to the great and the mighty. He knew me. I had been reluctant to speak of the Count's ambitions because of my son's close relationship with him. It was at that moment I realised that if I could not trust my son then all was lost. I nodded, "I fear that the Count has ambitions to be Duke of Normandy."

William smiled as though he was relieved. Perhaps he had been expecting something more worrying. "Of course he does. I thought it was something far more sinister."

"But it is not his title. If any it belongs to Henry Fitz Empress."

"True and he will attain that title when his father dies. Besides, it is right that Count Geoffrey becomes Duke. He has fought for this County and conquered much of it. The Empress is the Count's wife. She will still be Duchess of Normandy but the land will belong to Count Geoffrey and that is right. The people of Normandy want a leader they can follow... a man and Henry is too young. It is right that the man who has reconquered the land should reap the reward."

"You and I have done our part for him too."

He leaned forward and said each word slowly, "But not the Earl of Gloucester." Then he leaned back and waved an airy hand as though to dismiss the Earl, "Since his father's death the Earl has not set foot on this land."

"He fights in England."

"Father, you should know that there are many Angevin and Norman knights who wish to wash their hands of England. They see it as a war that cannot be won. The two armies cancel each other out. Lincoln should have been the end but it was not. It is here where we can win. If we take a few more castles then Normandy will be ours."

"And then England?"

"Why? What has England to offer us that we have not got here?"

"So when you said many Angevin and Norman knights wished to wash their hands of England you included yourself. You would not fight for England."

"I will be blunt, father, for I am now a man and not the squire who obeyed your every command. I am now Norman. You never were. You were Byzantine and then English. Everyone calls you the English knight. It is a good title and well deserved. I am not you. I never was. I will fight for England and for the Empress but my heart will not be in it. I cannot be any more honest than that."

I was stunned but I held my tongue and sipped my wine. It was understandable. He had lived almost as long in Normandy as he had in England. His wife was from this land. His children had been born here. He had a reputation here and he was well respected by both his peers and his liege lord.

"Father? Have I upset you?"

"No, but you have surprised me. I suppose I had a vision of this war ending and you returning home to Stockton."

"And what? Be given a manor like Elton of Hartburn? They are too small for me. Ouistreham is a fine manor. It is like Stockton, it is a port. The land about is rich and Caen itself is but a few miles away. That is the home of the Duke or will be. My future is here but I will continue to support the Empress and to support you but I am not English. I am Norman."

The words struck me like the blows of a hammer. In that short conversation my life changed. My firstborn was lost to me. His children would see me as a distant grandfather. They might struggle to even remember my name. It felt as though someone had reached in and torn my heart from me. My wife had died, the love of my life was denied me, and now my son was lost too. I finished my wine and stood. "Thank you for your honesty. I appreciate it and the confidence. I hope that you will keep my confidences too."

"Of course." He put his hand on my shoulder, "Father, I am still your son but I know how much you value honesty."

"And I do. But you know that your words were not the ones I wished to hear. I must think."And now I had better clean up. I daresay there will be a feast tonight."

"There is a feast here every night. We want for nothing in Normandy, neither game nor wine nor coin."

My son was now Norman.

Count Geoffrey arrived four days later. By then there were tents strewn around the castle. My men at arms and archers had been relegated there as barons were housed in the warrior hall. That was to be expected. It was a large army the Count was taking north. At the feast which was held for the barons and earls, the Count explained his strategy.

"It is now high summer. Mortain is the manor of Stephen of Blois given by my wife's father. We take that now and then, next year, we advance on Vire as a prelude to retaking Normandy!"

They were the words his men wanted to hear. I was seated on his right hand, the place of honour, and I heard three names called out by the knights: the Count's, my son's and mine. The Count had ensured that the cause for which we fought was his and not the Empress. Had I not given my word I would have headed back to La Flèche and taken ship back to England. The deciding factor was Henry who was allowed to attend and sat on the Count's left hand. I had a king to train. I had lost one son. I would not lose another.

Chapter 3

The castle at Mortain had been built by the Conqueror for his illegitimate son, Robert. The Count of Mortain had lost it when he fell out with Henry I. As the King had then given it to Stephen of Blois it was a juicy morsel to be taken. Strategically it was not as important as the Count thought but I agreed that we could take it.

It took two days to arrive at the castle. By that time the defenders knew that we were coming and had time to prepare their defences. The Count had learned his lessons from earlier campaigns and we had the parts for siege engines which we would construct once we had the castle surrounded. I rode next to Henry on the two-day journey. That was partly his choice and partly the fact that his father and my son spent the ride laughing together with their close friends. I did not mind. I was an outsider. I had not shared the experiences they had and, more importantly, I could get to know Henry a little better. Gilles rode on the other side of him. It was a little to ensure his security and safety but also because they got on well. That was strange for one would be a king and the other was the son of a poor archer.

"How will we take this castle, uncle? Will we charge the walls?"

"That would waste too many lives, and a good leader never wastes the lives of those who follow him. We will surround the castle and then begin to break down the weak points. They will have laid in a good quantity of supplies, of that, I have no doubt, but we have time. Your father is clever, Henry. He takes this now and then the rest of

Normandy in the spring. When Mortain falls it will make every other castle fear that they will be next. That sort of pressure tells."

He looked at me. "They will fear you, won't they?"

"What makes you say that?"

"I heard my father talking to your son. He said that now you were here the people would be terrified. They call you a wolf." He pointed at my surcoat with the emblem of my wolf sewn onto it. "Your son and my father are a mighty force but you... you are the champion of the Empress and the King." He leaned in and spoke quietly. "There are many men who wish to kill you."

I was surprised and asked, "How do you know?"

He shrugged, "I am young but I have ears. My father allows me to attend many feasts and I hear men when they are drunk." He suddenly looked at me. "Why do men become foolish when they drink?"

"Not all men do. If men wish to kill me that is something I understand." I pointed to Gilles. "Gilles and Richard know that too. They sleep with a dagger close to hand should anyone try to enter my chamber at night."

His eyes widened, "Truly?" I nodded. "Then where are you safe?"

"My castle in Stockton."

"And is that the only place?"

"Every man in that castle is oathsworn to me. Many years ago we had a spy and we paid the price. We will not make that mistake again. When I sleep in my castle it is the only deep sleep I enjoy."

"And yet you put yourself in danger for me, my mother and England." I nodded. "I did not know. I thought you did it for glory. I can see that I was wrong."

He became silent as we rode north. His fertile mind was working as he reassessed his world.

I am not sure if the Count and my son were trying to prove that they could outdo me but I was ignored as they planned the assault on the castle. They had, however, made good preparations. We spent a week encircling the castle so that no one could get in or out. Then the siege engines were

26

brought up. As July approached we were ready for the assault. One of the priests we had brought with us, Father Pierre, suggested that we might try to negotiate the surrender. I was brought into the discussion and asked my opinion. "Perhaps it might save lives. Our intent is to reduce this castle. If we can do that without too great a loss of life then it means we will have more men to assault Vire."

The three of us, the Count, my son and I approached the castle for a truce. The castellan was an Englishman, Sir John de Villiers. He leaned over the parapet. "What is it you want, Count?"

"I come to demand the surrender of this castle."

Sir John laughed, "And you have brought the wolf and his cub to make me fill my breeks. Do not worry, this castle will laugh away your siege. The tide is about to turn and you will be swept away with it. Enjoy the gains you have made for they will be short-lived."

I could see the Count becoming annoyed and before he could say something he might regret, such as no quarter, I spoke. "If we attack, Sir John, then many of your men will die. We have overwhelming numbers and the siege has you surrounded."

"And you would surrender as you did when the Scots surrounded your castle with equally overwhelming numbers? I think not. You held out and so shall we. Do your worst for we are prepared."

As we rode back my son, as astute as ever, said, "I was not expecting that. It was almost as though he knew something we did not."

The Count seemed not to be bothered by the attitude. It was the castle that was his focus. "Even if he is prepared it makes no difference. We break down his walls with the siege engines and we use arrows to slay those on the walls."

I was not so sure. When we reached our camp I sent for Griff of Gwent and James the Stout. "I have a task for you two."

Griff grinned, "I have missed this, my lord. Life on the Loir is very pleasant and very easy. Training new archers is

27

not challenging. As soon as you arrived I knew our lives would become more interesting."

"Perhaps not. It may be I am becoming an old man who worries needlessly. However, indulge me." They nodded. "I would have you scout to the east and south of us."

Griff frowned, "But the enemy lies to the north."

"The enemy we see lies there but as the hairs on the back of my neck are prickling I would have you go and see if they are caused by a foe who wishes to trap us against these walls."

"Aye, my lord."

"Take supplies with you. This may take a couple of days."

They turned and left. Gilles and Richard had been listening. Gilles asked, "But how could there be enemies behind us, lord?"

"How long have we known that we were coming here to attack Mortain?"

"Two, three weeks lord."

"And the Count knew for longer. My son knew for longer and that means men in both their households knew. Other lords were aware of it. This is too predictable, Gilles. The castellan's words had a warning in them. He was too confident in a castle with just a narrow moat around it and wooden towers. Our siege machines will make them kindling and we have more men than enough. Perhaps I am wrong. If this was England then we would expect an attack on our siege works, why should it be different here in Normandy?"

"Will you tell the Count and your son, lord?"

"I will wait until my archers return but you two need to be ready to go to war instantly. If others choose to become drunk and lax then do not emulate them. Now take my helmet back to my tent. I must speak with Brian and Padraig."

I went to my men at arms and told them to make sure that my men did not drink too much and that I wanted them alert. Unlike my squires, they did not question my command. They knew me of old when we had clung on to the Tees with our fingertips and fought against Scots and traitors.

As I had expected there was a relaxed atmosphere around the camp. Drink flowed although a watch was kept. What secretly pleased me was that my son and his conroi did not do as other lords did. They did not drink heavily and they kept weapons to hand. Like me my son was suspicious.

He spoke to me before we retired, "This is too easy, father. I expected the castellan to negotiate for time but he did not."

"Stay alert."

The next day we assembled the siege weapons and, under the protection of large shields pulled them into position. Before we sent the ram to batter down the gate we would weaken the walls as well as the resolve of the defenders. Stones were hurled at the gatehouse while our archers, fewer than I would have liked, sent arrows at those brave enough to show their heads above the walls. By the end of the day stones in the gatehouse had been loosened and one of the towers had been damaged. It had been at a cost. Two of the stone throwers had been damaged and would need to be repaired. We knew that the defenders would be working all night to repair the damage we had done. It was why sieges took time. It seemed you took three steps forward only to take two back but the Count was pleased with the progress.

He gathered his commanders together at his tent. Along with my son, there was Sir John of Nantes, Sir Hugh of Langeais and Sir Stephen of Azay. They had all been young knights when I had first met them. I had trained them to fight in the tourney and they were the close companions of the Count. They seemed confident as we gathered around the fire.

The Count was ebullient. "This will not take as long as I had thought. In two days we can send in the ram. We might even be able to advance on Vire before winter sets in!"

It was my son who advised caution, "Lord, the broken war machines need repair and Vire is a more challenging proposition. There is a river there."

The Count had been drinking and he waved a hand towards me, "We have your father with us! Did he not use the river at Lincoln to aid their attack?"

29

I shook my head, "With respect, Count, there we were relieving a siege. We had those within the walls to help us. There my archers from within helped to slay some of their key commanders and cause confusion."

William suddenly said, "Where were Griff and James today? I saw other archers but not the two finest in Normandy and Anjou."

I had been hoping that their absence would not be noted. I had to speak the truth or be seen as a disruptive force in the army, "I sent them to scout."

The Count swivelled his head towards me and his eyes narrowed, "Scout? But we know where the enemy lies." He pointed his goblet at the castle. Some wine spilt. "Where were they scouting?"

I watched his three close companions as I pointed south and east, "There."

"But that is a friendly country. The enemy lie before us."

"Then all that I have done is give my archers some discomfort. There is nothing lost."

"What do you think they will find, father?"

"I am not certain but I liked not Sir John's confidence. It was misplaced. You noted it too." My son nodded. "If our enemies knew where we were coming then they could have prepared an ambush."

Sir Hugh of Langeais said, "But that would mean one of our men conspires with the enemy."

Stephen of Azay shook his head, "Surely you cannot suspect any of us. We have followed the Count since the beginning."

Sir John of Nantes had drunk more than most and he spluttered, "I would vouch for all of my men!"

My son said, "As would we all but that does not mean there cannot be treachery."

Silence descended around the fire until I broke it. "The Earl of Chester was one of the Empress' closest supporters and then he changed to support the Usurper. Now he has changed back to support our cause. If the high and the mighty can do so then why not a baron who wishes a larger manor or a man at arms who wishes more gold?"

30

The Count had sobered slightly. "In which case you are wrong, Earl, for only those around this fire knew of our destination."

"A week ago you told the army, Count. A week is long enough if you have been planning this for some time."

"What mean you, Earl?"

"Summer is the time you campaign. The enemy may not be strong enough to meet you in the field but he can ambush you or attack you in the rear. Who knows what word passes between London and Cherbourg? It is but a short sea crossing."

My words had caused upset and dissension. Words rattled across the fire and I remained silent. Suddenly there was the sound of horses' hooves and I heard the cry, "Stand to!"

In the distance, I heard raised voices and then Raymond of Chinon appeared with Griff and James. "My lord, the Earl's men have news. I apologise for disturbing you."

The Count looked at me, "These are your scouts?" I nodded and the Count smiled, grimly, "It seems they have found something!"

Griff and James had dropped to their knees and I nodded when Griff looked up at me. He began, "My lord, we found a Norman army. It is camped a short march away to the east. We counted more than two hundred horses and at least forty banners and standards." He looked at me, "We saw the banner of Blois and that of Flanders."

Sir Hugh said, "But Theobald is busy fending off the French."

My son said, "There is another Blois. Stephen's son Eustace."

It showed that I had lost touch with the politics of this part of the world for I had forgotten the usurper's son. "He is but a child!"

William smiled, "He is thirteen or fourteen but he married the sister of the King of France two years since. I had heard he was in Boulogne."

Sir John said, loudly, "We have no need to fear a stripling boy!"

31

I smiled, "When first the Count went to war with me he was not much older, were you, my lord?"

"The Earl is right and besides if he is married to the sister of the King of France then he may have experienced leaders with him." He reached into his purse and threw two gold coins to Griff. "Thank you, you have done great service. I have no doubt your wise lord will reward you too but you have saved this army from disaster."

They took the coins, "Thank you, my lord."

"And now what? March to meet them?"

"First, Count, I think we need to ensure that no one leaves the camp. We do not wish the game to be startled. If they are camped a short way to the east then I am guessing they will attack during the morning when they think our efforts will be directed to the castle walls. We let them march here, unawares and meet them when they do not expect it. If they have many horses then they will try to use them. We meet them on foot with ground prepared before us."

My son said, "We should have scouts and archers to eliminate their scouts and to warn us." I nodded.

The Count said, "Sir William, arrange it." I could see that he was shaken. He had drunk too much to think clearly and he was delegating.

I rose and accompanied my son. He turned and said quietly, as we left the fire, "You still think that one of us betrayed the Count?"

"Not you but one of the others? Aye."

"And who would you guess?"

"If I was putting money on it then I would say Sir Stephen of Azay."

"Why?"

"He was the only one who did not appear surprised by my comments and he was the only one whose face betrayed nothing. I would have expected something: derision, shock, surprise but there was nothing."

We reached William's camp and his sergeant at arms stood, "My lord?"

"Henri, there is an enemy out there and they are going to attack on the morrow but there may be a spy in the camp. I

32

want our men at arms watching the horses. If anyone tries to leave then restrain them."

"Aye lord."

We went to Raymond of Chinon. "Raymond, I want the sentries on alert this night. No one is to leave. If any resist then slay them."

It says much for my son's authority that Raymond nodded and said, "Yes, my lord. None shall leave."

William turned to me, "I will have the archers put under the command of Griff of Gwent, " he smiled. "There is no one better and your men, above all others, are trustworthy."

"Thank you, William."

When I reached my camp my men were all alerted and awaiting me. "Griff, I want you to take the archers and those of my son to watch for the approach of this army. Stay hidden but stop their scouts from becoming aware of our preparations. We defend on foot."

"Aye, my lord."

"Get what sleep you can."

I slept but an hour and then I went, with my son, to begin to clear the ground and plant it with stakes. We wanted the land before us to be killing ground. I took my men at arms as William's were guarding the horses. Using whatever we could we cleared away the scrubby bushes and then chopped the upper halves of the trees leaving branches facing east and south. We used the branches we felled to make a spiked barrier that would deter horses. If the enemy had two hundred horses then they outnumbered us. We had but one hundred and fifty knights and men at arms. William and I were the only ones with mounted archers. Many of the Angevin lords had dismounted men at arms. Fighting on foot would play to our strengths. Finally, we dug small pits. They were not deep; many were but a hand span deep. Others were as deep as a man's arm. The purpose was simple. When a warrior charged at an enemy he looked for weapons and not his feet. Uneven ground could hurt as much as a weapon. By dawn we were ready.

William's Sergeant at Arms, Henri approached us. "Yes, Henri? Did anyone try to leave?"

He looked uncomfortable, "I think they tried, lord, but they did not succeed."

"Tried?"

"Louis heard the horses make a noise. When he reached them he saw a shadow disappearing back into the camp. I am sorry lord but we only had twenty men to watch the entire herd."

I nodded, "Do not worry, Henri. We will discover the traitor soon enough. We stopped word reaching the enemy and that was your appointed task. You and your men have done well."

He nodded and left us.

"He failed in his task, father. I would have reprimanded him."

"And had you been in command would you have discovered the traitor? Would you have seen in the dark?"

"I would have..."

I waited for him to think about it and then smiled as I said, "Looking back is easy, William. If we had had more men then we would have had a better guard. The traitor would not have even got close to the herd for he would have seen the guards. This is good. The enemy approach and know not what we know."

"A wise head as ever. How is the wound you received? It is but a month since you were hurt."

"I will be fine. The Empress had a good healer in Abelard." It was not quite the truth. The wound had been seeping but Gilles had not smelled anything that might suggest something sinister. I was a warrior and warriors ignored such inconveniences.

Our men were amongst the first to approach our new lines. Raymond of Chinon had reported to us that the Count had left a few men watching the two gates at the castle and the rest were preparing to join us. The men of William and I had mail and good weapons. The wheel had been used to grind sharp edges upon them and when we reached the killing ground they were there, ready. Our archers would be the last to arrive. I made sure our men ate and drank well. This could be a long day.

It was mid-morning when the archers began to arrive. It was Robert of Derby who brought us the news. "They come, my lord. We slew their five scouts. They will not know that we are ready. Griff and the others are hard on my heels."

William nodded, "Well done." He turned to Guy of Bayeux, "Find the Count and tell him the enemy comes."

We had arranged it so that our men held the centre. The Count's men would be to our left. They soon began to filter towards us. Each of our men at arms had a spear. William and I stood in the second rank with our squires and banners behind us. The Count appeared and frowned. "Why is my banner not in the centre, Sir William?"

I answered for him, "This way we guard your right, lord." I pointed to young Henry resplendent in a mail hauberk and open helmet. "The future King of England will be well protected by the English Knight and his son."

I decided to use the name given to me by the Normans and Angevin. It seemed to work. "Very well. Henry, go and stand by the Earl's squires." He looked at Gilles and Richard. "I charge you with the responsibility of watching over my son."

"We will, my lord."

I had no reason to doubt their ability or desire. They were as loyal and trustworthy as any. Strangely I did not think that Henry would be in any danger. It was the Count, his father, whom the enemy would wish to kill. William and I would have to stop that. We saw Griff of Gwent and the archers as they ran across the open fields some half a mile away. Then they disappeared into the trees before us. As soon as they picked their way through the traps, trees and stakes we were ready. We opened ranks to allow them to go behind us. I nodded to Griff. Thanks would come later; if we survived.

The ground fell away to the south and we saw their banners above the trees. They did not use horns and trumpets for they thought to surprise us but when we saw the tips of the banners and gonfanon stop moving then we knew they were forming lines. They appeared across the fields. They were closing with us. If the scouts had not warned and we had not prepared the ground then we would have been trapped between the wall and the ambushers.

Half the force, at least, looked to be knights. I had no doubt they saw us. This was the time when they could reconsider and withdraw. If they did so then it would be a victory for us. If I led them and knew we were expected then I would have pulled back. Whichever leader led them he was reckless for he sounded his trumpets now that there was no need for secrecy. I also suspected it was a pre-arranged signal for the defenders. Their time would come.

As with Griff and his archers they disappeared into the trees when they entered the dead ground below our eye line. They would be slowed down as they picked their way through them. We heard them before we saw them. Their hooves sounded and the branches they broke rustled and cracked.

Raymond of Chinon shouted, "Stand to! Ready spears. Archers, stand by!"

William looked at me and shook his head. Our archers needed no such command. Suddenly the line of horsemen appeared. The trees prevented them from riding knee to knee but they tried to form up at the other side of the felled trees. We had cleared a hundred and fifty paces of trees and undergrowth.

Griff of Gwent shouted, "Archers! Release!"

Forty arrows soared in the air. The riders were all mailed and we did not expect to kill many but their horses had no mail and they began to die. The wounded and injured ones reared and some turned to disrupt the lines, charging away from the missiles in fear. I heard cries as riders were thrown from their mounts. Some were trampled underfoot but still, the rest came on. When they reached the stakes and sharpened branches the riders had to take evasive action. Some collided with other riders. Some fell when hooves found holes and traps. Even so, twenty lucky riders managed to reach our lines. Their lances jabbed down at our men at arms. I flicked my shield up as a red and yellow chequered knight tried to spear me in the head. My right hand came over and I chopped the lance in two. The rider's horse was speared by Brian and as the rider fell Padraig speared him like a floundering fish.

The survivors of the attack fell back. Our men cheered but William shouted, "Silence! That was their first attack!"

Just then a man at arms ran up to the Count, "My lord, the castle has sallied forth! We can barely hold them!"

The trumpet had been a signal. That explained the castellan's confidence. We were now trapped between two armies!

Chapter 4

I saw indecision on the Count's face. William looked at me too. "Count, take your men and face this new foe. We will hold these here."

"But my banner!"

"Your banner will make them think we retreat and that their clever plan has succeeded. We will hold. Sir John and his men can fill the gap."

"Very well. Raymond!"

As a third of our army left the line we spread out so that we were just two ranks deep. The front rank was made up of knights and men at arms. The second was the archers. William and the other leaders had knights in their conroi but I had none. It did not matter. As far as I was concerned the men I fought with were the equal of any knights that we would face.

A trumpet sounded behind us. I knew it was a signal from the castle. A second one sounded from before us. Someone had made very careful plans to catch us unawares. This time they did not ride at us. They had dismounted and they charged on foot. Once again the mailed men led but now they had lightly armed men following. Griff of Gwent ordered the archers to release five flights of arrows as the men on foot negotiated the killing ground. It was just as tricky for men on foot as for those on horses. They held their shields above them for they feared my archers.

As soon as they were fifty paces from us Griff of Gwent shouted, "Choose your targets! Aim for the open helmets!"

Using a flat trajectory they began to send arrows at a ridiculously close range towards those knights and men at arms who still wore open helmets. They could not miss. Fifteen fell before the shields were pulled around to protect their faces. The protection was an illusion for it stopped them from seeing the pits and traps. Those who stumbled were rewarded with an arrow. By the time they were close enough to attack us they had lost half of their front rank and were not in a solid formation. However, they were all armed with spears and many of ours were broken or were embedded in horses and men. I was flanked by Brian and Padraig. They were like iron walls beside me. So long as I was surrounded by my men then I feared no one. The wind was from the north-west and my standard fluttered above us, occasionally catching my helmet. It drew the enemy to me. The knight who led his men towards me had a quartered fleur de lys on his surcoat. He was related to the French King. His helmet covered his face and I could not determine his age. He had four knights alongside him. They carried maces, axes and swords. That suited me.

I pulled my shield tighter. My wounded side still bothered me. My sword was the equal of any however this would be a test of my wound. My archers were releasing over our shoulders. It was effective for it meant that the approaching knights had to keep their shields up. They drew closer. Padraig had a long axe and he suddenly swung it not at the shield or the sword the knight carried but at the leg he saw below the shield. It sliced deep into the flesh to the bone. As blood-spattered us, he fell to the ground adding to the barrier of horses and men which lay before us. As a second knight stood on a horse and raised his sword to smite Brian, my man at arms darted his sword up under the arm. It broke the mail there driving deep within the knight's body and the sword fell to the ground. James the Stout sent an arrow almost at point-blank range through the mail of the next man at arms and into his chest.

The royal knight brought his sword down towards my shield. That was a mistake for my shield was well made. He brought his own shield up to defend against my blow. None was forthcoming. I was looking for a weakness. He swung again and struck at my shield. I took the hit and he prepared for my own strike. Each movement weakened him for he had had to walk a long way in his heavy mail. By the fourth strike, he had stopped raising his shield quite as high. Around us, others were exchanging blows. Mailed men fighting with similar weapons find it hard to kill. It was then I saw his shield drop a little. He swung again at my shield but this time I pulled my right arm back and stabbed upwards towards his helmet. His shield was too low and the tip caught the helmet as his head jerked back. His helmet fell from his head revealing the face of a warrior of an age with William. He had just a coif to protect him; there was no ventail.

For some reason, the loss of his helmet made him less cautious and he attacked me with renewed energy. This time the strikes showering my shield took effect. My left side had been wounded on the ride to Oxford and I felt the wound burst after another flurry of blows. I had to end this. I brought my sword sideways and sliced towards his knee. He had quick hands and he brought his shield down. I pulled my arm back for a second blow. He anticipated the move he thought I would make. As my sword swept towards his head he realised his error. My sword cut through the mail of his coif and into his skull. He fell, stunned. Those behind formed a wall around him while the two who remained from his knights hurled themselves at us. Their recklessness cost them. I took the blow from a knight's mace and stabbed forwards with every ounce of strength I had left. It tore through his mail and ripped into his gambeson and then his body. I twisted as I pulled and, gutted, he fell at my feet. The royal knight was dragged from the fray and just one of his knights remained. He was wounded.

"Yield for you have done your duty!"

"Never and I will fell the Wolf before I am taken!"

The brave young man charged towards me. As his sword struck my shield I did the unexpected. I stepped forward and punched him in the side of the head with the hilt of my sword. He stumbled backwards over a dead horse. The sword flew from his hand and I was on him with my sword at his throat before he could recover. "Yield!"

His hand reached out for his sword. Suddenly Henry Fitz Empress darted from behind Gilles and Richard to grab the sword. "Here, lord! He has to surrender now!"

Gilles and Richard raced to protect the future king but there was no danger now. The attack had faltered and they were falling back.

The knight nodded, "I yield! But that was a trick! That was not a fair blow!"

I laughed, "You are young and will soon discover that there is little that is fair in war. Richard, Henry, escort our prisoner back."

I looked down the line. Some of our men at arms lay dead or wounded but the line held. William was alive. Sir John and Sir Hugh had lost men too but, to my right, Sir Stephen of Azay and his conroi looked to have survived intact. In fact, they appeared to have lost barely a man. Behind us, I could hear the Count as he fought against the defenders. The battle was not yet over.

I turned, "How are you for arrows?"

"More than enough, lord!"

"Then on their next attack, I wish you to shower them. There will be fewer men with mail."

He nodded and I waved him to close with me. "Yes, my lord?"

"Watch our right during the next attack. If you see any danger then concentrate your arrows there."

"My lord?"

"Watch for treachery!" I walked over to William and spoke quietly to him, "I fear treachery. Sir Stephen was not attacked as heavily as we were. It may just be luck but..."

"But you do not trust him."

"No, I do not. The Count thinks his rear is protected. Take your conroi and go to his aid but leave your banner here. It will fool the enemy into thinking you remain here still."

"I will not let you down." He nodded his head to Henry.

"Gilles, Richard, Henry. Bring the prisoner and put him and our banner next to my son."

Henry said, "Why?"

"When you are King then you shall command. Your father placed you with me and you will obey my orders!"

"Yes, lord!"

Gilles hurried him to my son's banner and Richard helped the injured knight to join the standard-bearers. "Padraig, Brian, you will be on the right!"

"Aye, lord!"

"They come again!" Sir John's voice sounded from my left.

"Stay tight together. We must hold them and buy time for the Count!"

There was a chorus of, "Aye lord!"

I could feel something dripping down my back. I think it was blood. It was dripping slowly. I would live a while longer yet. As they approached I saw that they had weighted their line to come towards me. There were mailed men but I only saw five knights. I wondered where the rest were.

Griff of Gwent did not shout 'release' but he must have signalled, for arrows flew overhead. They were aiming at those without armour and at any bare flesh they saw. Men fell but still, the solid phalanx of mailed men came forwards. "Steady!"

They were thirty paces from us when Griff of Gwent shouted, "Treachery! 'Ware right!"

As we turned I saw that the men of Stephen of Azay had turned and were attacking us. Had I not had my archers watching for such treachery and if my men at arms were not so well trained then we would have died there and then. The archers slowed down their treacherous attack.

"Fall back right! On me! Sir John, Sir Hugh, charge!"

I gambled. They were counting on eliminating me. Sir Stephen and their best warriors showed that. It meant that their right was weak and a sudden attack by Sir John and Sir Hugh might break their will. It was all that I could think of.

Men still fell to my archers' arrows and the line echeloned back. There was no obstacle to the men who now

42

faced us. I was the corner. I had men from two sides coming at me. Three men came directly at me. There was a knight with a yellow and white surcoat and two of his men at arms. They wielded swords. Three to one were never good odds. I did not let them strike the first blow. I punched with my shield as I swung my sword at head height. They ducked and one man at arms reeled as my shield connected with his face. I felt a blade slide along the links of my mail. The knight brought his sword down to strike my head. I barely managed to block it with my shield and then I had to sweep my sword to deflect the second man at arm's sword. Out of the corner of my eye, I saw an enraged man at arms with a bloodied face launch himself at me. Even as he did so the knight stabbed at me again. I brought my shield around more in hope than expectation.

Suddenly a sword darted out from my left and the bloodied man at arms looked down at the sword which was in his middle. Even as Gilles pulled it out Richard jabbed the standard at the knight's face and Henry, with just a short sword, stabbed the second man at arms in the knee. I did not hesitate. I brought my sword across the knight's neck. I put all of my effort into it. My standard had stabbed his mouth and my blade broke his neck. He fell to the ground and I backhanded my sword into the wounded man at arms. It hit his head and stunned him. Richard did not hesitate. He stabbed him in his mouth, pinning his head to the ground.

"Get Henry behind me! Now!"

Sir Stephen had just slain Guy of Angers and he lunged at Henry just as they moved. I saw the red mist. I hurled myself at the treacherous knight. He had known Henry since he had been a child and yet he had been willing to slay him. His sword was almost next to me as I smashed his hand with my shield. I was so close that I could not swing my blade properly and so I punched towards his face with the hilt of my sword. The guard tore into his eye and he screamed. I twisted as I pulled back. Gore slid down his ventail. He tore the ventail from his mouth and spat. He stepped back and a man at arms swung at my right side. I turned his blade and then using the hands which Wulfstan had called the fastest in

England, brought the blade back around to slice across his throat.

Sir Stephen was trying to back away. I could see now that our archers had destroyed most of the men of Azay. Three of Sir Stephen's men were trying to extricate him. I took another step and swept my sword horizontally. They were so busy trying to protect the traitor that they didn't see it. I hit one on the side of the head and he stumbled. Robert son of Gilles darted forward to slay him. A second reeled back out of the way of my swinging blade and I brought my right leg around to kick his knee. I heard something crack and he fell to the ground. Before he could recover I had killed him.

To my left, I heard Sir John roar, "Victory! We have them!"

I hefted my shield higher as I advanced towards Sir Stephen and his last knight. Sir Guillaume was brave but he was young and lacked experience. He lunged at me and I blocked it with my shield. His lunge overbalanced him and as he fell forward I brought my sword down. His coif was poorly made or I was lucky for my sword broke the mail and cracked into the back of his neck. My sword was stuck, caught in his spine.

Sir Stephen saw, through his one remaining eye, his chance. "I might have missed the whelp but you shall die!"

I could not use my sword and so I punched him in the face with my shield. His sword stabbed into my left leg as my shield smacked into his face. He fell, unconscious at my feet. As blood began to flow from my leg I dropped to one knee. Richard, Gilles and Henry ran to me. I was safe for the enemy were fleeing. We had won. It was Gilles who saved my life. "Lie him down!" As I was laid on the ground he tore a piece of material from Sir Stephen's surcoat and applied a tourniquet to my leg. "Richard, find a healer. Henry put your sword at Sir Stephen's throat and if the traitor moves, kill him!"

I felt myself becoming dizzy and I closed my eyes. It helped. Sound faded as though it was far away. I fought sleep. If I slept then I would die. As the tourniquet bit into my leg, the pain made my back arch.

"Sorry, lord! Where is that healer?"

Sounds became distorted. I heard Henry Fitz Empress say, "Will he die? I pray not. I have never seen such courage."

Gilles' voice sounded thick with emotion as he replied, "I have many times; too many times. His mail is rent in so many places his leg might not be the only wound. Where is that healer?"

"Richard comes with a priest!"

I opened my eyes and saw that Sir John of Nantes was there. He saw my eyes open and said. "We have won, lord. The Count and your son are finishing off those who sortied."

I tried to speak but no words came out. "Out of the way! Quickly!" The priest's body bent over me. He released the tourniquet and I felt such a rush of pain that I must have blacked out.

As I came to I heard my son say, "Where is he? Where is my father?"

Henry shouted, "Here!"

As I opened my eyes the priest's face filled the sky. "Open your mouth, lord. This will help you sleep. We need to move you."

I did not want to sleep and as I opened my mouth to tell him so I felt a warm bitter liquid in my mouth. I had swallowed it before I knew. I saw William, Henry and Gilles above me but soon they faded as I fell asleep.

I heard the voices and knew that I lived. "Lord, he stirs!"

I opened my eyes as I heard Gilles' voice. It was dark and we were in my tent. A candle threw shadows on the canvas. My son looked worried. He came over to me, "You had me worried, father. The wound in your back had burst." I nodded. "And yet you fought on."

"If I had stopped fighting so would my men. How are they?"

His head dropped. Henry's face appeared, "Your men at arms were all slain. They protected your side until the end but all are dead."

I looked up at William. I could see the pain on his face, "Brian and Padraig?"

"They died together and were the last to fall. Even as you fought that traitor and his brood they held off the rest of the conroi. They saw you fall and fought on. They died of their wounds. The healer could not save them." I tried to rise. "And you will be going nowhere for a while! The healer has said that there will be no fighting for a month at least."

I lay back and closed my eyes, "We will see. I will decide when I am fit to rise." I opened my eyes, "The Count?"

Henry said, "My father lives. He is questioning the traitor. I think they are torturing him."

"For his treachery and dishonour, it is just. To change sides during a battle is the most dishonourable thing a man can do." I smiled, "I forgot to thank you for disobeying my orders and saving my life."

He grinned, "My mother would never have forgiven me if I had allowed her champion to be killed. Besides Gilles and Richard did more."

"And they shall be rewarded." I looked up at my son, "The castle?"

"No one can leave and the castellan died in the fighting. I slew him."

"Then tomorrow we go and ask for their surrender."

"You shall lie here."

"No, I will not. Do you not see that I have to be there? I have no doubt someone will have seen me fall and reported that to the garrison. They will say that the Warlord is dead. When they see me it will be as though I have risen from the grave. Use me, my son. Use my name. You say they fear the wolf then let them think that the wolf cannot be killed. We know it is not true but it is what they believe which is important."

"Come, Henry, we will leave them." He turned, "We have sent for the ransom for Richard d'Eveque. He is the knight you captured. His father is rich."

I nodded, "But the gold cannot buy me oathsworn can it?" I thought I would be alone when they left but Gilles and Richard entered. "Thank you for what you did on the battlefield. You behaved well and acquitted yourselves as future knights. Our conroi is becoming smaller, is it not?"

46

Richard said, in an awed voice. "Brian and Padraig were cut so much I know not how they fought on."

Gilles added, "And you, my lord had three bad wounds. You too had many wounds, lord. The one you received near Oxford is still the worst. The healer had to use fire."

"I cannot feel it."

"He put something into a flask of wine and your son poured it down your throat. It dulls the pain. He said it was a very mild dose of leopard's bane. The priest said it would hurt on the morrow as would your knee."

"See if you can find a smith to repair my mail. I would not like to go abroad without it."

I felt worse when I awoke for the pain was there. It was the paroxysms that wracked my body that had woken me for it was still night. It was a constant throbbing in both my back and my leg. I knew that both would ease eventually but I would not be able to get much sleep for the next few days. As I forced myself up, Gilles and Richard who had flanked me while I slept, leapt to their feet. "Lord, you were told to rest."

"And I need to make water." Richard held out a bowl. "If you think I shall use that then you had better find another master." I swung my legs off the cot and tried to stand.

"Your leg cannot carry the weight, lord. Put your arms around us."

Gilles was the stronger and he took my left side. I hopped using the two of them as a crutch. It was a cold night and the chill air hit me. They helped me to a secluded part of the camp and I relieved myself. As we hopped back two figures rose from the ground.

"You are alive, lord. Your son would not let us disturb you."

"I am just pleased that two of my men, at least, live." It was Griff of Gwent and James the Stout.

Griff nodded, "All of our archers live but the men at arms... They died with their swords in their hands. It was the old way. I knew them as well as any and I know that they would be happy. I think the last few years were too comfortable for them. We spoke before the battle and they were looking forward to the fray. They took many enemies with them."

"And I am grateful to you and the archers. Had you not done as you did then I might have joined them."

"You had too few men, lord. You needed your whole retinue. You are the Earl of Cleveland. You should have men to protect you."

"I came here not to fight. It is just the way things turned out."

I sat on a log by the fire and waited until dawn. I talked to my squires and my archers. It distracted me from my pain. I did not want to lie down for I knew I would have to get up and that was not a pleasant prospect.

The dawn brought sun and my son and the Count. I was not certain that they had had much sleep. The Count gave me a wan smile. "I am sorry you were left with a traitor at your back. You suspected did you not?"

"I did, Count, but until they turned I could not have sworn who the traitor was."

"All these years that viper has been trusted by me."

"Did we find his master?"

"He was working for Eustace of Boulogne and King Louis. It was Eustace who brought the army."

"But he is a boy!"

"He has ambitions and he was angry with you. He knows that it was you who captured his father at Lincoln. King Louis promised him, Blois."

"Louis is a clever man. Blois belongs to Theobald and is not yet captured."

"And that is how it worked. With us gone, they could surround Blois and force Theobald to give up his lands. Are you still determined to speak to the garrison?"

"Let us end this now. I have the *'Adela'* coming to Ouistreham. I am anxious for news from England."

Count Geoffrey gave me a sharp look. "You gave your word that you would be here until September! It is not yet August."

"I will give my word but I would like to see my son's wife and my grandchildren. Yesterday showed me that I am

48

not immortal. Gilles, fetch a horse. I cannot walk but I can ride."

We reached the walls some hours after dawn. Raymond of Chinon carried Sir Stephen of Azay's head. He held it by the hair. We brought the whole army. Our dead had been taken away but the bodies of the garrison lay where they had fallen and our horses picked their way between them. The Count nodded to Raymond who rode forward and threw the head onto the bridge over the moat. It thudded upon it and rolled so that the one eye stared up, lifelessly, at the gatehouse.

A head appeared and then another. Banners were raised to show that the garrison still fought. The Count shouted, "There is the traitor that was bought. Your castellan lies dead with more than half of your men. The relief army has fled. Surrender!"

"I am Philippe of Arras. I command here now. I was charged by Sir John with holding the walls and I will continue to do so."

I turned, "Griff of Gwent, come forward with me."

My archer obeyed and I rode towards the bridge. I wore no mail but I had my surcoat and my shield hung from my saddle.

"Know you who I am?"

Philippe of Arras nodded, "You are the Earl of Cleveland, the Champion of the Empress and the Queen. They call you the wolf. I have heard of you but you are far from home, my lord."

"They call me a warlord at home. That is what I do, I make war and I never lose. I have the finest men at arms and archers at my command." I turned and said to Griff, "The standard split it!" In one motion he raised his bow and released an arrow. It sped towards the largest standard. It was only a hundred and fifty paces away. His arrow split it in twain and the standard fluttered slowly to the ground. All but Philippe of Arras ducked. He was a brave man.

"Know you that I can clear your walls as easily as I felled your standard but if I do so and enter this town I will give no quarter. I will slaughter all within these walls. Would you have that on your conscience?"

"And what of your conscience, my lord?"

"My conscience is clear for I did not break my word to my liege lord, Henry Duke of Normandy and King of England. You did! I am not foresworn, you are! I will not rot in hell. You will!"

I had built up my shouts and the last one seemed to echo around the castle. The air was filled with silence.

"And if we surrender?"

"Then you may march out with your weapons but not your horses."

It took a heartbeat for him to say, "We surrender. Mortain is yours."

We had won. But my men had paid the ultimate price. They had paid the price of the oathsworn. They had thought me dead and they had died protecting my body. They were faithful to the grave. Such men were irreplaceable. I had my squires and my archers bury them with their weapons and mail. They would sleep together until the ending of time.

Chapter 5

We spent a week at the castle. My son and the healers made sure that I moved as little as possible. My squires let me know what was going on outside the castle walls. Other knights had been captured, apart from the one I had taken, and we had to wait for the ransoms. Although I was anxious to get to William's home it allowed my wounds to heal and for the smith to repair my mail. The Count placed a strong garrison in Mortain and I left with William for Ouistreham. Henry returned to Angers with his father. That ensured that I would not be able to leave for England on the *'Adela'*. I think that the Count knew I would if given the opportunity. It did not take long to travel north to the port my son called home. Despite the fact that we travelled across enemy territory the journey was peaceful. Our victory had made the rebels hide in their castles. They were safe. Campaigning had ended with the capture of the key stronghold. The next year would see the end of the war in Normandy.

On the journey, my son treated me like an invalid. To be honest the wound in my back and side did not bother me much. It had been worse before the battle. My knee ached and I had a feeling that it would be even more painful in wet weather. Wulfric and Erre, both old soldiers, had told me as much. I was both excited and nervous. I would be meeting my son's wife, Eliane, and my grandchildren. After what my son had said I had a feeling that this might be my only opportunity to see them. It was obvious to me now that he would not come to England. There was only one country in which I wished to live.

William and his men rode in a protective ring around me and my squires. They were taking no chances. After the battle of Mortain, the Count had made it quite clear that my life was as important as his. The fact that he had been deceived for so many years had unnerved him. I think I was the only one who was not surprised by such deception. Ranulf of Chester was still a straw that blew in the breeze. I had been betrayed by the first knight I had taken on. He had almost killed me not far from here on the road to Caen. He had died at my hands. Since then I had been wary of all.

We gave Caen and its huge and formidable keep, a wide berth. The Empress had given my son Ouistreham for it guarded the river which led to Caen. The city of the Conqueror was now cut off from England. It could be taken easily but there was little point for it served no purpose save as the place William The Bastard was buried. The manor of Ouistreham was not a large one. It relied more on the sea than the land but it was prosperous. When the war ended it would become even more prosperous. As we rode west William told me of his plans. Farms would be built behind sea defences and he would build roads. He had a vision. He reminded me of myself. It was what my father and I had done with the manors of Norton, Stockton and Hartburn when we had first come. I could barely remember those days of peace so many years ago.

He only had a wooden walled castle but it was bigger than a simple motte and bailey. The builder had used the sea and the river to defend two sides. The square keep was made of stone and it looked to be a hard place to take. It would be harder than was Mortain for here it could be supplied by sea. As we neared it I saw the masts of three or four ships bobbing up and down in the gentle swell. I hoped that one was my ship. I was anxious for news.

As we neared the gate I spied *'Adela'*. She was at anchor in the river. I would have news. That news was delayed for I was welcomed warmly by a family I had never seen. William and Gilles helped me dismount. The wound in my leg sent paroxysms of pain shooting up my body. I gritted my teeth. I would have to bear it. The pain would pass.

"Are you in pain, father? We have a draught from the priest."

"No, my son, for it dulls my wits and makes me sleepy. I would stay awake. I have a new family to meet." I forced the smile upon my lips. I looked to the small group who awaited us. There looked to be a nurse with a babe in arms and a toddler holding his mother's hand.

"This is my wife, Eliane." He took his son's hand from his wife's so that Eliane could do obeisance.

She was a dark-haired beauty and I could see why my son had fallen for her. She had dark eyes and a vivacious smile. She curtsied. "I have waited for this moment since I first married Guillaume." I raised her up and kissed her on both cheeks. "I am sorry you were not at the wedding."

"As am I but that is the past. And is this fine young man my grandson?"

My son led him forward, "It is. Say hello to your grandfather, William."

He had a puzzled look on his face, "I thought he was a wolf!"

We all laughed and I bent to pick him up. It was a mistake for the pain in my side stabbed like a knife but it was worth it for the child threw his arms around my neck. "They call me the wolf for it is the design on my shield."

My son saw my pain and took my grandson from me. "And this babe in arms is your granddaughter, Adele."

I peered into the swaddled baby. She was sleeping. My only daughter had been taken by the plague. I prayed that my granddaughter would escape that terror.

"Come, father, you have had a long ride and I can see that your wounds are causing you pain."

Eliane face clouded, "You are hurt?" She glared at my son. "And you have kept your father standing outside!" Shaking her head she shouted, "Raymond! Food and wine to the Great Hall."

I smiled for I could see that my son might be a great warrior and leader but here, in his home, there was a mistress who ruled his domestic world. They were right for each other. Adela would have been happy at the match if not the manner in which it came about. I was grateful for the chair into which I almost collapsed. My knee had barely carried me into the hall. Had not Gilles and Richard supported me then I would have fallen. The stairs to the Great Hall on the first floor were almost the straw that broke me.

The wine revived me somewhat. I drank a goblet and held my hand out for another. Gilles and Richard carried my chests to the quarters William had given me. His keep was well appointed. Eliane returned with furs. I smiled, "I am not an invalid. My leg aches. That is all. I am an old warrior and warriors suffer wounds. It is in the nature of what we do. I am fine but I thank you for your consideration and hospitality." I took her hand. "I am pleased that my son has had the good sense to find such a good woman as you."

For some reason, my words made her burst into tears and run from the room. I looked up at my son in surprise.

He smiled, "She has been worried about this meeting. She was certain that you would not like her and disapprove. She is not high born."

"You know I am not like that!"

"I know but you know women." Just then a servant appeared. "Yes, Henri?"

"Lord, there is a sailor outside. He says he must speak with the Earl." His tone suggested that Henri would rather the sailor waited without.

William looked at me and I nodded, "I need this news."

"Admit him."

It was William of Kingston. His face looked pained. "What is it, William? Is there trouble on the Tees?"

"No, my lord, it is worse. There has been a disastrous battle."

All the fears I had suppressed since coming across the sea now burst forth. I knew that I should not have come. "What is it?"

"The Empress and the Earl of Gloucester travelled to Winchester with their army to confront the Bishop of Winchester about his failure to support them. While they were there Queen Matilda and William of Ypres arrived with an army. There was a battle. The Empress' forces were

54

defeated. She and Sir Miles fled to Devizes but the Earl was captured. He is held by Queen Matilda and the Empress' forces are routed."

I looked at my son, "And I was here helping the Count when I could have been helping my Empress."

My son looked at William of Kingston, "When was this?"

"The start of July."

My son turned triumphantly, "You could have done nothing for you had not long arrived in Anjou."

He was right but that did not help. "I need to get back to England." I suddenly remembered the task appointed me by the Empress. "With Henry Fitz Empress."

My son shook his head, "The Count will not allow it!"

I smiled, "I gave my word and I have kept it. Surely the Count will keep his word?"

Nodding he said, "Perhaps."

I looked at my captain, "Tell me, have the Scots taken advantage of this? Is my home safe?"

"It is, lord. When I left your knights were aggressively patrolling your borders."

I smiled. I knew what that meant. They had mailed men approaching the enemy strongholds to let them know that they were watching. "What of Mandeville and the Earl of Chester?"

"The Earl of Essex fights still against Queen Matilda in the east." I could see that I had misjudged him. "The Earl of Chester now debates which side of the fence is his. He sits in the castle of Lincoln."

"Then I will have much to do once I reach England. I need to be there as soon as possible. Captain, when can you sail?"

"On the morning tide, lord. But to where?"

"Angers. The ride would take too long and with my wound, it would be both difficult and painful. I must speak with the Count and collect Henry. How long will it take us to reach it?"

"It could take a week perhaps longer."

That was too long but the journey by horse would be even longer. "And when we reach there it will be almost September."

My son shook his head, "I know what you are thinking! I just hope that the Count listens to you. I know what you are like. You would be just as likely to kidnap Henry."

"The rules by which I live are simple, William. I give and keep my word. I expect others to do the same. If all men lived that way then life would be easier for all." I turned to William of Kingston. "Take my chests aboard. We have gold and coin which must be secured. It will be even more important now than it was!"

When my captain had returned to my ship I sat with William. We had much to talk about. "So, father, the war you thought was over is about to burst into flames again."

"It is worse than that. Lincoln held meant that we had the usurper and his forces trapped in the south and east. That harpy of a wife can now control all but the west. We have Oxford, Wallingford, Gloucester and Bristol. That is a tiny island surrounded by enemies. My men on the Tees cannot go to the Empress' aid. The war could end now. Henry is our only hope."

"But he is but a boy!"

"You were not much older when I first brought you here as my squire. You were left here at the age of sixteen. You did not turn out so bad. Eustace of Boulogne is barely fourteen and yet he can direct a treacherous attack. I had the luxury of growing up before I went to war. You and Henry do not have that opportunity. If Henry wishes to be king then he must go to England."

He nodded, "I can see that. Would you wish me to accompany you?"

Shaking my head I said, "No. The Count will not campaign again this year but next year he will and you are part of his army. Enjoy your family. I know that I regret not having more time with you, your mother and your sister. You know not what the future holds. Make each precious moment count."

The brevity of my visit made the time we had together even more important. I stayed up talking with Eliane and William far longer than I really wished but I did not know when or if I would ever see them again. I wanted them both to know how much I cared for them and my grandchildren. William had made his decision about his life and his future. I was the one who would have to adapt to that.

The next morning I stood at the quayside and hugged my grandson. "I will return, William, son of William, and perhaps, one day, you shall come to stay with me in my castle."

"I would like that. But do you have to go so soon? There is so much I wish to show you."

"I am an Earl and I have duties."

I embraced Eliane. Salt tears coursed down her cheeks. "Like my son, I wish that you could stay. I want to know more about you. I hear William's stories and having met you I can see that they are more than stories. You have done enough for this Empress of yours. When is it your turn for life?"

I stepped back and smiled, "I am afraid the answer is never. Until Henry is on the throne I cannot stop in my endeavours. The future may seem black now but I have to believe that God is on our side for we are in the right. Honour will prevail. On that day I shall return here and enjoy your home once more."

William clasped my arm, "I will visit Leofric whenever I can. You will need more men in England. I will help him recruit and train them. Brian and Padraig were good judges of warriors."

"Thank you." Impulsively I hugged him. "I am proud of you, my son. I am sorry I was not a better father to you. I will try to make it up to you. You are right to live your life the way you wish to."

Before he could reply and before I looked foolish I turned and stepped aboard my ship. William of Kingston had been anxious to leave and even as I stepped aboard the ropes were cast and the sail unfurled. We headed down the Orne towards the sea. William and his family huddled together and waved as I left. I stood watching them until they were indistinguishable from the town and it was only when the coast became a thin line that I turned and went to stand by my captain. I waited to regain my composure before I spoke for I was uncertain if I would ever see my son and his family again.

"What was the mood in England then, William?"

"If I am to be honest, lord, despair. I did not speak with the Empress. Her letter is still in my cabin. I remembered your words. I hope I did right."

"You did. My letter was rendered redundant by the disaster at Winchester." I had wanted to know how the battle had been lost but my captain knew the sea and not battles. The problem with the Earl of Gloucester was that he wanted glory and he listened to those who flattered him. I had butted heads with him more times than enough for I did not go along with his plans unless they were sound.

We had a long voyage ahead of us. Gilles fetched me a chair so that I could sit on the deck and watch the land slip by. I began to plan how to help the Empress. At the moment there was an impasse but I thought it favoured us. The king was more valuable than a mere earl. The Empress would be safe in Devizes but it was imperative that I get there. The presence of Henry was even more vital. He could become the figurehead. If the clergy would not sanction the Empress as ruler then perhaps they would allow Henry to be king and she the regent. As the ship rolled south my plans began to ferment in my mind. I needed men to protect Henry. I would have to take them from Leofric. I was reluctant to take any from Angers after the defection of Stephen of Azay. Had I not lost all of my men at arms then I would not be in this dilemma. I would take Griff, James and the rest of my archers. Sir Leofric would have to train more.

The ship had hammocks and the rolling motion of the ship actually helped me to sleep each night. I hung my leg from the side and the pain lessened. As we headed south I had a better nights' sleep and, one morning woke to see the Loire estuary. We had made good time during the night. It was a cold breakfast but a hearty one. Henri the Breton brought me wine, cheese and bread we had brought from my son's baker. Gilles and Richard were both thoughtful squires and it was Gilles who approached me as we passed Nantes.

"Lord, is the war lost? The crew say that we lost a major battle and the Earl of Gloucester is captured."

"It is a setback. When we fought the French last week we lost a skirmish but won the battle. A warrior does not give in when obstacles are put in his way. We have far to travel. It is best we take it one step at a time."

He nodded, satisfied, "Your mail is repaired but the smith said you had best have a spare one made. The blows you took weakened some of the links."

"When William returns to Stockton I will have Alf begin one. He knows my size well enough by now. And you two are growing. When we return home it will be time for you to have new mail. If Henry comes back with us Alf can make him a hauberk too."

"Will his father allow it, lord?"

"That will be a test of my skills of persuasion." I watched every bend and island in the mighty Loire as we headed slowly east. We tacked and we turned. We never had the wind completely in our favour and twice we had to get the crew to haul us for we were trying to navigate a loop where the wind was against us. Coming downstream was easier. It took more than three days to reach the confluence of the Maine and the Loire. There the Count kept a watch tower and when we were spied as we approached. I saw a rider heading to warn the Count of our arrival.

In a week it would be September. I hoped that the Count would allow us to leave early. I began to have my doubts for while I always kept my word others appeared to be more flexible.

As we approached the quay I said to Gilles, "I want you and Richard to go to my manor. I will give you a letter. I need Griff of Gwent and all my archers and as many trustworthy men at arms, Sir Leofric can spare."

He looked at me, "Trustworthy?"

"You will need to tell him about Sir Stephen. He may have heard stories. You were there and you know the truth."

"Thank you for entrusting me with this task, lord."

"You are ready. You showed that at Mortain."

When we reached the castle I could tell that the news from England, although six weeks old, had not reached Angers. I wondered why. I did not wait for a summons from Count Geoffrey but took it upon myself to find him. He was in his Great Hall and was listening to cases brought to him by his landowners. He looked bored. His face brightened when he spied me. "I will hear the rest of the cases tomorrow. Clear the hall!"

I waited while the crowds which had been there grumbled their way out.

"I had not expected to see you so soon. Is your wound healed?"

"Count, I bring grave news. In July the Empress and her brother were defeated at the battle of Winchester. The Earl of Gloucester was taken prisoner and the Empress is holed up in Devizes." I told him all.

There were just guards and Raymond of Chinon in the hall. "All of you, leave us. Raymond, guard the doors!" Alone he said, "You know England better than I. Should we fetch the Empress home?"

"No, Count. This is a setback but that is all. I will return to England with your son as arranged and..."

"Are you mad! That is out of the question! He would be a hostage to fortune! I will not allow it."

"You gave your word, my lord."

"That was a different set of circumstances. The Empress was free then."

I took a deep breath. As usual, the Count could not see further than the end of his nose. "The Empress sent me for Henry in June. If I had travelled back then who knows what the outcome of the battle would have been? Who knows what effect the presence of King Henry's grandson would have meant? But I gave you my word that I would help you at Mortain, which I did, even though it cost me dear. I lost men I cannot replace. I kept my word. I ask you to honour your promise and keep your word."

"But my son!"

"Do you honestly think I would allow any harm to befall him?"

"But how do you know that you can protect him?"

"I have been protecting the Empress for twenty years. Even though there have been attempts on her life none has got even close. If I say your son will be safe then he will be. You have my word."

"But what good can he do?"

"More now than before. If the clergy will not crown the Empress and Stephen of Blois is in Bristol castle then Henry may be the only alternative." I could see him thinking over my words. "When we reach the Empress if she does not agree with my suggestion then we will return, forthwith, and your wife and son will be returned to you."

He sat in silence for a while. Then he nodded, "Nothing that you do is for yourself. If this was anyone else then I would suspect ulterior motives. I will give you guards to..."

I shook my head, "Count, remember Stephen of Azay? Are these guards cut from the same cloth as he? We have no Swabians now. I have sent my squires to fetch men from my manor. Your son will be safe."

"When will you sail?"

"It could take three or four days for my squires to return. Let us say five days from now."

He smiled, "And that will be September."

I nodded, "Aye, it will be. I only hope I am in time."

He rose, "Give me your word that my son and my wife will be safe."

I clasped his arm, "I swear that they will be safe."

"Then let us go find him. I daresay he will be delighted to be on an adventure with his Uncle Alfraed!"

Chapter 6

We left on the last day of August. I had ten archers and six men at arms. They were all Angevin soldiers but the fact that they were there to protect Henry seemed to make them even keener to serve me. Henry was, as his father had said, ecstatic. He had not stopped talking about the battle of Mortain. He and his brothers had refought it with wooden swords each day since his return. As we sailed down the Loire I had Richard and Gilles work with the new guards and Henry. Their English needed improvement. I spent the voyage writing letters and studying maps.

We would have to sail to Bristol and take horses from there. The journey down the Loire might only take two days for the current was with us but we had to cross the Channel and that could take another week or so. We had Cornwall to round and those waters were treacherous. I hoped that the situation would still be the same and not have worsened when I eventually reached the Empress.

The weather was against us. We struck a storm as we reached Ushant. At the back of my mind was the thought that this whole civil war had been started when the heir to the throne had drowned in the White Ship when it had sunk in these very waters. How ironic it would be if Henry suffered the same fate. I could protect him from human danger but Nature was a different matter. Our ship was so badly damaged that we had to put back into Ouistreham. Both my son and his wife were surprised to see us but delighted that we had this extra and unexpected time together. It took three days to make the repairs and we had our farewells once more.

With winds against us, we had to tack, take in sail, let out sail, so many times that the crew were exhausted. It took another week to reach Cornwall and five more days to finally make Bristol.

We had been at sea so long that we left the ship like drunks. It was dark when we reached the port. We would not be travelling further that night. "William, sail to Stockton. I have letters for my knights and for Alf. One of them and their men will return south with you unless the danger from the Scots is too great. I know your men are exhausted but this is important."

"Aye, my lord."

I took a purse of gold from my ransom chest, "Take this instead of cargo."

"My lord! This is your ship!"

"And you have your livelihood to think of. Take it!"

He reluctantly took it, "Aye lord, and do you wish me to return here?"

"If you would be so kind."

I took my squires and Henry to the Castle. My men would sleep aboard the cog. The castellan was surprised to see me. "We heard that you had died in Normandy, my lord."

"A slight wound, nothing more. We will be staying but one night."

He nodded, "That will not be a problem, lord. Would you dine alone?"

"Alone?"

"King Stephen and I normally dine together. I did not wish to offend you."

"We shall dine with him. We can be civilised about this."

When I told Henry that he was to dine with his mother's cousin he looked intrigued. "You captured him did you not, uncle?"

"I did but he had fought many men and he was tired. He is a good warrior."

"But you are better."

I did not like boasting. "On the day, yes, I was. On another? Who knows?"

My leg was bothering me less these days but I still walked with a limp. Stephen noticed it as I came in with Henry and my squires. He frowned, "You have been in the wars again?"

Henry blurted out, "He captured Mortain and killed the traitor Stephen of Azay!"

Stephen laughed loudly, "Thank God for some entertaining company! You are a frightening foe, Cleveland, but you have something about you. I shall enjoy this meal!" He turned to the castellan, "No offence, Robert, but the Earl's stories will be far more interesting than yours."

The castellan smiled, "I look forward to hearing them myself.

After so long at sea, the food tasted like nectar but I watched how much wine I drank. I made sure that my squires and Henry took heavily watered wine. Stephen questioned me about the battle. It was obvious he had had no knowledge of Azay's treachery nor the plot involving the French. When we had finished he grinned, "It seems that, like you, Earl, I have raised a cockerel to crow in the farmyard!"

"If he moves in French company then we both know how dangerous that is."

"True. This new Louis is as tricky as the old one I fear!"

Henry stared at Stephen, "Why do you not let my mother have the crown? It is hers and not yours you know!"

Stephen nodded, "I can see how you would see that Fitz Empress, but is your mother strong enough to defend this land?"

"She is strong enough to defeat you and have you held in this castle!"

That took me and the castellan by surprise but Stephen laughed loudly, "And it seems there is another cockerel here! It was not your mother who beat me but the man seated opposite. If the Earl had been on my side then your mother and father would be in Normandy and I would be fighting them there. The Earl is the only reason that England is at war."

That was not true and it was trite of him to say so but I would not argue for it was pointless.

"When I am old enough I will fight you for this kingdom. We will have the Duchy by then for the Earl of Cleveland will help my father to conquer it!"

Stephen seemed amused by the precocious youth, "We shall see, we shall see. And would you be a good king?"

He nodded, "I would be like the earl and give the Scots a good thrashing and the Welsh! I would make England bigger and stronger." He jabbed an accusing finger at Stephen, "You have lost parts of England; the Palatinate, Cumbria as well as Wales! You have given away my mother's land!"

"You are knowledgeable for one so young. I think you might make a good king. Sadly for you, however, my son, Eustace will be the king after me."

I sipped my wine, "Your son who colludes and conspires with England and Normandy's enemies does not seem a good choice to me."

For the first time, Stephen's good humour left him. It seemed I had touched a nerve. Perhaps he had not thought deeply enough about his son's actions. He stood, "I thank you for your company. Remember me kindly to your mother Henry and it has been a genuine pleasure to meet and speak with you." He came to grasp my hand, "And once again I am mindful of the difference we could have made had we fought alongside each other."

When he and the castellan had gone I said, "Come, we have a busy day tomorrow. It is time for rest."

"You two like each other, Uncle Alfraed."

"I think it is respect. He is a fine warrior but I do not like the way he rules. It is not honest."

"Then when I am king I shall be honest and rule so that I have your approval."

"Is that important?"

He nodded, "It is to me." He looked up at me. "Earl, could I be your squire? I mean while we are in England can I be attired as Richard and Gilles? It will be safer for me and I could learn to be a warrior. I know that I have much to learn. My father does not take me to war but you can. You will keep me safe."

He was right. He would be safer wearing my livery and masked with a helmet. He would not be sought out in battle. They would come for me. If you wished to hide a valuable sword then you place it among other swords.

I nodded, "But if you are squire to me then you obey me and my commands." He nodded. "I will instruct Richard on the morrow. He will be your tutor."

We left early the next day. The leaves were falling, the wind was blowing and the land was muddy. In Anjou, you barely noticed autumn, here it was a warning of what was to be unleashed by winter which roared in like a wolf. I had used more of my precious ransom gold to buy horses for us all. It was a wise investment. The war had quietened down of late but it would flare up again. Now was the time to buy horses for they were cheaper. We bought enough sumpters to carry armour, weapons, arrows and supplies. Bristol had plenty; who knew what we would find at Devizes.

We found barely twenty men at arms and no archers. Miles of Gloucester commanded those along with half a dozen of his knights. I could not believe how poorly prepared they were.

The Empress burst into tears when we approached. I think there would have been tears for any of a dozen reasons but the combination of her son, me and the fact that the war was close to being lost made the iron lady break. It made Henry run to her to comfort her. "It is fine mother, your champion is here now. The war will change. We have the Warlord of the North with us!"

Miles clasped my arm, "It is good that you are here!"

"Where are the rest of our forces?"

He waved a hand, "Wallingford, Gloucester, Bristol and Oxford; it is all that we hold."

"Where is Reginald, Earl of Cornwall?"

He looked at me and then the Empress, "Come Henry, I will show you your new quarters."

My squires knew when to show discretion and they led my men and Henry Fitz Empress to the upstairs chambers glad to be away from the wind, the rain and the chill atmosphere.

We walked into the antechamber of the Great Hall and I closed the door for privacy. The Empress had her head bowed, "I did not know you would come."

I shook my head, "The sun will rise, the moon will set and if I say I will return with your son then I will do so." Her tone and her body told me that she had done something which she knew would annoy and anger me. "What have you done?"

I realised that I was talking to my ruler but to me, she was the woman who had stolen my heart. We both knew that she had done something she should not have done. She raised her head and jutted her jaw, "We thought you dead! Word came from Normandy that you had been badly wounded."

"I was wounded but those who spread those lies are those who support Eustace of Boulogne the Usurper's son. What have you done?"

"The Earl of Cornwall is with the Bishop of Winchester. He is arranging an exchange of my brother for Stephen."

I sat down. My knee ached but, more importantly, I saw now that the war which was close to being ended would now last until Henry was a man.

She saw my despair and put her hand on my shoulder. I felt her fingers squeeze. "I thought it for the best. We need Robert!"

"No, my lady, you need men who are resolute and keep their heads: Brian Fitz Count, Miles of Gloucester, me! You do not need your brother. We sacrificed our greatest prize for..."

"For my brother! He is the son of the king as am I!"

I closed my eyes as I tried to come up with a plan which might still regain the throne for the Empress. I found none.

Her hand stroked my hair, "Alfraed, I thought you were gone."

I opened my eyes, "In your heart did you?"

She shook her head, "No, you are right. In my heart, I knew that you lived yet." She smiled. "You are clever. There must be a way out of this."

"We need to leave Devizes tomorrow! As soon as the exchange is made Queen Matilda and William of Ypres will send horsemen to capture you and your son! This is no place to hold off an enemy. I should not have brought him! Had I known what you intended I would have stayed in Normandy and kept our son safe!"

For the first time ever there was anger in my voice and Maud recoiled. My father's voice came into my head. I was losing my temper and he had told me that was always the way to failure.

"I am sorry. That was wrong of me. Tomorrow we go to Oxford. It is strong and easy to defend. The garrison is loyal and I have sent for my men." She brightened, "But I fear you will never be crowned. This was our only chance and London will support Stephen, they always have. We must now work to make your son King. You need to let your supporters know that we now fight for Henry and not the Empress."

She nodded and then said, "What about my brother?"

The mention of Robert set my blood to boil once more. "I do not give a fig for your brother! I care for England and Henry! He will be King of England or I will die ensuring that he does!" I realised I was shouting for Margaret and Judith, her two women, burst in.

"The Earl is just becoming a little over-excited. Prepare our bags we leave tomorrow morning."

They nodded and backed out. Once alone she put her arms around me and buried her face in my chest. "I am lucky that my father entrusted you with my life so long ago. I know I am a trial."

"We must plan how to raise an army to fend off our foes. Winter draws on and campaigning will be hard." In my mind, I knew that was not true. We had fought the battle at Lincoln in February. If a leader was determined then he would find a way to fight. My only hope lay in a paucity of numbers. The enemy had lost many men at Lincoln and we had at Winchester. The only sizeable numbers lay in my castle at Stockton. I dared not bring them all for that would open the gates to the Scots and they would tear my home apart. I had to keep that safe. If disaster struck again we had somewhere we could use as a refuge.

The Empress sighed, "I have to tell you that I have come to an arrangement with King David of Scotland. There is peace between us."

I knew then that the day could not get any worse. "Then, for the first time since I became a knight I must disobey you for there is no peace between the Scots and me so long as they hold one hide of England."

Before she could answer there was a knock at the door and Margaret put her head through, "We have food in the Great Hall, my lady. Perhaps it will put the Earl in a better mood. He is obviously not himself."

I smiled. Margaret was loyal to the Empress and she was reprimanding me for my outburst. "You are right, Margaret; I was rude earlier. I am sorry."

As I stood there was a twinge of pain in my leg. I winced. The Empress grabbed my arm, "You are wounded!"

"It aches that is all. I have been travelling. It is nothing."

Miles, my squires and Henry looked up as we entered. The Constable of Gloucester had known what my reaction would be to the news. I could not believe that he was happy about it. They had left two seats for us between Henry and Miles of Gloucester. When we were seated I turned, "We must leave tomorrow. This castle is too close to the enemy and too small to defend."

"Where do we go, my lord?"

I leaned in and said quietly, "Oxford." He nodded. During the meal, I told him of the perfidy of Stephen of Azay and the trap into which we had nearly fallen. "So you see the war which could have been over in Normandy now limps on to another year and I cannot see the end of the one in England. It took years to bring Stephen to battle and to capture him and now he is free. Perhaps I should have slain him in battle."

Miles shook his head, "Regicide is a heinous sin, my lord. It would deny you heaven."

He was right but it did not stop me from thinking that I might have ended the war had I slain him in combat.

I spoke with Griff of Gwent and James the Stout as we prepared to ride to Oxford. "I know it goes against your natures but we need to watch our allies until we are certain that they are on our side. I trust those we brought from Anjou. If you suspect any then let me know and I will deal with them."

"We will, lord."

I mounted the horse which the castellan had provided. It was a good horse but it was not mine. I was wearing my repaired mail for the first time since the battle. It felt oddly heavy. I knew that I would need it. My shield hung over my cantle and protected my left knee. I now had a weak side. I would need to build up my muscles over the winter. An enemy soon learned your weaknesses and used them against you.

I rode with Miles and my squires guarded Henry. Despite the objection of the knights who accompanied us I had my six men at arms guarding the Empress and her ladies. I cared not for the delicacy of their feelings. I seemed to be the only one who knew the dangers we faced. It was fifty miles, no more and yet the half-day journey seemed to take forever. I had thought we had reached safety when I spied the distant towers of the castle. It was but six miles away.

Robert of Derby had been tasked with ensuring that we were not being followed. He suddenly galloped up, "My lord, there are knights following. They ride hard and they follow a Flemish banner!"

William of Ypres led Flemish warriors.

"Sir Miles, take my men at arms and escort the ladies to Oxford. Richard, guard Henry. Gilles, you come with me." I turned to the knights, "Now we shall see your mettle. We will meet these warriors and bloody their noses! Are you with me?"

"Aye, my lord!"

Henry opened his mouth to object and Richard snapped, "If you wish to be the Earl's squire then obey him in all things!"

I whipped around the head of the borrowed horse. I would have preferred a horse I knew but this one would do. I left my shield hanging. I would pull it up when we went into combat. The six knights I led were young and all came from Gloucester. The fact that they had escorted the Empress from the rout at Winchester told me that they were not reckless and would obey orders but as that was their only battle it did not say much for their skills. My archers who followed us and the ten men at arms from Gloucester were my only support if the knights failed. I glanced at Gilles. He was no longer the half-trained son of an archer. He had fought in the line and slain knights. I could rely on him.

This was not a Roman road over which we travelled but one built in the time of King Alfred. It was not straight and only had ditches in places. Had the leaves not fallen from the trees in the recent storms then we might have stumbled upon the column of knights but Robert of Derby had sharp eyes and he shouted, "Lord! They are four hundred paces away!"

I pulled up my shield, ignoring the pain in my shoulder, and drew my sword. The six knights had lances and they couched them. Gilles carried my banner in his left hand behind his shield and he carried a sword. I hoped that the sight of my banner might unnerve the enemy. If the Empress had thought me dead then it might come as a shock to the enemy.

"Griff, have the archers support us. Go for their horses!"

A knight without a horse could neither fight us nor follow us. We were not seeking glory, I just wanted to get the Empress to Oxford! As we came around a bend in the road and through a small stand of trees I saw them. There were forty of fifty men at arms and knights. Robert's cry had given us an advantage and I would not lose it. "Charge!"

I held my sword before me and, along with Gilles, we led the six knights and ten men at arms into the mailed wall of men. In the initial contact, my shield and my horse unhorsed one knight and my sword hacked into the arm of a second

71

who was slow to pull up his shield. As the ones at the rear began to react to the danger arrows fell like raindrops amongst them. I saw horses, pierced by arrows, rearing and flailing their hooves. Our sudden attack had caught them napping. We plunged through their column. A large Flemish man at arms brought his sword around to smash into my shield. Normally I would have stood in my stirrups and brought my sword down on his head. My weak knee prevented that and, instead, I whipped around my horse's head to the left and brought my sword around into the middle of his back. It tore through his mail and into his flesh. Hanging on to his reins the warrior headed away from me.

I saw an opportunity. The warrior's flight created a hole in the enemy lines and I exploited it. "Follow me!" I wheeled back through the enemy ranks. The backs of the men at arms and knights were now to us. As they turned they put their formation into further chaos. I stabbed through the gap between coif and helmet to end the life of one knight and then we were through. I glanced around and saw that four knights and six men at arms still followed me. The road was littered with the bodies of horses and men.

"Griff! Hold them awhile and then follow."

"Aye, lord!"

As we cantered down the road I shouted, "Well done! You have saved the Empress' life this day!"

One young knight, Ralph of Cirencester, shouted, "Aye and we have ridden with the Warlord too!" They cheered. Here were four knights I could trust. It was a start!

Chapter 7

We passed beneath Oxford's walls and headed for the castle. Surrounded by water and only accessible over a double bridge and a barbican, this was a strong castle. Sir Robert D'Oyly was pleased to see my banner as we rode through his gates. He rushed to greet us. I had persuaded him to defect to us a year since and he had loyally held this crucial castle since then. As the gates slammed behind us I breathed a little easier. These walls were more secure than those of Devizes. Once we were safe we sent messengers to tell the Empress' supporters where we were. I would have to rely on my ship to take the news north. The enemy knew and there was little reason to hide. If Oxford could not be defended then the war was over.

At the end of October, we received news that the exchange had been arranged and made by Reginald of Cornwall and the Bishop of Winchester. It would take place in November. On the last day of the month, a column of horsemen was spied approaching down the Leicester road. The garrison was stood to but it was just Dick and his archers. They had received my summons. It meant I could send my Angevin archers and men at arms back to Leofric. I had felt guilty, having deprived him of the best warriors. I said farewell to them and they headed down the road to Bristol. With Brian, Padraig and the others dead, Leofric had just my archers who were English. Would he become Angevin as my son had become Norman?

With Dick and his conroi, I now had the finest archers in England and the most dependable men at arms. I could face our enemy. *'Adela'* had docked again at Bristol and was waiting for my men so that they could return to Anjou and my ship could trade once more. If I was to fight on I needed finances to do so. War is expensive!

"What news from Stockton, Dick?"

"The Scots have become increasingly active since your departure, lord. They raided the lands around Appleby a month since. Sir Hugh sent a message that many families had been enslaved and villages destroyed. There is a new constable at Carlisle. He is related to the Mormaer of Athol. He is young and seems to wish to impress Prince Henry, his liege lord. Sir Edward sends patrols to the north to keep them at bay but it is wearing. Wulfric is all for attacking them and putting them in their place but Sir Edward holds him in check. He finds it too peaceful at Pickering. We are awaiting your return, lord."

There was just the faintest hint of criticism in Dick's voice. I understood it. I had been away for far too long. "Wulfric is right as is Edward. If I was there I would lead our men and bloody the Scots' noses however so long as the situation here is as it is then I will agree with Sir Edward."

We were alone and we could talk. "The land is restless, lord. As I came south I saw many new castles being built."

That was ominous although I had done it myself. If there was a king then you sought his approval. While Stephen had been in captivity there was no king and the new castles which had proliferated would be a problem I would have to deal with. "When the Earl of Gloucester returns then we shall plan our campaign. We are weak but the enemy must be as weak as we."

"Aye, lord, but my men and I will be glad for a week or two of rest. We have been in the saddle almost daily since April. I fear our horses are as weary as we are."

"Then we will get more. I still have ransom gold from Normandy and gold from Count Geoffrey. He was generous."

While the Empress fretted about her brother I went with Dick, my three squires and my men to procure horses. We bought up every mount within twenty miles of Oxford however that yielded us but ten. As we rode back with the last of them I said to Dick, "If we cannot buy them then we will have to take them from our enemies."

Henry, who hung on our every word, asked, "Is that honourable, lord?"

"No, but it is both pragmatic and practical, Henry. We cannot prosecute the war without horses and if we cannot buy them then we take them. If we have them and the enemy do not then we are stronger."

Dick said, "Besides, my lord, if we take them from our foes we restrict the war that they can wage." My archer was aware that we were teaching a future king. His classroom was the back of a saddle.

The Earl of Gloucester and the other prisoners arrived at Oxford in the middle of November. He arrived on a stormy day which matched his stormy mood. His face was filled with anger. He was looking for a fight from the moment he arrived. Foolishly I gave him one. I regret it now but sometimes these things are meant to be. However, it could have resulted in disaster.

It was the sight of Henry which sparked the row, "What in God's name is he doing here? He should be in Anjou with his father. If Stephen captured him then the war would be truly over."

His mother bowed her head. It was up to me to defend her decision. "The Empress thought that he should be in the land he will rule eventually and I brought him. His father approves. If the clergy and the people will not accept Matilda as Queen then perhaps they will accept Henry as king."

His eyes narrowed, "But I see your fingers all over this, Cleveland! You see yourself as someone who can manipulate the boy! Is that why he wears your wolf?"

Henry, to his credit, stood up to his uncle, "I asked the Earl if I could be his squire! It was my choice and no one makes me do things I wish not to do."

"Quiet, boy, and speak when you are spoken to!"

"And you, Earl Robert, curb your tongue and give the man who will be your lord one day some respect!" I would not have my son spoken to like that.

"And who are you to speak thus to me?"

I was angry but it was a wave of cold anger. "I am the man who fought the Scots at the Standard and captured Stephen at Lincoln. I am the man who rescued the Empress at Devizes and helped her husband capture Mortain." I paused. "I am not the man who caused the rout of Winchester."

His hand went to his sword. I kept mine at my side. "I could have you killed for that!"

"Why? Are you king here or just the bastard son of one? A word of advice, Robert of Gloucester, either take your hand from your sword or I will draw mine and the exchange with Stephen will be a complete waste for you will lie dead!"

He glared at me for a moment. I saw that the Empress was white and the room was deadly silent. Without looking around I knew that Dick and his men had their weapons ready. I was not afraid. If violence broke out there would be but one winner. However, a battle between us would only harm the Empress and her cause.

He took his hand from his sword. He turned to Sir Richard D'Oyly. "I am your liege lord, D'Oyly, and I wish this man and his rabble ejected from this castle!"

Maud said, "We cannot fight amongst ourselves! We do the work of Stephen. You are both angry and have said that which should not have been said. Make peace for my sake."

I held out my hand, "For my part, I regret my hasty words. Take the hand of friendship."

The Earl of Gloucester kept his hands by his side, "D'Oyly! You heard my command or shall I strip you of this castle too?"

He turned to me, "I am sorry, Earl. I owe you much but..."

I nodded, "It is not your doing, Richard. Take care of the Empress for me. I know I can trust you." I stared at the Earl daring him to do something about my insult but he just stared back. "Let us go. We shall return north where there

76

are men I can trust. I am sorry to leave you, my lady, but you are quite correct a war only serves our enemies. When your brother has calmed then send for me and I will return." She nodded and I saw that she was crying. I turned to Henry, "Look after your mother, Henry."

He shook his head, "I am your squire, my lord, and I will follow your banner." He glared at his uncle, "Besides, I will be safer in your company!"

"No!" I saw Matilda's face and it was as though she had woken from some dreadful nightmare.

"I must, mother, and you are safe here. This castle is as strong as any. I will return a better and wiser youth for I can learn more from the Earl than I can here. Unlike my uncle, he knows how to win battles."

"Why you little..." The Earl moved his hand back to strike him.

My hand had my dagger at the Earl's throat in an instant, "Speak again and you shall lose your tongue! Gilles, take Henry and Richard and get the horses. Dick!"

"You can lower your sword, my lord."

I looked around and saw Henry Warbow and Ralph of Wales. Their taut bows were aimed at the Earl while Rafe and Long Tom were covering the others. Everyone knew the power of my archers' bows and no one moved. By the time we reached the outer bailey, the horses were ready and our chests were packed upon the spare horses we had bought.

My archers mounted and the Earl of Gloucester pointed at me. "I will not forget this insult, Cleveland!"

"Good for I want our parting to haunt you! You are sending away the only chance you have of defeating Stephen. I once followed you for I thought you a leader. I was wrong. You are self-centred and shallow. Your father was a true leader and he would be ashamed of you!"

He roared, "I shall kill you for that!"

"You may try but I suspect you will use the hands of others to do your dirty work. Farewell, my lady. You know where I shall be."

"Farewell; you are ever the Knight of the Empress. I will end this conflict. Take care of my son." Her voice sounded frail and weak against the wind and I left the woman I loved once more. I dug my spurs into the flanks of my horse and he leapt forward.

We were at Bicester before any dared speak with me. Dick asked, "Where to, my lord? The days are short and we have no tents."

"We push on to Lincoln. We will ride through the night." I turned to Henry, "You may regret your choice, young Henry, for this will be hard for even my most hardened veterans."

He nodded, "If you and your wounds can endure then so can I."

"Lincoln, lord?"

"Aye, Dick. It may be that I can persuade the vacillating Chester to remain in the camp of the Empress. I might salvage something from this disaster."

The road along which we travelled was the old Roman Road called the Fosse Way. The biggest obstacle we would have would be the castle at Leicester. It was not a large castle and the garrison belonged to Ranulf, Earl of Chester but I did not want to take any chances. It was dark when we passed by the castle and we skirted its walls so that none saw us. It was almost midnight when we reached Lincoln. I did not attempt to enter the town but rode, instead, to the main gates.

"Who goes there?"

"It is the Earl of Cleveland and I would have a conference with the Earl of Chester. Admit us."

"The watch is set and the Earl is not here. I will not wake the Countess!"

The ride had aggravated my leg and my shoulder and I was not in the best of humours. "I demand that you let us in."

"Demand away for..."

I recognised the voice straight away as, Maud, Countess of Chester shouted, "Robert, open the gates; now!"

As we rode beneath the gatehouse I glimpsed the cloaked figure of Maud approaching across the outer bailey. "I am sorry, Alfraed. My husband took the better men with him to London."

"London?"

"Aye, he goes to attend the coronation of Stephen and Matilda."

I was too late. "He changes sides again?" I dismounted and handed my reins to Gilles.

She took my arm and led me across the bailey, "Come into my hall. We will speak where it is warmer."

Her servants had banked the fire and we were struck by a wall of heat once the door to the Great Hall was shut. She looked questioningly at Dick and my squires, "You can speak before them besides this is Henry Fitz Empress. I think he has some interest in this conversation."

She smiled, "It is good to see you, my lord, and you are right. It does concern him. My husband is pragmatic. He attends the coronation but he does not yet side with Stephen. Does that make sense?"

"To me? No. But then I never understood your husband. Tell me, Maud, why do you stay with him?"

"He is my lord and...I know not." I saw her shake her head, "And how is my father?"

I would not lie to her, "We have had a falling out. He has threatened to kill me."

She laughed, "You two butt heads like Billy goats. You cannot have two such bulls in the same field. There can be only one. So, you return to Stockton?"

"Aye, we do. We will stay here tomorrow unless you feel it would be wrong."

"Of course not. I am happy for the company and I can get to know my cousin Henry here!"

It was a good decision. A November storm blew in from the north. A month later and it would have been filled with snow. As it was it was filled with sharp raindrops which chilled to the bone. My knee ached! Maud insisted that we stay another day and I was grateful. Dick took the opportunity to try to buy more horses. He managed to buy four and Maud sent her steward into the town to buy bolts of cloth for our surcoats. The battles and the seas had taken

79

their toll. When we reached Stockton then Alice would have to make new ones for my squires and me.

In the two days we were there Gilles and Richard took the opportunity of teaching Henry how to be a squire. They also gave him lessons with the sword. Both were accomplished swordsmen despite the fact that Gilles had had humble origins and Richard's training had been badly neglected by his lord. I could see that Henry would become proficient for he had a natural ability. It came through his mother's line and, I liked to think, through his father. If he was to ride with my men then he needed to be able to handle himself.

We left when the weather abated. Maud was a little tearful as we left. I think she was fond of me. I had known her since she had been a child. "Take care of yourself, Earl. Do not let your honour lead you to an early grave. Farewell, cuz. I look forward to the day that you are king."

"And when I am, cousin, I will not forget your kindness and your loyalty."

In times past we would have halted at York and enjoyed the hospitality of Archbishop Thurstan. The old man was now dead and the gates would be barred to us. I headed, instead, for Helmsley and Wulfric. We would travel to the east of York. It was less than a hundred miles and we could do it in daylight if we rode hard and changed horses.

It was no surprise to me that we were spotted not far from Malton. Wulfric controlled his land aggressively. His men did not wait for trouble; like their master, they sought it. William Longshank led the horsemen who met us, "A bitter day for a ride, my lord."

"Aye, and your fire will be all the more welcome. How goes it, William?"

"Quiet and that does not suit Sir Wulfric. He will be pleased to see you for he has been like a bear with a sore head without heads to cleave. Your return makes that more likely."

I remained silent. It would be best if my news were given directly to Wulfric.

His hall was not huge but it suited him for he was unmarried and had no household knights. He normally

80

shared his table with some of his men at arms but that night he dined with Dick and our squires. As we ate I told him all from the victory at Mortain to the rout of Winchester.

He shook his head sadly, "Brian and Padraig and the others had a good death but it is sad that so many of our old comrades are gone. It seems that apart from Wilfred and Dick here, there is just Sir Edward and me left from the beginning of this adventure."

"I am afraid so. My men at arms are growing smaller in number."

"So, lord, we are alone?"

Henry piped up, "We have my father's armies in Normandy!"

Wulfric smiled but Gilles flashed an angry look at him. Squires, even of royal lineage, kept silent before their betters.

"It is worse than that, Wulfric. The Empress has made peace with the Scots. When we fight them we disobey her. I will truly be a warlord, beholden to none."

For some reason that seemed to please him. "All the better. There are no rules when it comes to fighting the Scots. It is a pity winter is upon us else we could punish them this year!"

"We are banished until the Empress can send for us. We build our forces up until spring and then we ride to war." I had spent the journey north brooding about the losses at Appleby. I was angry and I wished to punish someone. It would be the Scots.

Wulfric insisted upon escorting us up through the valleys of the Cleveland hills to our home. "I have killed many bandits and brigands, lord, but there are always more. They are like fleas on a dog. I am surprised that the monks at Fountains Abbey and Rievaulx are not bothered more. We visit them to make sure that they are safe but they seem to like their isolation."

"The brigands fear hell. The Scots do not mind slaying monks but homegrown bandits do."

Stockton was like a welcoming beacon as we waited by the river for Ethelred and the ferry. We were home. As we stepped aboard I saw that it was new and larger. "You have invested in a new ferry, Ethelred?"

He grinned, "It is worth the investment, lord. Many people use this for it saves a long journey west. Besides, I did not waste the old one. I can use that too."

December proved to be a cold, harsh month. It was a rude welcome to the north for young Henry who had been brought up in balmy Anjou where even the worst winter was like a cool day in a Stockton summer. He was made to feel welcome by all and there was so much for him to learn. Edgar and his brother, along with Aiden taught him about animals and hunting. Aiden took my three squires out each day to give them skills. It was good training for a knight and they were as safe in Aiden's hands as any. I had much to contend with in my castle. There were cases to be heard and John, my steward, had a long list of jobs he wished me to undertake and complete. I was also aware that my castle needed improvement. I had my mason, William, build new warrior quarters attached to the west wall.

Those tasks completed, I visited with Alf and the people of my town. I confided in Alf for I trusted him. He had to know that we were now a rebel kingdom even within England. He was pleased to see me. He felt like we were now related for his daughter had married Sir John of Stockton, one of my household knights. I told him of the setbacks. I had learned that honesty paid.

"It will pass, lord. Even here we have heard of Lincoln, Winchester and Mortain. We know that we have had victories and we have had reverses. We know that Stephen will be crowned King once more. Here, in your valley, we prosper still. Goods arrive and leave. We all grow richer. I now have six forges and they work every moment of each day. It is good that we have iron so close to us. More settlers come to our fertile valley and there is work for all those who come." He grinned, "And I am to be a grandfather. Sir John has strong seed in him. I feel it in my bones that it will be a boy!"

Speaking with Alf the Blacksmith was like taking a bath in warm feelings. I left his company feeling hopeful. With folk like that, we could not lose and it made me even more determined that the Scots would be sent packing. I could do nothing about Stephen and his Queen. The Earl of Chester would do what he wished but I could wage my war. When Spring came then we would ride forth with mail and fine horses. We would have more archers and men at arms. I might not be able to help the Empress but I could make up to my people for my absence. We would punish the Scots for their depredations. This new mormaer would be brought to book.

When the snows of January arrived we were trapped within our castle and town. The only news came from the *'Adela'*. The river had not frozen and so when William of Kingston arrived he was greeted with great joy for he brought spices, wine and other luxuries from Anjou. We had swords and weapons to send back to Leofric and my son but his greatest cargo was the news he brought. Stephen's coronation was confirmed as well as the rumour that he was travelling north to speak with Ranulf of Chester. I knew that meant the slippery Earl would be given a gift and he would change sides once more. When William left with my ship, at the end of the month I knew that we would be isolated for some time to come. Visitors and travellers were rare at the best of times. In winter they were nonexistent.

I took Henry to visit the manors close to Stockton. Barnard Castle was too far away in winter but the others were just an hour or two away. I had not seen Sir Richard of Yarm since he had lost his hand and I was unprepared for his appearance and the deterioration in his health. It was as though his spirit had been removed along with his hand. Lady Anne was also grey. But they brightened when they met the future king. They saw it as a great honour to their humble home. Yarm was still a wooden castle. It was a throwback to the time of the first Normans who came north but it was their home and it was safe enough.

I had taken Sir Tristan with me and as we left I asked, "Why did you not tell me of the change in your father?"

"I am sorry, lord. I hope, each time I visit, that he will be his old self but he is always worse. He is growing old and now he cannot be a warrior he sees no purpose in life."

Even though he did not know Sir William the visit visibly upset Henry. "Your father was hurt fighting for me and my mother."

"He was."

"So we are to blame for his condition?"

I stopped Rolf and looked at Henry, "You cannot think like that. You will be the anointed king. If you worry about those warriors who might be hurt fighting for you then you would never go to war. A king has to make hard choices. I also have to make difficult decisions, even Sir Tristan here does. It comes with the responsibility of being a knight. A king just has more responsibility. You need to think about the men you lead but you cannot worry that they will live or die. If you have made the right plan then more of them will live than perish in your cause."

"I have much to learn."

"I think that is why your mother sent you here. On the frontier, it is a harsh world and lessons learned are clearer and easier to see."

My new mail was ready by February and so was Henry's. He was more excited about his hauberk than even my squires. I had paid for them both although Alf would have done it for nothing. Henry paraded around in it, obviously pleased with the effect.

"Thank you, smith. When I am king you shall make all of my mail."

"I would be honoured, sir."

"I would also like you to make me a sword. You made the Earl's did you not?"

"I did, sir."

"Then can you make me one too?"

"I could but you are not yet fully grown. You would barely get the benefit from it." Gilles and Richard were with me. "Young Master Gilles here he is about to have his first man's sword. I have been making it since he left for France.

When he goes to war this year he will have a fine blade but he has had to wait years for it."

"Then I will wait too." Another lesson was learned, patience.

We did not have many visitors but we received one a week or so after we had collected our mail. It was a priest from York. Although the new Archbishop was no friend of mine and, indeed, had been appointed by Stephen, there were still priests who had been close to us when Thurstan ruled. It was one such priest, Father Thomas. He rode an ass and was wrapped up against the cold wind. Father Henry brought him into my keep.

"Father Thomas has news, Earl. I believe you will wish to hear it."

Sir Tristan, Sir John and Sir Harold were in my hall and they leaned forward to hear the news. Any news was welcome but from a friend, it was doubly so.

"We are eager to hear what you have to say. Does the Archbishop know you are here?"

He smiled, "I was sent with a sealed message for Durham. I was one of Archbishop Thurstan's priests. I am not popular and the long ride north through this wintery land was a suitable punishment for siding with the venerable Archbishop. I mind not for the ride helps me to think and to contemplate."

"Your news?"

"King Stephen is ill. Some say he is close to death!"

The news was both unexpected and shocking. "How?"

"He became unwell and then a fever took over. Some say he contracted the disease in Bristol Castle. There are rumours that the Empress poisoned him."

"That is a lie!"

Father Thomas looked up in surprise at Henry's outburst. I smiled, "You will have to forgive my squire. He is still learning but it is understandable for the Empress is his mother. However I agree with him, the Empress would never stoop to such an act. It is more likely the damp conditions in his quarters."

"What does this mean, lord?"

85

"It means, Gilles, that perhaps God is on our side but so long as Stephen lives it cannot affect us. Thank you for your news, Father Thomas. The roads north of here are dangerous. Sir Harold and a company of my men at arms will escort you to Durham and bring you back here."

"Is that not dangerous for your men? I would not wish them to come to harm on my account."

Sir Harold laughed, "The winter has been dull. For our sake, I hope something interesting happens on the journey!"

By Easter, we had heard no more and preparations were underway for our spring offensive. I sent Aiden down to York for news. He was able to mix with those in the city and pick up the news. When he returned he told us that the Usurper had worsened and might die. Henry was torn when he heard the news. Stephen was his cousin and he wished that he was no longer king but, like me, the thought of death by disease did not seem right for a warrior. We delayed our proposed attack on Carlisle. If the King died then, summons or not, I would head south and see that the Empress or her son was crowned this time. I would take every knight and man at arms to ensure that it happened. If the Earl of Gloucester objected then I cared not.

When Aiden returned I sent him, Edward and Edgar to the west to spy out the land around Carlisle. We had fought there before but if this new constable was determined to impress then he might have made changes to his defences. My intent was not to reduce Carlisle. That was a costly business as Carlisle was built of stone and had a river and a moat to defend it. Instead, we would ride north of the Eden and Esk rivers. The land which lay beyond the Roman Wall in the west was Scottish. I would reduce the castles there.

It was William of Kingston who brought the news, in early May, that Stephen the Usurper had recovered and was now in good health. My feelings were mixed but it meant that we could not do as I had wished. I could not return to the Empress. I was still a banished knight and without a lord. We could go to war.

The Borders 1242

North

Berwick

Bamburgh

Jedburgh

Alnwick

Warkworth

Otterburn

Elsdon

Morpeth

Bellingham

Ponteland

Newcastle

Hautwesel

Prudhoe

Carlisle

Alston

Durham

Barnard Castle

Stockton

12 miles

Griff 2019

Chapter 8

We headed west towards Carlisle. Sir William had stayed on his manor. He could not fight and I needed his men to watch my valley. All the rest accompanied me save Erre and his men at Norton. With Sir Phillip and Sir Richard, I had two companies of archers who could decide any battle for me. Sir Wulfric and Sir Edward had men at arms who were the equal of mine and we had a force which, thanks to our horse breeding and purchases, were all mounted with fifty remounts. I intended to shock the Scots and show them that the peace treaty meant nothing. Each castle had a small garrison left to defend it and I had ponies and young boy riders ready to fetch me in case Prince Henry of Scotland took it upon himself to attack us in the east.

My knights were all in good spirits. Those who had seemed young once, like John, Harold and Tristan were now full-grown men with children. Some would ride to war with us as squires. One of Sir Edward's sons, John, would be ready for his spurs in a year or so. He carried his father's banner. Sir Edward was very proud of him.

When we reached Barnard Castle we would collect Sir Hugh's men and I would be leading the largest number of men I had yet commanded alone against the Scots. Here I did not need to ask permission or to seek approval. I did not have to worry about the delicacies of position, authority or feelings. I was a warlord and I made such decisions. If I had the same power further south then Stephen would still lie in Bristol!

On the journey across the old Roman Road, Henry Fitz Empress was assaulted by questions. He was the grandson of a king. Most of my knights and their families were low born. Henry seemed to have been born in a rarefied atmosphere. His mother was named Empress. They asked question after question. I was going to intervene and silence them when Gilles said, "I would not interfere, lord. If you do he will be seen as being different. He wishes to be a squire and learn as the others do. This way they will be satisfied and he will be accepted. When you go into battle he and the other squires will have to work as one. Besides he has as many questions for them. He will cope."

I smiled, "You have grown wise, Gilles." I followed my squire's advice and soon the questions stopped and it was Henry's turn to ask questions of them. Some of the answers surprised him for not all of my knights were surrounded by servants, slaves and vast halls. Gilles of Normanby had only recently been knighted and his squire, Henry too, had been the son of a swineherd killed by Sir Edward Mandeville's men in a raid. Their conversation was illuminating for all of them.

We camped outside Barnard Castle. The knights and squires were housed in the huge keep there. It was the first time we had all been gathered together as one mailed family. It was a large gathering. With nine knights and eleven squires, we filled the hall with both bodies and noise. The healer we would take with us, Father James also joined us and he blessed the food before we ate. I saw and listened and watched. These men would be fighting for me and it was at times like this that I learned more about them. They had, with one or two exceptions, been squires first and they were still growing into their role as a knight.

Sir Hugh told us in more detail of the attacks. They had been deliberate, brutal and in force. Sir Hugh used, like all of us, those men who lived by the lonely ways, as scouts. They had huts in the forests and raised their families there. They had been slain and their families slaughtered before they could warn us. Then bands of men had attacked the small villages and isolated farmsteads at the same time. They had not burned them for that would have alerted Sir Hugh but the men had been slaughtered and dismembered while the women and children along with the animals had been driven into captivity. It was only a chance patrol by some of Sir Hugh's men which had stopped them emptying the land of the English. Sir Hugh had chased shadows all the way to the Eden valley. The one they had slain had been a Scot and wore the surcoat of Moray. It confirmed that they were Scots.

When he had finished I stood. "I know the Empress has signed a peace treaty but we cannot let this raid go unpunished. If we do so then they will return and encroach further east. We will hurt them so badly that they do not even think of a return." I looked down at Henry. "That may not be until my new squire becomes king but it will happen!"

He nodded firmly and my men banged the table and chanted. Their faces told me all that I needed to know. They were resolute. I looked around the table at my loyal band of brothers. The youngest knight was Gilles of Normanby. He had been Sir Edward's squire. Serving with Wulfric he kept the south of the Tees safe. Wulfric and Edward, in contrast, were now both grey. They had been men at arms and had served with me the longest. They were the most experienced of my knights. Dick and Sir Philip were my archer knights while the rest, Tristan, Harold, Hugh and John had all served as squires together. The four of them were more like brothers than any brothers I had ever met. I enjoyed listening to them.

Sir Harold turned to me. "Lord, you are quiet this night. Does something lie on your mind?"

"No, Harold, I am just enjoying the company of men that I can trust. It has been rare of late. Here men speak what is in their hearts. I have missed this."

Sir Edward asked, "Why did the Empress make peace with the Scots, lord?"

The room became silent. I was acutely aware that Henry Fitz Empress was watching my face and listening for my words. I had just told Harold that men could speak what was in their hearts. I had to do the same.

"I was not with her when she made the peace. The Earl of Gloucester was. I think that the north is far from Gloucester. It was a political act intended to put pressure on Stephen's forces in York. Sometimes these decisions and sacrifices have to be made."

"But you would not have done so, would you, lord? You do not bend. You have a vision and you try to shape the world around you to that vision. My great grandfather was the same."

I looked at the Empress' son. His words were more mature than other boys his age. The main difference between him and the other squires was his education. He could read well and had access to books. He had had tutors and could understand complicated arguments. He was no cleverer than the other squires but he was better educated. It showed.

"No, Henry, I would not have made the treaty. King David pretends to be thinking of your mother's interests. He is a relation but if he was thinking of your mother he would not try to take pieces of England. If he attacked York, even if he said it was to rid England of Stephen the Usurper, he would keep what he took. He took Carlisle and the land south of the Wear. He is like a disease and it is spreading south, insidiously. The problem is that England is ruled from London and Winchester. They are far to the south and they do not bother overmuch with what happens here. It is seen as a wild and dangerous land with little profit. They are happy to let the dogs of war nibble pieces from the carcass of the north. We do not grow much wheat here and the manors are poorer. To them, it matters not."

"Yet my great grandfather conquered as far as the Clyde and the Forth."

"He was a great warrior and your grandfather was embroiled in the wars against your paternal grandfather, Fulk. When you are king you will need to keep a close watch on all of your land. You watch your borders. That is where the enemy will try to take pieces of your lands and encroach, insidiously. Use strength to guard them and your heartland will have peace. You need castles like Oxford, Wallingford and Stockton. When England and Normandy are yours you will have a larger Empire than any save the Byzantine Emperor. Think about that!"

My men began banging the table with their daggers and chanting, "Henry! Henry!" It was at that moment that the future king was truly born. He was going to war and, for the first time, it was to reclaim England. He nodded at me and I saw the resolution and steel in his eyes.

We had the finest of scouts with us. Aiden and his men had already reported that there were new castles appearing along the Esk. They were made of wood and earth but there were many of them. From what I gathered from his news they were trying to do as I had done and have castles less than ten miles from each other so that they could give mutual support. Malcolm mac Athol was not to be dismissed because of his youth. Others had made that mistake with me. We were heading for a new castle in the middle of the line. Arthuret lay on the south side of the Esk and guarded the bridge there. I intended to surprise the garrison with a dawn attack while I swam horses across the river to prevent news of our attack reaching Carlisle. Once I held the bridge and the castle we would sweep through the hinterland. I intended to draw Malcolm mac Athol into battle where I would use my archers to destroy his army. I could not reduce Carlisle but I could stop his men from raiding. My other intention was to gather as many animals as I could. Now that we were isolated we had to increase our herds of horses, cattle and sheep. This would be the easiest way.

If we could have travelled the way the crow flies it would have been a journey of no more than sixty or so miles, less than half a day for we were all mounted. As it was we would have to travel the greenways and valleys. Until we reached the wall which the Romans had built the largest place where we might find some Scots was Aldeneby. The Baron Veteriponte ruled there but I had never met him. On the way there we passed through small villages and hamlets. Middleton had been ravaged by the Scots on their recent attack and was a pitiful sight to behold. Sir Hugh's men had buried the dead but the burned out buildings were testament to the ferocity of the Scottish attack. They had been shocked at the bodies they had found.

The road passed along the valley sides and we were hidden from view. Aiden rode back as we halted some four miles from the small manor of Aldeneby. "Lord, there is a small garrison at the manor. There is no motte."

"How many men?"

"Ten, perhaps twelve."

"Is there a way to get around the hall and approach unseen?"

Aiden nodded, "The river is wooded and shallow. I could lead your archers thence."

I waved Dick forward. "Take your archers and go with Aiden. Take the hall."

"Aye lord."

I dismounted, "Feed and water the animals."

Henry would have to get used to this. We looked after our mounts and carried grain with us. Although they would eat grass when they halted we also made sure they had grain too. I heard Richard say, "Come, Henry, let us fetch water from the river."

"Why can we not lead the horses there?"

He laughed, "Because we are squires and that is our task."

When the horses had been watered we mounted and headed along the road. I had given Dick enough time to get into position and begin his attack. As we crested the rise I could hear the sounds of men dying and people fleeing. A family ran straight at us. As soon as they saw my banner they cowered before us. Behind I saw the bodies of the garrison. All had been slain by arrows.

Others joined those whose flight had been stopped by our arrival. One man with a withered arm said, "Spare us, Warlord! We are poor people."

"I know and you will be spared but you cannot stay here in Aldeneby. You have a choice. Return to Scotland and ask King David for protection."

"We are not Scottish!" he held up his withered arm. "I was hurt at the Battle of the Standard."

I nodded, "Then head south. The Scots ravaged and emptied the village close to Barnard Castle. Sir Hugh is the Lord of the Manor. If you farm there then we will give you protection. You have my word."

I spurred Rolf. They would debate and they would argue. Some would take me up on my offer and others would not. Life on the frontier was hard and the decisions you made could be fatal. My archers had already collected the weapons and the three horses which were there. I could see that it had been a sergeant at arms and eleven men who had protected the manor. Of the lord and his family, there was no sign.

"Burn it!"

Sir Hugh said, "But, lord, that will tell them where we are! I thought we came in secret."

"By the time they spy the fire we will be north of the wall. If it draws some of the garrison of Carlisle here then so much the better. The folk who are here will tell them where we have gone. We move swiftly. Let us ride!"

My archers set about setting fire to the hall. The huts and farms would be unharmed. If any chose to stay there I would not harm them but they had had a warning. As we headed towards the Roman Wall Henry asked, "Was that manor in England or Scotland, Warlord?"

"It was England but your cousin, Stephen, gave it to the Scots. Until you are King it will remain Scottish."

He was silent. Wondering, I have no doubt if he would ever become king. It seemed that too many others were making their best efforts to deny him that opportunity. We reached the wall just after dusk. We headed for the Roman fort close to the deserted farmstead of Gilstad. There were water and walls. More importantly, it was just a short ride to Arthuret.

Henry had never campaigned in England. He had stayed in castles and manor houses with his mother. This was a rude awakening for him. Sleeping on the hard cold ground this far north was never pleasant. Gilles came from Normandy and he showed Henry how to use his cloak and horse blanket to make an improvised bed. He pointed to the other squires who put their blankets close together so that they would be warmer. He would learn.

I sat with my knights as we planned our campaign. "How many men were there in the raiding party, Sir Hugh?"

"It was hard to tell, lord. We cut their trail and counted forty horses but that could have been just men at arms. We caught none alive."

I noticed Wulfric shaking his head. He was thinking that he would have caught at least one and made them talk. The trouble was Sir Hugh was clinging on to his part of England which was closer now to Scotland than anywhere else. He was not as aggressive a lord as Sir Wulfric. I knew we had to get the border back to the wall, hold that, and then push on further north. The days when we had held Hexham, Norham and Morpeth were a distant memory.

"Then we cannot know the size of the garrison at Carlisle."I waved Aiden over, "Tomorrow, Aiden, I would have you scout Carlisle. I need to know the numbers of knights and men at arms there."

"Would you wish me to enter the walls, lord?"

"There will be little to be gained by such a risk. Just rough numbers will do."

Sir Gilles had not been in this part of the world before. "And Arthuret, lord, what can we expect there?"

We had attacked it once before but that was some years earlier. "It may be that they have built a castle there but if so it will be wooden and not stone. We use speed." I nodded to Wulfric, "I think Sir Wulfric here wishes to hack his way through the wooden walls anyway."

Wulfric nodded, "Wooden walls are no match for my axe and the lads I have are handy with them too. So long as Sir Dick and Sir Philip keep them from the fighting platform on the walls then we shall get us in." He sniffed, "I think it will be poor returns though for these border Scots have little worth taking."

Sir Edward who knew Wulfric as well as I did, smiled, "I think the Earl knows that, old friend, which is why he hopes to draw the enemy from Carlisle on to our spear points."

"Sir Edward is right. Even without a castle, we can use the natural defences of the river and the town to make it a killing ground. My aim with this raid is to make the enemy bleed and to take his horses and mail."

I sent Dick's scouts out before dawn. We had fifteen miles to go. Although there were few roads the land was forgiving. It rolled gently to the west. We rose mailed and ready for war. Henry had asked if he could carry the standard into battle. Richard had chided him, "When you have been to war and seen how I carry it then we shall see. I watched Gilles many times before I was ready."

"But what is there to it?"

Gilles laughed, "You carry your standard and shield as well as your reins in your left hand. You ride your horse with your knees. When the banner blows into your face so that you cannot see and you are attacked we will see just then how easy it is. Watch Richard. Holding the standard is a vital task. If it falls then the army loses heart. You have to be where the Warlord goes. It is a sign of our success or failure in battle. If it goes deep into the enemy ranks we are winning and if it quits the field then we have lost. If Richard falls then your task will be to take up the standard and stay by our lord."

Suitably chastened he rode in silence and I smiled. I had never carried the standard but Wulfstan had often taken me to task for something I had done which displeased him. In the end, it paid off. You learned not to make mistakes.

The scouts returned as dawn broke. "They have a ditch and a palisade, lord."

"A castle?"

"I would not call it one. Rolf could jump the wall in one bound. It is on this side of the river. There are many cattle, pigs and sheep. They have built it up since last we were here. The river is very shallow. A man could ford it and keep his backside dry."

"Thank you, Ralph." I turned in my saddle, "Sir Wulfric, take your men and force the bridge. Sir Philip, have your men cover them. Sir Tristan, Sir John and Sir Harold take your men to the south and ford the river. Capture as many animals as you can. Sir Hugh and Sir Gilles, take your men north, ford the river and capture as many animals as you can."

"And do we stop the people fleeing?"

"Let the people go but slay any with weapons."

I pulled up my shield and loosened my sword as we cantered down the road. There was just Sir Edward, Sir Richard and myself left with our three columns of men. If things went awry we would be the reserve but I did not think it would. We rode at the rear so that I could view the castle and the river. As we crested the rise I saw the magnificent sight of three columns of mailed men charging towards the river and the castle. The two flanking columns were already splashing across the shallow Esk while Wulfric and his men reined in as Sir Philip and his archers dismounted and prepared to release their arrows. I think whoever commanded miscalculated for he looked only at the sixty men who had dismounted. He could not see the two flanking columns and we must have been too far away to see numbers. I saw men racing to the walls.

Even though Sir Philip only had twenty-two archers they were superb bowmen and the range was less than a hundred and fifty paces. I watched as five flights of arrows soared towards the gate and the walls. Where there had been a line of helmeted men holding spears there was now nothing. It was as though a wave had washed them away. Wulfric led his men across the bridge to the gate. As we closed with the walls I could hear the sounds of their axes striking the wood. They were thick timbers but Wulfric's men's axes were sharp.

I saw two riders leave by the rear gate. They might escape my men for the two columns were still sweeping around. It did not matter for I had planned for that. I heard a roar as the gate was shattered asunder and Wulfric and his wild warriors burst into the castle. There was a flood of men, women and children from the rear gate. Their route to safety was now barred by two lines of knights and men at arms. I just caught sight of swords slicing down and then they were hidden from me as we crossed over the bridge and into the castle. The garrison was slain. The townspeople and farmers who remained stood fearfully together.

I pointed to the damaged and open gate, "Go! I give you your lives and the clothes on your back! Any who remain here will be enslaved!"

There was hesitation and then Wulfric shouted, "Go!" They fled through the gate.

It took until afternoon for my men to return with captured cattle, horses, sheep and pigs. We slaughtered a heifer and a pig for our food and set sentries on the walls. There was little in the way of treasure and their granaries were empty but we found beans ready for sowing as well as much wool ready to be spun. Sir Harold discovered two carts.

I gathered my knights. "The constable of Carlisle may come tomorrow but I think he is more likely to scout tomorrow. He will not know our numbers. If he does come tomorrow then that will mean he is reckless and that is a good thing. Sir Gilles, I want you to take your men and load the two carts. Drive the animals, along with the captured supplies, back to Barnard Castle and then return here."

He looked disappointed. Wulfric, his mentor said, "Do not worry, Gilles, there is still fighting to be done. I promise you that."

"He is right. Tomorrow Sir Edward and I will see what other morsels are waiting for us to pick from them."

Aiden rode in late at night. He was smiling. "The hen house is full of activity this night, Warlord. I watched the people flee into the walls after your raid. The gates are barred and they await your attack. Those who passed me spoke your name as though you were the devil himself. They call you the wolf!"

"Good. That means they will not come tomorrow. And how many men?"

"It has a large number of men. The walls were filled with helmets and shields. I would say there are three hundred men within the walls. They sent riders north as soon as the first two horsemen reached the fortress."

"You have done well. Rest." Turning to my knights I said, "Then we have time to prepare for them. Sir Edward and I will ride north tomorrow. Sir Wulfric, take the rest of our men. There is a hill north of Carlisle. It is more of a knoll than a hill but it is less than a mile from the river and the castle. Two of its sides are protected by two small becks. We will wait in the lee of the hill. Do not array all our forces in plain view. Keep most hidden. Sir Edward and I may be able to intercept the reinforcements they have requested."

"You know how you will attack them, lord?"

My men all knew but then we had done this many times. Young Henry did not. "I do, Henry. We use the arrows from Sir Richard and Sir Philip to attack their flanks and keep them in the middle and then we charge with two lines of men. They will have the river at their back and a narrow bridge to safety. If I time the charge correctly then we can hurt them."

"And if they stay within their walls?"

"Then we will enjoy ourselves collecting animals and food from their farms. When we have taken all we will return home and they will starve."

Sir Edward nodded, "And that is why this Malcolm mac Athol will come forth. He showed, when he attacked Sir Hugh, that he is aggressive and wishes to make a name for himself. What better name than the knight who defeated the Warlord of the North?"

It was only eight miles to Carlisle and just over seven to the hill. Wulfric would have plenty of time to reach it. Gilles would be arriving at Barnard Castle even as Wulfric arrayed his forces and by the next day, he would be returned. We would have all our men available then. Sir Edward and I headed north. We would have no archers with us for I needed them to prepare their defences on the hill. It was not much of a hill but it had a slope and that was important. Dick and Sir Philip knew their business.

Taking our spears, we went northwest. I knew that there was a small settlement there. It had been Viking but now it was Scottish even though it retained its Viking name. Loc-hard's by was a prosperous place for there were many sheep and the wool spun there was considered valuable. It was seventeen miles away but if there was a relief force heading for Carlisle then it would use that road. Although I did not have archers I had Edgar and Edward. They were my eyes and ears ahead of us. We were five miles from Loc-hard's by when Edgar galloped in on his small horse. "Lord, there is a column of men. Half are on foot. They are two miles ahead. Edward is watching them."

"Do they have scouts?"

"No, lord, but they march close together as though they expect an ambush."

"How many men are there?"

"Forty on horses and forty on foot. We counted three banners."

I turned to Sir Edward. "This is a relief column for Carlisle. We ride at them. Edgar, is there a bend close by us?"

"Just over the rise, lord. It twists and rises up to this ridge."

"Then place yourself where you can signal when they are at the bottom of the slope and heading up." He turned and galloped up the road. "Gilles, watch for his signal."

"Aye lord."

"Wilfred and Theobald. You will ride next to me and Sir Edward. Gilles, you and the squires will form the rear rank."

Sir Edward said, "My son, John, is ready for the front rank. He will be on my right. That way we will fill the road." Sir Edward was keen for his son to be knighted. By giving him the chance to fight in the front rank he was giving him the opportunity to impress me.

We formed ourselves and waited for Gilles to shout. I had no idea where Edgar waited but Gilles could see him.

"Now, my lord."

I spurred Rolf and he began to head towards the crest. The Scots should have had scouts out but then they were used to my tricks and ambushes. Travelling in a solid column made ambush less effective. They could have a wall of shields ready in an instant. They would form a shield wall if we attacked with arrows. As we reached the top of the road I saw them a couple of hundred paces below us. They were halfway up the slope. It was not steep but they would

100

struggle to gain momentum. In contrast, we were galloping. I reined Rolf back a little so that we stayed in a straight line. We had to reach them together. Two arrows arced from the woods at the side of the road and found two bodies. The effect, however, was far greater than just two arrows. They thought it was an ambush rather than just my two scouts. They turned the spears on their right to face the woods. More importantly, the men on foot stopped moving.

I had not used a lance for some time and it felt a little unbalanced. I adjusted my grip as I approached the leading knights. I leaned forward as I pulled back my weapon. The Scots had not lowered their lances yet and there was confusion as they did so. We struck them when they were almost stationary. I punched my lance at the chest of a knight wearing a variation of the De Brus livery. Although he managed to get his shield up my blow was so powerful that it knocked him from the saddle. Rolf was a big horse and he shouldered aside the next two mounts. My spear struck a man at arms in the shoulder. The steel head of the spear penetrated his mail and threw him to the ground. The head broke off, embedded in his flesh. I threw the stump of the spear at the next man at arms and drew my sword. He flinched when the spear haft came towards him and I was able to slash down at him with my sword. It came away bloody and we were through the horsemen.

Men on foot who are not prepared are terrified of horsemen. I pulled back on Rolf's reins and stood a little. My horse reared and that was enough to make five men on foot try to flee. It was too late for two of them. His mighty hooves crushed their skulls. As the blood, brains and bone spattered the others Sir Edward and my men at arms arrived. It proved the final straw and the men on foot fled.

I whipped Rolf's head around, "Finish the horsemen!"

I could not see John of Thornaby but my men at arms and Sir Edward were still with me. The Scottish horsemen who were still mounted were beset on all sides. I saw Gilles and Richard fighting one knight while Henry was as close to me as he could. Sir Edward was flailing around with his sword like a Viking Berserker. He seemed oblivious to the blows being rained upon him. He was in danger of being too reckless and I spurred Rolf towards him. I stood in my stirrups and brought my blade down on the back of one of his enemies. He arced and then fell to the ground. As Sir Edward took the head of a second the last four knights held their swords by the blades. They were yielding.

I looked around and saw that at least one of my men was unhorsed. Sir Edward threw himself from his horse and knelt by his son who lay on the ground.

I shouted, "Wilfred! Secure the horses! Gilles, you and the squires take charge of the prisoners. Make sure they are safe!"

"Aye lord."

I dismounted and hung my shield from my cantle. I knelt next to Sir Edward. His son was not moving. "How is he?"

"He took a blow to the head. I am not sure."

"Hold him while I remove his helmet." I took off his helmet and then untied the ventail and removed his coif as gently as I could.

Once his helmet was removed I could see a tendril of blood dripping from the side of his mouth and, as I cradled his head, my hand came away bloody. I saw, however, that he breathed. "He is alive. Let us get him back to Father James. There is little point in having a healer and not using him."

Sir Edward had regained some of his composure now. "You are right. I will mount and carry him." He turned to one of my men at arms. "Put our helmets and shields on his horse, Theobald."

He climbed on his horse and then Raymond of Le Mans and I gently lifted the squire up to his father. Sir Edward looked down at me with pain etched upon his face, "This is my fault. He was not ready."

There were no words of mine that would change his dark thoughts. I knew that. I slapped the rump of his horse. "Four of Sir Edward's men, escort your lord. The rest, collect weapons and treasure."

I mounted Rolf. Wilfred rode up with a string of eight horses. "A good haul, lord."

"Did we lose any?"

He shook his head, "We surprised them and it showed. We have men who will need the healer but they can fight again soon. Young Master John is another matter. It was a blow from a mace." He pointed to a dead knight. "Sir Edward finished him off."

I nodded, "Ride ahead with the horses and my squires. I will form a rearguard." I turned to Alan son of Alan of Osmotherley, "Collect any standards and banners that you can. Fetch them with us."

He found four, including the one from the leader. I guessed that he was the lord of Loc-hard's by. I had thought to take their heads with me but that act could wait for a more appropriate occasion. I waved my arm and led my rearguard up the road. With my two scouts and eight men at arms, we rode after the rest of my men. I did not think that the Scots would attack us but I was taking no chances. I allowed a gap of half a mile but we made it safely back to the hill overlooking Carlisle as the sun set. We had two victories. Would God grant me a third?

Chapter 9

Father James spent all night ministering to John and his wound. The other wounded were seen to by my men. We knew how to fix cuts and small breaks. Our scarred bodies were evidence of that. While Sir Edward watched the priest and his son I went to the brow of the ridge to look down at Carlisle. It was just a shadow on the far side of the river but the flicker of fires which could be seen as doors in the huts opened and closed gave us an idea of their location. Wulfric came with me. He pointed across the river. "A small boat left there not long after you had left this morning, lord. Aiden spied it. He has sharp eyes that one."

I had expected this. The Scots had armed forces on the west coast. They protected against Irish raids as well as giving support to Carlisle. "He is sending to Dumfries for help."

"That is what I would do. He will have a shock when the column of men you scattered does not arrive."

I shook my head, "The men we scattered came from the north. Someone must have escaped that way too. It matters not. We watch this morning and then, at noon, I shall ride down to give him the news that his friends are scattered to the four winds."

"Do you think they will surrender?"

"Do not sound disappointed, Wulfric. No, I do not. It is a strong castle. Had not Stephen given it to the Scots we would hold it yet. I hope to put doubts in his mind but I need to see his face. I want to see the measure of this man who challenges me. Will he allow me free rein to capture every animal in his valley? If he does we have won but I think that the people we allowed to flee the farms and villages will have filled his walls. He will have many hungry mouths to feed."

"He might send them from his walls."

"He might, Wulfric, and if he does then that tells me something about him."

Wulfric jerked his thumb back at the camp, "Young Henry has the blood of his grandfather coursing through his veins. Sir Edward's men told mine that he was as close to the fighting as he could get and he did not shirk when the Scots closed. He held his sword boldly."

"But if he falls then the hope for England is gone. I fear the Empress will never be crowned. If Henry dies then all is finished. Stephen's son, Eustace, will be king."

"And what will you do if that happens, lord?"

I hesitated. The thoughts had flickered through my mind like something I had forgotten and then remembered. I had spoken of it to none but since I had returned to England it had been lurking there in the dark recesses I kept hidden from all. Wulfric was owed honesty, "Then we would have a new kingdom. I would take back England's losses here in the north and make my own domain between the Scottish firths and the Tees. We would have a land which went from coast to coast. If Henry does not rule then I follow no man. I will be Warlord of the North in the Kingdom of Cleveland."

Wulfric was silent, "Could we do that?"

"What other choices would there be?"

"You could go back to Miklagård, lord. You have a home there and you would be welcomed. They have need for men such as you to fight for the Emperor. Erre has told me as much."

"And if I did would I be able to take all those who have supported me? Alf, Ethelred? My knights and their families? No, my friend, I could not and I would not desert them. We are in this together. However, so long as Henry lives then there is hope."

"Then I will make sure that the lad is safe in battle!"

"If he is meant to fall and not become king then that will happen no matter what we do. We have to trust in God."

"Aye and Gilles and Richard! They are good squires. They are his best hope of survival."

We left sentries on the ridge and returned to the camp. The priest was talking with Sir Edward. "How is young John?"

Sir Edward said, "The priest has bled his skull. He seems to breathe easier. I fear it is in God's hands now. I have prayed." He shook his head, "His mother will blame me!"

"It is war, Edward." Wulfric put his arm around the shoulder of his old friend, "I have no children of my own but I have watched John grow. He is tough. He has been bred in northern winters and he comes of good stock. He will come through this and be stronger for it."

I nodded, "Rest. You have been up all night and we may be called to arms soon."

"Do not worry, lord, I will be ready!" Sir Edward was like me. Inactivity was the worst of punishments. He wanted to do something rather than helplessly watch his son.

I went to my squires. They had sharpened my weapons and groomed Rolf. "We will be riding to the town at noon. Richard, you will carry the captured banners. Gilles, have the names of the captured knights ready."

"What do we do, lord?"

I owed Henry an explanation. I was training him not just to become a knight but to become a leader. "We go to put fear in the heart of Malcolm mac Athol. Doubts are a deadly enemy. I want this Scot to be fearful before we begin our attack. His raid into England made him confident. He escaped Sir Hugh and he thought he had won. Our first victory has put doubts in his mind, We go to aggravate those doubts."

"We attack the walls?"

"No, Henry, for I still believe he will try to shift us from our hilltop perch."

"Even with doubts?"

"Even with doubts for I will go bareheaded and this young Scottish cockerel will see an old, tired man and, more

106

importantly, he will see you and you will be the bait which draws him to our blades. And the other reason is that he cannot sit behind his walls with fields untilled and animals taken by us."

One of our sentries rode back to bring us news. "Lord, a boat has just pulled in close to the castle."

"Thank you." I turned to Wulfric. You had better have the men prepare. I want them below the ridge until I signal and then bring them forward in one line."

"Aye lord."

"Squires, let us go to speak with our foes. Keep your shields close. They may not honour the truce. Dick." My archer knew what I meant.

Dick nodded and mounted. He would bring his bow but keep it from sight. I slung my shield across my back. The Scots would see two knights and a squire. Dick had more to him than most knights. When we were ready I slipped my coif from my head so that I was bareheaded and I led my men down to the river. We would not cross and I hoped that Malcolm mac Athol would see this as an opportunity to talk. If he did not then I would unleash my men to raid his land.

I heard the horns from within the walls as we approached. My reputation preceded me. They would suspect some sort of trap or trick. We halted at the river. Here the river looped so that the five of us had water on three sides. There was a bridge some hundred paces to our right. It had no tower but crossbows and bows could cover it from the gatehouse of Carlisle Castle which stood on a manmade mound. It was a well-sited castle. When we reached the river we waited.

Dick and I chatted while we waited. I knew my squires would be nervous and an easy conversation would put them at their ease. "When we win back this castle we should not give it away so easily, lord. With my archers alone I could defend this against an army"

"You are right and Stephen made a blunder when he did so. What galls me is that he did so when the Empress was in Anjou and the only danger to him were my knights."

Dick said, "That is a measure of how much he fears you, lord."

Henry said, "But he is king."

Dick laughed, "That means nothing for men will follow the Warlord and that makes him a dangerous enemy."

"My lord, they come."

Gilles' voice brought our attention to the gate. As convention dictated five men rode from the gates. I guessed that one would be Malcolm mac Athol. They had one squire with them carrying the standard of Scotland. The fact that he did not bring his personal standard told me that he was acting on the authority of the Earl of Northumbria, Prince Henry of Scotland.

They halted on the other side of the river. Malcolm mac Athol was of an age with my son William. He had been given a high honour at an early age. I waited. He broke the silence, "I see by the wolf your squire bears that you are the Earl of Cleveland. What brings you to Scotland?"

"This land is England but Scotland, for the moment, controls this castle. I came here to repay your visit to the lands around Barnard however unlike the carrion you sent we do not make war on the weak." A grizzled warrior next to him bristled and snorted. I guessed that he had led the raid. "And who would you be?" I pointed. "You, the one with the face like a bear's behind!"

He roared, "I am the Mormaer of Bute and I will have your tongue for that insult!"

"The only one I have insulted is the bear but if you wish satisfaction then come and try a lance or two with me. I have slain enough Scotsmen to know that it will not exert me overmuch!"

Malcolm held out a hand, "Peace, Donaldbain. Did you come here to insult my men or is there another purpose for your visit?"

I held my hand out and Gilles and Richard threw down the standards we had captured. "I met some of your knights on the road yesterday. I have some four or five waiting for ransom but these lords will need no ransom. Perhaps you were expecting them?"

I saw his face fall. "I was, old man, but fear not I have men enough within my walls to drive you hence."

"Really? And yet I dine on Scottish beef and enjoy the land hereabouts. I see no one trying to shift me. Perhaps the fact that we are armed and will fight back has something to do with it. It may be that this horde you have waiting within your walls is better suited to killing women and children!"

"Lord, let me fight him!" I had annoyed this Donaldbain and that was my intent.

"Do not be foolish, Lord Bute. It is what he wants. He is a champion at tourney. You are a brave fighter but this man is a King's Champion. Your day will come!" The Mormaer subsided and Malcolm turned to me, "As will your day, Warlord. Prepare to die for we come for you."

I turned to Gilles, "We had better take back these standards. It seems that the constable is not willing to surrender his castle, yet!"

As we turned to ride away Henry said, "Will they not attack us?"

"I doubt it but my shield is about my back. It shows we fear them not."

"Were you not afraid that huge warrior would take you up on your challenge?"

"I hoped that he would for he looks to me the sort who charges recklessly into battle. They are the easiest to defeat in single combat."

My knights had been watching from the small ridge. "Will they fight, lord?"

Dick laughed, "There is certainly one Scotsman who wishes to take the Earl's head. As for the rest? Probably."

I dismounted and handed my shield to Gilles. "It will not be for some time. I am guessing that the boat brought news of reinforcements from the west. Have the men rest and make sure that the horses have enough water. For England, this could be a warm day. Keep a sharp lookout, especially to the west. Aiden, take your scouts and watch for the arrival of these Scots."

I saw a large rock and I went to sit upon it. "Richard, fetch me some food and some ale. I have an appetite."

Henry brought water for the horses while Gille took the captured standards to the rear. My men left me alone and when Richard brought me the half leg of cold mutton and ale I began to devour them. Henry sat close by, "How can you eat, lord, and be so calm when we could be fighting in a short time?"

I waved him closer and swallowed some ale to wash down the greasy cold mutton. "When you lead men, whether a few or an army, it is important that they think you are calm and in control. Inside your heart may be beating like a galloping steed but to the world, you are cold and calm. When we fight this battle I will need to have eyes everywhere and to make decisions in the heat of the moment. Being calm will help me. "

"Do you never lose your temper?"

"Of course I do." I pointed to where Sir Edward was bathing his son's head, "Sir Edward lost his temper and his blood boiled when his son was hurt. If aught happened to my kin or my oathsworn I would be as angry. The blood might rush to my head. It happens. Harold, Tristan and John have all been my squires. Just as the three of you are special to me, so were they."

Just then there was a shout. "Riders come!"

I looked to the west but Sir John said, "No lord, it is from the east. It is Sir Gilles of Normanby. He is returned."

I rose from the rock and put the half-chewed bone and goblet there. I was eager to hear his news. He dismounted and dropped to one knee. "Lord, I returned as soon as I could."

"I hope you did not tax your horses overmuch, we shall need them."

"No lord, we used remounts from Sir Hugh's castle." He pointed east. "We had a skirmish with a conroi heading towards Carlisle. We might have pursued them but I came here instead. Did I do right?"

"You did. Your news is welcome." I pointed to Sir Edward, "Your former lord may need you, Gilles. His new squire has been wounded."

"Not John!" He turned and ran to the squire he had helped train.

I took in his news. He had not defeated the conroi and that meant there were reinforcements from the east or possibly the south. I looked up at the sky. If there were men coming from the east and from the west then the battle would take place either in the late afternoon or early in the morning. I strode to the ridge and peered down at the bridge. The Constable would not wish to have to cross the bridge with his whole army. We could make it a bridge of death. When the forces came from the west he would emerge. It would be this afternoon. That way his reinforcements could hold the bridgehead and deny it to us. I did not want it. Now that I had made my guess I knew what to do.

"Gilles, summon my knights, not Sir Edward, he can stay with his son for a while."

When my knights were gathered Wulfric rubbed his hands, "You are ready eh, lord?"

"I am. I have made my guess. If I am wrong then so be it but a battle will be fought here. Malcolm will cross the bridge when his reinforcements arrive from the west. They will use men on foot to charge us and knock us from the hill. He thinks he has counted our forces but he did not see Sir Gilles' men nor Sir Edward's. However, he will still outnumber us. Sir Richard, your archers will cut stakes and make a barrier on the west side of the ridge. Sir Philip, you will do the same but it will be further back. I wish you to stay hidden. He knows we use archers. I want him to see Dick and not Sir Philip. Sir John and Sir Harold, I will attack whoever comes at us with our three companies." I saw the disappointment on Sir Wulfric's face. "You know me better than that, Sir Wulfric. I wish you and the rest of my men to form a shield wall at the top of the ridge. I intend to break their attack with the sixty of us and then do as Henry's great grandfather did at Hastings. We will fall back. I would draw them onto our arrows and your blades. We will pass through your lines. Sir Gilles, you and your horsemen will wait behind the lines. When we pass through you will join me and we will make a flank attack on their left while Sir Harold and Sir Tristan do the same from the east. Sir Wulfric and the archers hold them and we round them up."

111

Their nods and smiles told me that they thought it was a good plan. We would now have to wait for Aiden to bring us news. I walked over to Sir Edward. I saw that Father James was praying. Sir Edward looked up. He suddenly looked old beyond his years. "We have made our plan of attack. You and your men will stand in a shield wall on the ridge."

He nodded, "I will be there."

"Your son is strong and God will not let you lose him. The Father here is a good healer."

Father James said, "He grows no weaker and that is a good sign. His breathing is regular and his colour is better. I have been feeding him soup made from mutton bones. It will aid him."

Sir Edward smiled, "I have faith in God and the priest. I will be ready to fight and I will not let you down."

"I never doubted it for an instant."

In the middle of the afternoon, my three scouts rode in. "Lord, there are a hundred warriors marching along the river and two boats with more men in them."

"Horsemen?"

Aiden shook his head, "They are led by a horseman. He has a standard with a lion upon it. There look to be ten mounted knights and the rest are men on foot." He shook his head, "Some are farmers with bill hooks and hunting bows."

"You have done well. Choose your own place to kill."

He looked around and spied Dick behind his stakes, "Sir Richard and his men will do us, lord."

I walked to Rolf and mounted him. "Sir Hugh, I want to make sure that our enemy makes mistakes. Take your men at arms and as soon as you spy the men coming from the west make them believe that you are going to attack the bridge. I want them to sally forth. Do not risk any of your men and when you ride then do so loosely as though you have little control over your men."

He grinned, "I will, lord. This will be a grand jest."

He gathered his men and rode to the edge of the ridge. It was a gentle slope and there would be little danger of the horses being injured in their descent. I hoped that we could spark a charge by some of the wilder Scots.

"They come!"

We saw their banners as they marched along the river. They were a tight formation for they knew the threat our horses posed.

"Now, Sir Hugh!"

He raised his arm and made his horse rear, "Let us avenge the folk of the Tees Dale! Ride forth!"

He spurred his horse and led his sixteen men and his squire towards the bridge. A trumpet sounded inside the walls showing that they had seen the danger. At the same time, the column of men heading east began to run. It was foolish for there was little chance that they would reach the bridge before the horsemen. Those inside the castle, however, would. The Constable sent mailed men with long spears to hold the bridge. Had Sir Hugh wished it then they could have reached the bridge and fought with the men there but that was not their task.

The defenders stepped from the bridge and their spears bristled before them. Suddenly Sir Hugh charged alone at them. He must have instructed his men for they did not move. The hedgehog of spears tightened. In a superb feat of horsemanship, he wheeled his horse to the left just out of reach of a jabbing spear and he hurled his own spear at a warrior in the centre. The spear impaled him and he fell backwards. Sir Hugh's men cheered and the men with spears raced forward to get to grips with the arrogant horseman. Sir Hugh was too clever for that and his men wheeled in formation and followed him back up the slope. He did not gallop but kept at a speed that tempted the spearmen to carry on up the slope. I saw that the relief column had almost reached the bridge.

When the charging spearmen were in range Dick shouted, "Release!" Sixty arrows soared. The spearmen raised their shields but even so some found their marks. I saw men with pierced legs and arms and, as they began to descend they left two bodies. Sir Hugh and Dick had done as I had asked. The Scots would now be keen for revenge. They would regard my men as being without honour for retreating and the

113

slaying of three of their men would rankle. They would brood about it. The Scots were like that.

My men all cheered Sir Hugh and his men as they reined in and dismounted. Sir Tristan said, "A fine hit."

Sir Hugh nodded, "I had the spear especially sharpened but their mail is not as good as ours. I was confident."

"Now rest your men for soon they will come." I pointed and we saw the garrison as it emerged from the castle to cross the bridge. There were just thirty horses with them and I knew that they would not waste them. They did not outnumber our horse but they did with their spears. They would use their strengths and their numbers to try to overwhelm us. I knew from the long spears held by the men at arms at the bridge that they had made them to counter our horses. They were longer than ours. It would be suicidal for us to make a frontal attack.

I motioned for Sir Harold and Sir John, "Change your lances for spears. We will do as Sir Hugh has shown us. Copy me when I charge. Leave thirty paces between the lines. If there are enough of the shorter spears have your men carry two."

As they left I rode towards my men at arms who waited patiently. They were already armed with the shorter spears. "When we charge we will halt just short of their long spears. I want them to think we are foolish enough to hit their line. Have your spear couched until the last moment. It takes two hands to carry their longer spears and they only have a small shield. Aim for the neck and the face. Follow in my steps and go no closer."

"Aye lord." Wilfred pointed to the bridge. "They are using the wild men from the west behind the spearmen, lord."

"I counted eighty of the long spears and they are in two ranks. Then if only half of our spears strike home we will have seen off a quarter of the spearmen. Gilles, you ride in the line. Richard, you guard Henry and Henry you ride on my left so that they see my banner."

They all nodded their assent.

I waited until all of the Scots were arrayed in a solid phalanx. They waited. It suited me. My father had said that it was unwise to interrupt an enemy when he was making a mistake. They had chased off Sir Hugh and, from their position they outnumbered us greatly. Their spears stopped us from charging them. I could see that the Scots were eager to get to grips with us. Their barons and mormaer were having to restrain them. It was almost time. Sir John and Sir Harold returned, rearmed, and joined me in the line.

I rode a little way away from my men, "For God, the Empress and our future king, Henry!"

Henry obliged by rearing his horse and the whole army chanted, "Henry! Henry! Henry!" It was a good start.

I wheeled Rolf around and my men formed up on me. Wilfred was to my right and Henry to my left with Richard close behind. We cantered down the hill. There was no need to ride boot to boot for we would not strike home. The men who had arrived from the west had bows but they were not the war bows my archers used; they were hunting bows and hunting arrows. Against animals and men without mail, they could be deadly. Against mail and shields, they were useless. They began to release them when we were fifty paces from them. Hunters rarely get to send an arrow at an animal coming hurtling towards them and most of the arrows flew over us. One hit my shield and a second clanged off my helmet. From the Scottish cheer, one would have thought I was dead.

When I was twenty paces from the spears I wheeled Rolf to my left. Henry had been watching my wrist and his horse mirrored mine. I do not think that the Scots knew what we were doing until I raised my spear and hurled it. Unlike Hugh's spear, ours were thrown along the line. There were more targets. Mine hit a warrior in his left shoulder. I heard cries and shouts as our spears struck home.

Henry had my standard fluttering high in the breeze and he shouted, "England and the Warlord!"

When I reached the end of the Scottish line I wheeled left. I felt an arrow strike my mail but it did not penetrate. I watched Sir Harold and his men as they hurled their spears.

The effect was dramatic. The men with the long spears had to bear it. If they moved then they risked us cutting them down once they became isolated. I drew my sword. I was leading my men in the opposite direction from Sir Harold but I was able to see the effect of his spears and Sir John's. When I was almost at the end of Sir John's line five warriors decided they had had enough. They burst from behind the men with the long spears. I had been waiting for such a rash move. I pulled Rolf's head around as I swung my sword sideways. Behind me, Wilfred and Gilles did the same. The five men ran and jumped up at us. They were half-naked and held a sword in one hand and a small buckler in the other. My sword smashed into one sword, bending it and then slashed across a naked chest. Wilfred's sword split the skull of the second and Gilles sliced across the throat of the third. Sir Harold and his squire hurled their spears into the chests of the last two.

We had done what I had intended and I shouted, "Fall back! Henry, the standard!"

I had worried that in the excitement of battle he would have forgotten his instruction but he had not. He waved it three times and followed me as I led the three companies back up the slope. The sight of our horse's rumps seemed to ignite and inflame the Scots' passion and the comrades of the five dead men raced after us, intent on revenge. More followed and soon the whole of the Scottish line was racing up the hill. We could not afford to slow up for they were swift. I saw Wulfric and my men as they opened their ranks to admit us through them. When Dick's arrows began to fall amongst them they veered away from the left towards our right. We passed through our men and I reined in Rolf. He was tired.

I watched as the Scots saw their opportunity to flank us and then Sir Philip and his men appeared and began releasing arrow after arrow into their unprotected bodies. The rest of my men arrived and Wilfred said, "Do we attack them now, lord?"

116

"No, let them waste themselves on our line for a while. I want the Constable to commit all of his men first. Have the men form up on the flank in preparation."

"Aye lord."

"You did well, Henry, you all did well."

"Lord, their horsemen are forming up."

I glanced down the slope as Alan son of Alan pointed. "I see them. Are you ready, Sir Gilles?"

"Aye lord."

I headed for my men. Richard handed me my lance and I saw that men all had their lances ready. "Gilles, you stay with Richard and Henry. They will try to take my banner. Stay behind our first line."

We rode down behind Dick's archers. We were hidden from view. I knew that for I could not see the enemy either. We formed our line on the slope and I shouted, "Forward!" I led my men west following the ridge down to the shallow beck at the bottom. When we were fifty paces from it I shouted, "Wheel!" and turned Rolf to our left. I could not see the enemy but I knew that they would be charging my archers and their staked position. As we came up the shallow rise I saw them ahead of us. The Constable had a line of horsemen with lances charging towards Dick and his archers. They were less than forty paces from us and saw us too late. We crashed into their flank.

My first blow was lucky, my lance struck a knight with a blue and green surcoat. It hit his shield and then slid up to the top of his arm. The head of the lance went into his shoulder and Rolf's power pushed him to the ground. His horse was dragged by the rider's reins and by Rolf's force and he too fell. Their line was disrupted. They tried to wheel and face us but we had more powerful horses which were taller and stronger than those we faced.

"My lord! Watch out!"

I glanced to my right in time to see an axe slicing down towards my lance. Richard's cry had managed to give me enough time to swing the lance sideways towards the knight. At the same time, Richard kicked on his horse and he hit the warrior with his spear. The combination of a lance and spear

117

striking him tumbled him from his horse. It was now a confused mêlée. I drew my sword. This was where my squires would show their true worth. They had to guard my back. That was easier said than done for four knights, led by the Constable, saw me and my banner. They spurred their horses towards me.

One of the knights was the wild warrior, Lord Bute, whom I had insulted. His spear was shattered and he had a war axe. He closed with me ahead of the others. I reined Rolf back a little to gain more control and I readied my sword. He was charging to strike at my shield side. At the last moment, as he was pulling back his mighty arm to send me into the next world I jerked Rolf to the left. The Scot was moving so quickly he could not turn. I brought my sword in a scything sweep and hacked through his upper arm. The tendons severed, the axe fell from his hand. Richard's spear found his throat.

The other three Scots had reached me and I was almost stationary. The Constable was flanked by his squire and a mounted man at arms. The Constable had the best hauberk and only his eyes could be seen above his ventail. The man at arms had a short hauberk as did his squire. Both had a coif only. I fended the blow from the squire's sword as I smashed my sword against that of the Constable. The man at arms tried to get around the Constable's horse. Gilles still had his spear and he punched at the man at arms. It was a good blow but the man at arms was strong and he reeled as the spear broke.

As the squire raised his sword to hit me he was smashed in the face by the head of my standard as Henry came to my aid. It was not a powerful blow for it had been delivered by his left hand but it bloodied the squire and made his eyes stream. The Constable was, briefly, isolated, and I stood in my stirrups to smash down once more. Our swords rang together but the Scot had been fending off my strike and his did not have the power of my hit. His sword began to bend.

Richard came to the aid of Henry and his sword slashed the squire's leg. The squire wheeled away. Gilles was having to defend against the man at arms' powerful blows and his

118

horse was backing off. I stood again to hit the Constable and he began to raise his sword. I stabbed instead and my sword slid through his mail, into his gambeson and sliced his flesh. He wheeled away as Gilles was knocked from his horse. I pulled Rolf's head around and brought my sword backhanded at the man at arms. The Scot was leaning down to stab a recumbent Gilles. My sword struck him in the back of the neck. He fell dead from his horse.

"Richard, Henry, stay by Gilles! Wilfred!"

I spurred Rolf and took off after the Constable who was following his squire back to the castle. The men on foot were streaming from the low ridge pursued by Wulfric. The Scots had seen the flight of their leader and they were following. I had not expected to capture Carlisle Castle but if I could capture the Constable then I would be able to do so. Rolf's exertions that day were my undoing. As we picked our way through the corpse littered field the Constable began to pull away. As we neared the narrow bridge it became congested with soldiers trying to get into the safety of the walls. They closed around the Constable's horse giving him protection. If we followed it would be suicide. We would be swamped and pulled from our horses.

"Wilfred, back!" As I turned Rolf around a wild warrior saw his chance for glory and ran at me. He leapt from the body of a dead horse to rise in the air like a sea bird. My quick hands came to my aid. I held my sword before me and he impaled himself on my trusty and true blade. His body, greasy with sweat and with blood, slid from my sword to lie across the dead horse.

"Dick, Sir Philip, bring your archers!"

I heard my command repeated. The Scots had jammed the bridge. They were a tempting target for arrows. Our horsemen picked off those isolated at the periphery and then the arrows fell and the slaughter began. Those without mail hurled themselves in the river. Some could swim and made it to the other bank. Others were swept down the Esk to feed the fishes. My archers were tired but they kept at their task. They knew that the more we killed now the fewer we would have to face in the future. War was a cruel world.

Sir Edward and Sir Wulfric, both bloody with dead men's blood rode up to me. "Keep up the arrows and the slaughter until they are within the walls. Let us make this lesson a good one and worth the price."

"Aye, lord, a great victory. They fell upon our swords and spears as though they were embracing death. They died well but they were ill-prepared to be facing mailed men. I fear the treasure will be poor."

"We came for the victory and we have that. We can loot the land at our leisure now for there will be no one close to threaten us."

I turned my horse and headed back to Gilles and my standard. He was rising and I breathed a sigh of relief. He was merely dazed, "I am sorry, lord. I should not have fallen."

"You did well as you all did. We shall have to tip the standard for you if you wish to use it as a spear, Henry."

I recognised that look on his face. I had seen it on the face of William after he had carried my standard into battle. It was a mixture of joy, awe and terror at what he had done. He just nodded. Later he would talk. For now, he stood next to Gilles gripping the standard and staring at the field.

"When you are recovered, Gilles, I want you and the squires to collect the horses which are roaming free. Search the knights for swords and treasure. There may not be much but we will have to be frugal now that we are cut adrift from the Empress and her army."

Chapter 10

It was dark by the time the last of the Scottish warriors had made the walls of Carlisle. We were too weary to clear the field and so we retreated to our ridge where, by firelight, Father James tended to the wounded. Men asked for comrades who had not returned and the stories emerged of where men at arms had fallen. Sir Hugh had received a bad wound to his leg and Sir Gilles had had a horse slain from beneath him. He had broken some bones in his left hand falling. Others like Sir Harold and Sir John had more scars to show their wives but my knights had survived. Sir Edward's son was still our most serious casualty.

Sir Edward returned to his vigil and his son. Sir Gilles joined him; he would be doing no fighting for a while. We ate the cold remains of the meat we had slaughtered the previous day and I set a good watch. As we sat around our fire Henry began to chatter about the battle. He gave us an account, blow by blow, of what he had seen. Richard and Gilles smiled for they had done the same thing. I did not mind for Henry had acquitted himself well. I was proud of him. I did not know yet if he would be a good leader but I knew that he had the courage and would not flinch in battle. It was a start for the boy who would be king.

In the night we heard the sound of rustling, squeaking and yelping below us. The foxes, rats and creatures of the night were feasting on flesh. We could do nothing about it. The sentries hurled stones into the dark which sent them scurrying away from the feast briefly but they would return.

As soon as the sun rose I sent men down to recover the bodies of our dead while I rode with my knights and my squires to the gates of Carlisle. From the gaunt looks of those on the gates, they had kept watch for an attack all night. We halted before their gates. They made no attempt to harm us.

I shouted to them, "We will clear our dead from the field. When we have done I give you truce until noon to reclaim your bodies. I will return, after noon, to speak with your Constable."

The old Scottish knight who leaned over said, "Aye, well the Mormaer is still with the healers. You hurt him, Warlord." He shook his head, "Those of us who had fought you before warned him and that hot head, Robert of Bute, but they wouldna listen. Well, the Mormaer of Bute has paid with his life. I thank you for the courtesy. We lost some fine warriors yesterday."

I nodded, "We all did."

My men stripped the bodies of the fallen of anything of value and then we quitted the field. I sent Sir Tristan, and Sir Wulfric with their companies to ride north, east and west to gather as many animals as they could. I made sure they knew not to harm the farmers and the people. It was animals we needed and I wanted the Scots to suffer for their attack. It was the only way they would learn.

As I dismounted Richard ran over, "Great news, lord! John, Sir Edward's son has awoken."

"Has he spoken?"

Richard looked at me as though I had not understood him, "Lord?"

I spoke quietly, "Sometimes men awake from a blow to the head, Richard, but they are not in this world. They cannot speak and as men they are useless. Oft times it is as well to end their suffering. Has he spoken?"

"I know not."

"Come then, let us go for either way Sir Edward will need us."

John was being fed watered wine by his father when I reached him. I had a smile carved onto my face in case this was bad news. Sir Edward smiled, "He lives."

"Good."

"And he speaks. He is weak, that is all."

I was relieved, "Then we will give thanks to God and Father James!"

We had made a pyre of our dead and they were burned at the top of the hill where Wulfric had held the enemy at bay. The Scots had taken their dead back across the river and buried them. As the smoke drifted east the air was filled with the smell of burning human flesh. It was not a pleasant smell. "Wilfred, have the dead horses butchered and cooked. That is a better smell to fill a man's nostrils."

"Aye lord."

I rode with my squires, Sir Harold, and Sir John as well as my archer knight, back to the gates. We would speak with the Constable. It was the grizzled old Scot who greeted us.

"Thank you for allowing us to bury our dead. They died bravely."

"They did indeed. And I take it that the Constable is still with the healers?"

"He is but I have the authority to speak with you. What would you have with us, Warlord? I am an old warrior so speak plain."

I liked this man and I did him the service of speaking honestly with him. "I would have the Scots go from Carlisle but I know that the Constable will not agree to that and I value my men too highly to waste their lives in a fruitless attack on your walls. I would take it but it would be a pyrrhic victory so send this message to your Constable. I will take every animal I can find between here and Barnard Castle. If ever he dares to try to take one life in England then I will return and every man I meet will die. That is a promise. If you know me then you know I keep my word."

"Aye Warlord, it is true. Until he recovers you have my word, Angus of Menteith, that we will respect the border."

"Farewell, Angus. I wish you a long life."

He laughed, "Aye well that is out of my hands is it not?"

By the time our hunters returned with cattle and sheep as well as some horses which had fled the battle the funeral pyres were smoking ash and the horse meat was ready for eating. My knights were in good humour. "The castles are locked up tighter than a reeves' purse and we collected many animals. The people fled when they saw our banners."

"Are there more animals to be had, Wulfric?"

"I think another six days should see us clear the fields."

"We have five. I have no doubt that if we tarry longer then Prince Henry will cause mischief in the east."

The next day I sent back Sir Edward, his son and Sir Gilles along with their men. They drove the animals we had gathered. They would leave them at Stockton. Over the next few days, as more animals were recovered from the Scots I sent other knights and their men to return with our booty. Sir Hugh was the second to leave. He would retain the animals he drove for his people had suffered already.

At the end of the five days, the rest of the army left. There were just five knights. I rode with Dick, Sir Harold, Sir Tristan and Sir John. We had the fewest animals but I wanted to ensure that we travelled safely. Aiden and his scouts ranged far and wide seeking enemies. They found none. We reached home by the middle of summer. My valley was peaceful and my people prospered. The new animals increased our wealth. The treasure, mail and weapons we had recovered would make every man richer and the people of Stockton would prosper. All of my men now had remounts and we had a good herd of horses from sumpters and rounceys to palfreys and destrier.

As I sat in my Great Hall eating with my household knights, squires and my constable, John of Craven, Sir Harold said, "Perhaps we should stay apart from the rest of the Empress' army, lord. Being a Warlord is far more profitable."

I was about to censure Sir Harold when Henry Fitz Empress said, "The Earl serves my mother, the Empress. This is a minor disagreement. He will soon be fighting alongside her once more."

Sir Harold looked at me and I shrugged. He was right but so was the future king. "We shall need all the coin we can and soon. John of Craven, see if you can get two of your Frisians to sail home and recruit more of their fellows. They are good warriors."

"They are, my lord. They will never be horsemen but they can stand a watch on a wall and can defend ramparts like no warrior I have ever commanded."

Sir John said, "Alf will appreciate the business."

Sir Tristan laughed, "It is more money for the family coffers eh, John?"

Sir John blushed, "He makes good mail and excellent swords."

"I was only having fun at your expense."

"We have much to spend the coin on and we have the animals to fairly distribute. I am mindful of the fact that Erre and his men had no opportunity to capture animals for themselves."

John of Craven said, "The people say that you do not take as much as you ought, Earl. They are right."

"I am happy for my share to benefit Stockton. If Stockton is rich then I profit from the taxes. Is that not so, Steward?"

"We have a healthy surplus. That is true."

Sir Harold roared with laughter, "Do my ears deceive me? Is John the parsimonious steward happy with our income?"

John was known for being tight-fisted and he had the good grace to acknowledge it. He shrugged. "I confess that you have all done far better than I could have hoped. We will need to build a bigger workshop for my father." William the Moneyer made our coins. Since the Civil War had begun we had had to produce many more coins and they were in high demand. Their value could be trusted. As we had discovered in some of the ransoms for the Scots many of their coins had base metal mixed with bronze, silver and gold. It was another reason why we were able to trade so far afield. Our coins were known to be true. The sign of the wolf was a good one when it came to money.

The good humour of the hall continued over the next weeks as wounds healed and coins were spent. *'Adela'* docked twice more taking back with her, on one voyage, Günter the Frisian who sailed to his home to hire more mercenaries. Gilles and Richard continued to train Henry to become a better squire and I fretted that I had no news from the Empress. Since Stephen had recovered from his illness we had heard nothing.

A rider arrived in August. He was one of Miles of Gloucester's men. He had a letter for me and one for Henry. Both were from the Empress. I was selfish and wished to read my letter alone. I tucked it in my tunic for later. Henry devoured his and I questioned Richard, the messenger, about his news.

"Ranulf of Chester has allied himself with Stephen once more. My journey here took longer than it should. I had to avoid Lincoln."

"And what of the Usurper?"

"He is trying to take the new castles of Cirencester, Bampton and Wareham. The noose tightens around the Empress' lands."

I nodded, "And the Earl of Gloucester?"

He hesitated and then said, "He hunts a great deal, my lord." He looked at me with as an honest a look as I could remember. "The Constable told me to be honest with you." He pointed towards the unopened letter, "I am guessing the letter tells you more. I was told to destroy it if any threatened to take it."

"Sir Miles must trust you."

"I am his cousin, lord, and he does."

"If you would wait a week or two I can offer you a voyage home on the *'Adela'*."

"Thank you, Earl, but I am anxious to return home. I find it cold this far north."

"But it is summer!"

"I know!"

When he left us I turned to Henry, "What does your mother say?"

He looked disappointed, "Nothing! She asks about my health and hopes that I am eating well!"

"That is mothers for you. You had better go to Gilles. He has your new sword ready from Alf."

His eyes lit up and he raced from my presence. He was almost a youth but there was still enough of the child in him to forget his manners. I did not mind and I took a jug of wine up to my solar to read the letter from the Empress. Despite Miles' trust in his cousin, I had no doubt that the Empress would be discreet and I would have to read between the lines but knowing that she had penned this herself made it seem like I held her in my hands once more.

Alfraed,

The manner of your departure and the ugly words which were exchanged have weighed heavily upon my mind. I have had sleepless nights and I have paced the floor. My soldiers and servants believe it is because my son is absent but I know that you care for him and will watch over him as carefully as if you were his father.

My brother is cold towards me. I know not why for I sided with him over you. Perhaps it is because the Earl of Chester has defected again. He is untrustworthy and yet his wife is so brave. My brother hunts. I have heard a rumour that he intends to join my husband in Normandy. Margaret overheard a conversation between two of his men. He sees more chance of victory and glory there. On a more positive note, if he does leave for Normandy, then I shall be able to send for you. Prepare to join me.

I know we can reverse the gains made by Stephen.

I have no doubts that Henry will prosper with you but ask him to write to me, please.
Your friend,
Maud

I read and re-read the letter a number of times. She must have trusted Miles' cousin for the letter was more open than I expected. I sent for Sir Richard. "We may be travelling back to Oxford soon. Prepare your men. I will travel light with just archers if the summons comes."

"You have had word, lord?"

"I have had a hint. However it may be next week, next month...."

"We shall be ready. The new horses have been schooled and we have arrows aplenty. Half of my archers now have a short mail vest. They can form a shield wall if needs be."

"Good. You anticipate my every wish."

We were all in good humour for a long week and then a party of Churchmen arrived from the south. We had received news that Sir Edward's squire, John had fully recovered. He would walk, talk move and, most importantly, laugh. It seemed a sign. The men who came wore the garb of the men of Winchester. What had Henry of Blois to do with me? I might be Warlord but even I had to be civil to the clergy no matter what their politics. I respected honest priests like Father James and Father Henry. In fact, I held none in higher regard for they placed themselves in danger without any weapon save their faith. I could not do that. These robed prelates with rings on their fingers were as far removed from priests as I was from a swineherd. They were pampered young men who had chosen the church rather than knighthood. The Templars and Hospitallers showed that you could be both but the party of eight who awaited me in my Great Hall were too well fed to be poor priests. My knights and squires waited behind me.

I smiled at them and watched as they fell upon the food and wine Alice had brought as though they had not eaten for a week. I had no doubt that their arrival heralded something unpleasant in my life. I wondered what sin or crime I had committed which demanded such a gaggle of clergy. I waited until they had finished. The Canon who led them looked at me sternly. "Thank you for your hospitality, Earl. The north, it seems, has rather less in the way of lodgings and fine food. "

A younger priest said, "And the monks of Fountain's Abbey served us porridge!"

I nodded and kept a serious expression. "It is the war. We have many raiders and bandits. I am sure that when we have peace then the fare will improve."

The Canon jabbed a podgy finger at me, "It is this peace of which we need to speak. We have had representation from King David and the Archbishop of Glasgow. The Empress made peace with the Scots and you have broken it!"

I flashed a warning look to my knights and squires. They too remained impassive. "I am sorry but what has this to do with you? The last time I was in Oxford it was said that the church would not support the Empress or her son's claim to the throne."

"The Church is neutral in these matters but the Archbishop of Glasgow has sent word to the Pope. He wishes you excommunicated."

I could keep a straight face no longer. "If every warrior who made war on another was excommunicated then there would be few indeed who would escape that judgement." They looked stunned. I think they expected a more penitent response. "What did you think would result from this visit?"

"We thought that you would apologise to the King of Scotland and then make a pilgrimage to Rome to beg the Pope's forgiveness. That is not unreasonable. The Archbishop and the King have assured us that this would be an acceptable penitence."

I nodded. I could see now that this was a plot. King David or, more likely, Prince Henry, wished me far from the Tees. Then they would attack and use the treaty with the

Empress as an excuse. I was just amazed that Henry of Blois had been taken in by this. There was something I was missing. I waved forward Henry Fitz Empress. "This is my squire. He is the son of Empress Matilda." I could see that they did not know of this. I guessed that they had not even bothered to speak to Henry's mother before travelling north. "Henry, tell the priests from Winchester why we went to war with the Scots."

He said, firmly, "They raided and killed many Englishmen from around Barnard Castle. They stole animals, burned farms and enslaved women and children. I saw the bodies and burned farms."

"So perhaps you, as churchmen of England, should write a letter to the Pope demanding that the Scottish lords should be excommunicated."

"We have no proof of that!"

"You have my word and that of the future King of England. And what proof has the Archbishop of Glasgow!"

"The word of the Constable of Carlisle."

"Ah, so an English priest believes a Scottish lord over an English one. Interesting." I turned to Henry, "You will have some interesting decisions to make when you are king, Henry." He nodded and I winked at him. He joined the others. "Will you be returning south tomorrow, gentlemen or visiting the Scots?"

I had confused them. They had expected the threat of ex-communication to have had more effect. They were bluffing. Pope Innocent was too crafty to side with one side or the other in the Civil War. The outcome was still in doubt. He was a practical and pragmatic Pope. He would side with the winning side... at a price, of course.

"We will return south tomorrow."

"Good, then tonight we will serve you fare which is more representative of this valley. My steward will show you to your quarters."

When they had left us Sir Richard asked, "What was that about? Excommunication? Are you not afraid for your soul, lord?"

"Did we do anything wrong? Did we do anything which others have not done?" They all shook their heads. "This was an attempt to make me leave my valley. I will delay my visit south until after the harvest is in. I do not trust the Scots."

Henry said, "Visit south, lord?"

"Yes, Henry. It seems I may well be welcome at your mother's court soon. I did intend to go before the month was out but now I shall wait. We will use this time to send scouts and determine what the Scots are up to. I had thought our expedition would have taught them a lesson but it seems not." I turned to Richard. "Fetch Alice to me."

When my knights and squires had departed I spoke to Alice, "I want tonight's feast to be fit for a king. I want these priests to leave here thinking that this is the land of milk and honey and we are overflowing with food and ale."

"But we are well off, my lord!"

"I know and I want them to talk of this feast for months to come." She went away confused but I was becoming crafty too. I wanted them to think that I would not leave my valley at all. When I did return to the Empress' side I would sneak away in the night. I could plot too. I had been brought up in the court of the Byzantine Emperor.

I dressed in my finest clothes. I had silks I had brought from the east. I wore gold on my fingers and around my neck. After I had bathed I used expensive oils. I made sure that my squires and knights all wore the new surcoats which Alice had just had made for us and we used expensive candles not the tallow ones. The Great Hall looked as festive and as glorious as it ever had. Adela would have been proud although she would have frowned at my motives.

We had a wild boar as the centrepiece for the meal. Even the gaggle of priests could not consume it all and my men at arms would feast well upon it. A brace of swans began the meal as well as four stuffed salmon. I ate sparingly but they seemed not to notice. The wine was a heady one from Chinon. Rich and powerful, it proved too much for two of the priests who had to have their sleeping forms pulled from the food. The dessert was a plum pudding. It was heavily spiced and was a speciality of Alice.

131

Canon Theobald beamed at me, "You eat well here, Earl. I have not tasted finer food since... I have never tasted food so fine and the wine is superb. Why even the Bishop's table is poorer than this and yet you said that the north is poor."

"It is, your grace, but not for those who support the Empress."

He seemed to see, as though for the first time, my clothes and my gold. He glanced around and saw the tapestries on the walls and the fine goblets used for the wine. "You must have few men then if you can afford all of this."

My natural honesty almost undid me for I would not actually lie nor would I exaggerate. All that I had said was the truth it was just that this was not the normal feast. "I have over three hundred knights, men at arms and archers under my command. Every one of us has at least two horses and every man at arms has a full hauberk. I have every castle garrisoned by dedicated warriors and we make swords and weapons so highly prized that they bring much gold to this land."

I smiled as I saw him sit back. I knew what he would do. He would tell the Bishop what I had said. He would tell Stephen and Queen Matilda. I have no doubt that there would be Scottish spies and they would be told too. The result would be that my enemies would be fearful of attacking us. They would all have the numbers and they would be given to them by a canon. They would be believed. If I was to be away from the valley then I wanted all to fear attacking us.

They left the next day. Some of the priests were a little unsteady on their feet but the Canon had much on which to ponder. I knew that they would visit York. There had been two nominations for Archbishop to replace Thurstan: Waltheof of Melrose had had his nomination quashed by Stephen while Henry de Sully had had his nomination quashed by Pope Innocence. There was a religious void there now and the Canon struck me as a clever man who might try to exploit the situation. Such conspiracies suited me as I now trusted no one in York and the more confusion which reigned there the better.

After they had left I began to plan my response to Prince Henry, the Earl of Northumbria. This would not be an act of war but it would be a threat to Northumbria. I told my knights that we would leave at the start of September and then I wrote a letter to the Empress. When *'Adela'* docked my captain would deliver it.

Chapter 11

Aiden and his men rode north. I had visited with Sir Hugh to ask him to keep a good watch on his borders to the west. It was the north where I feared treachery. With more new men for my walls, I was confident that all my entire ring of castles could be well garrisoned. I would take such a large army north that Prince Henry would have to think twice before venturing south. It was when he feared an attack by me that I would be able to ride south and join the Empress.

I was kept very busy but I noticed Henry Fitz Empress keeping a close eye on me. The visit of the clergy had set him to thinking. "My lord, if you ride north do you not risk ex-communication? That risks your soul."

Gilles and Richard were also interested but they had feared to raise the issue. A warrior's beliefs were his own. They knew that some of my men were barely Christian. Sven the Rus and the Frisians were only Christians because it enabled them to gain work. I had seen Sven's hammer of Thor around his neck. They could reconcile their new choice with the fact that amongst the pantheon of gods they worshipped there was one Allfather.

"Do you know where I was born, Henry?"

"Yes, my lord, in the Eastern Empire; the city of Constantinopolis or as Erre calls it Miklagård."

"That is so and they are Christian. However, they follow not Rome for they began their church before the church in Rome. They are Christian but a different branch. They are called Orthodox and they follow the teachings of the Patriarch. I would not wish to be excommunicated but that would mean I could not take communion in a Church of Rome. If that unlikely event happened then I would send to the east and hire a priest to serve here. I could build another church." I saw the three of them and their faces. I had shocked them. "But it will not come to that. This is a conspiracy concocted by the churches, the Scots and, I believe, Stephen or his wife, to force me from this country. They thought I would either stop my war or go to Rome to seek forgiveness from the Pope. That will not happen."

"But you risk your soul for my mother, me and for England."

"I do not think that my soul was ever in danger but I would have risked it if it was necessary. In my heart, I know that what I do is right and if I am wrong then I will face my punishment on judgement day."

When Aiden returned it was with dire news. "The Scots have gathered an army, lord. It is north of the Tyne by the bridges at the New Castle. They have improved the defences there since we raided."

We had captured the New Castle and held it for a while. The Scots, it seemed, had learned their lesson. The last time we had come, when we had avenged the death of Sir Hugh Manningham we had come from the west, through Hexham. I had no doubt they would have made the west end of the town walls and the gate there even stronger and would rely on the bridge across the Tyne for defence.

By the end of August, my men were gathered at my castle. Sir Hugh and ten men of arms joined me but the vast bulk of his men remained at his castle. I needed Sir Hugh's banner. We had new men and so I was able to take north even more men than had raided Carlisle. All depended on how much I could convince Prince Henry that I would attack him.

We left at the beginning of September and took our spare horses but disguised them as sumpters carrying supplies for a long campaign. We rode quickly north up the Durham Road. We crossed the Wear upstream of Durham but I knew that the garrison or their scouts would have seen us. They were Scottish but were not the game I sought. We swung northeast and reached the ridge overlooking the gate at the head of the bridge leading to the New Castle.

Although we had travelled quickly we had been seen and riders had warned Prince Henry of our imminent arrival. Refugees were fleeing over the bridge as we crested the ridge which paralleled the Tyne. These were not native English. These were Scottish incomers who had taken over the lands of our people. They took only that which they could carry upon their backs. The Warlord of the North was coming and that was the time to flee!

As I lined my men up on the ridge I spied great activity both at the bridge gate and within the walls. Wulfric laughed and pointed west. I could see banners as men rode from their camps there, "They thought we would do as we did the last time and attack from Hexham. You have upset their plans for the defence of the north, my lord."

"Good. If they think they know my mind then they are wrong. Have the servants we brought set up the tents and the camp. Aiden, take your scouts and hunt us something. Dick, go with Sir Philip and capture as many animals as you can."

"Aye lord."

"You know what to do when you have them."

The line of men who faced the Scots did not alter but a third of the men we had brought were now engaged in other activities. I, too, could deceive. Time passed and still, we did not move. Each man stood next to their horse and stared at the walls of the castle. As the smoke from our fires rose in the skies the gates leading to the bridge opened and three men, bareheaded and without shields, rode forth.

I mounted. "Henry, bring my banner. Sir Edward, come with me." I took off my helmet and gave it to Gilles. We rode down the cobbled surface towards the bridge. They had abandoned the gatehouse at the southern end. We had taken it so easily the last time that there was little point in defending it. We rode under the arch towards the middle of the bridge where the three riders awaited us. I smiled when I saw that one was a Templar. They were using a priest albeit an armed one. The other two were Scottish knights and one had a Scottish lion on his shield.

We halted close to them. I saw them frown as they spied Henry. The Constable of Carlisle would have told his lord and master of the presence of the future king. The knight with the lion spoke first. "I am Alexander of Moray and I am Prince Henry's kin. I speak for the Earl of this land you have violated."

"Then you know that I have punished the Constable of Carlisle for his effrontery and despoliation of the west." I smiled, "How is he, by the way? Has he recovered?"

"My cousin will fight you again, Warlord."

"Good. I need the exercise!"

I could see that my words had irritated the Mormaer. "I did not come to bandy words with an enemy of the Church! What is it that you want?"

I had been right. This had been a Scottish plot. "I come to speak with Prince Henry, the one who has usurped the title of Earl of Northumbria."

"I will see if he will deign to converse with you." He looked up at the sky. "It is late and I do not trust you in the night. If the Prince will speak then we will sound the horn in the morning and meet back here."

While he had been speaking the smell of cooking meat had drifted over. This was not accidental. Aiden and Dick had put two of the animals on the fires and men were using sheets of old canvas to waft the smell across the river. Aided by a breeze from the southeast the smell of beef being roasted was unmistakable.

"There is no hurry, mormaer, we dine well on the fare from the fields to the south of us. My men enjoy beef; especially when it is free. Take all the time you wish. We are going nowhere." I leaned forward and added, ominously, "Nor I think, are you!"

We turned and rode back up the side of the river to our waiting men. "Sir Wulfric, place guards here. Sir Harold and Sir John, take your men upstream and watch for them crossing with boats. We did it the last time we were here. They may try to copy us."

The weather was clement. The breeze from the southeast brought warm air. I wondered if it brought it all the way

137

from Anjou. The squires tied the horses to lines and we sat around the fires and stuffed ourselves with the two deer Aiden and his men had caught and the two old cows Dick had slaughtered. The people had left so quickly that we found a great quantity of ale, food and grain. Our horses grazed and then had a second meal of oats. What we took the Scots could not consume.

Sir Edward said, "I wondered at your strategy, Earl. It seemed overly complicated."

Wulfric threw the gnawed bone onto the fire and wiped his hands on his surcoat, "You should have known that the Earl thinks things through. You and I Edward, are old warhorses. You point us towards an enemy and say kill! The Earl thinks two moves ahead of the enemy. That is why we win more than we lose."

Henry piped up, "But what if the Prince fights?"

"Then we have already won but I fear that he will not be as compliant as the Constable of Carlisle. I have been defeating the Prince since the battle of the Standards. He will not risk a battle with me. This is a gesture merely so that we can travel to Oxford unseen. Tomorrow will be a time of threats and counter-threats. I will see if I can make him blink first." I waved a hand at the knights seated around the fire. "He fears me but he also fears these men. It is many years since a Scot took one of my valley knights. Aiden has reported that it is a huge army that is gathered. It is a measure of how much he fears all of you."

The first time I had fought Prince Henry he had showed me his character. He was brave and he was clever. He had almost won the battle at Northallerton but when the tide had turned he had shown that he had a keen sense of self-preservation. He had fled the field and arrived at Carlisle with but one retainer. All the rest were abandoned and captured or killed. He would be king. He feared anything which might stop that and one more major defeat might bring out a rival. That was my gamble. He wanted the crown more than he wanted a battle.

The next morning I sent half of my men, archers, men at arms and squires led by knights to range up and down the

Tyne. Already the crops were being harvested and some had been collected in. We would take it. Hungry men would have enough to worry about feeding their families and would be reluctant to try our walls.

The horn sound as I had expected and I rode with Sir Edward and Henry to meet with the Prince. Since his son's recovery, Edward had been his old pugnacious self. He laughed as we headed across the bridge. "I would gamble a suit of armour that this king has witches trying to lay spells upon you warlord. You, truly are the bane of his life."

We waited in the middle of the bridge for the gates of the castle to open. "What do you mean, Sir Edward?" Henry was curious.

"If it were not for the Earl here then Prince Henry would have all of England as far south as Lincoln and Chester. Those two castles would be the northern border of the County of Northumbria. Each time he has tried to gain more territory it has been the Earl who has thwarted him."

The gates opened and Prince Henry, his standard-bearer and Alexander of Moray rode out to meet me. The Prince had put on weight since I had last seen him. He had eaten more than he had fought. Warriors should have a lean and hungry look about them. I pointed to the castle, "I see you re-invested the castle after I left."

"It is my castle."

"For the moment."

"The Empress has signed a treaty with my father. You are outside the law."

"True and that should worry you for if I am outside the law then who restrains me?"

"The Church," he jabbed an accusing finger at me. "You have broken the treaty!"

"I signed no treaty. I was not consulted about a treaty and my lands are ruled by me!" I pointed to Henry. "Until the rightful heir, Henry Fitz Empress becomes King of England and Duke of Normandy I have no King to give me orders."

I had not given him the answer he expected. "But the Empress...."

Henry said, "My mother told the Earl to defend the Valley of the Tees." He pointed a finger at the Prince. "It was your man, Malcolm, who raided England and we punished him. The Earl has done no wrong and I approve of his actions."

For some reason, it seemed to amuse the Prince who chuckled, "A young cockerel crowing in the farmyard eh? Before you can become King you need to rid your land of Stephen, and his son, and his wife and then gain the approval of the Church!"

Henry raised his voice to the Prince. "Do not tell me what to do! You are a Scot and as such bend the knee to the King of England!"

I think it was his tone that annoyed the Prince so much. "I have no time to bandy words with a child! What will you, Earl? I have pressing matters."

"I come here to tell you that your plot has failed. I am ignoring the Pope. I was baptised not in the Church of Rome but the Church of Constantinople. If the patriarch wishes to summon me then so be it but I fear your gold does not reach that far. I will be in my valley and we will watch. I know you have an army north of the Tyne. Come south and the rats will feast on your men's bones all the way back to Din Burgh! And I would not look to the land south of the river of food. We will collect it all before we return to my valley."

The Prince was beaten. His shoulders slumped. "You will be defeated one day, Warlord. Of that, I have no doubt."

"True but I guarantee one thing... it will not be by you or any Scotsman!"

He whipped his horse's head around and they returned to the castle. As we rode back Sir Edward said, "That was well done, lord."

"It will be well done if I can slip away unseen. Now let us do as I said and return south. We collect every animal and every grain and fruit as we do so. We shall do as your great grandfather did without the slaughter of people. We shall make the land south of the Tyne empty of life!"

We spent four days ranging as far west as Hexham and as far east as South Shields. We drove the animals south. When we reached our valley the first signs of autumn were upon us. The apple and pear trees were dropping their fruit and the fields had all been harvested of oats, barley and, on the south-facing slopes, wheat. It was just afternoon as we reached Stockton, my home. Even as I entered my gates John of Craven shouted from my east tower, "Lord, the *'Adela'* has been sighted. She will be docking within the hour."

I waved my acknowledgement. I had wondered why I had not heard from the Empress. Had the Earl not gone to France? I changed out of my mail. These days the relief from shedding my iron skin was huge. I had to wear it once I left my valley. I was surrounded by foes.

I summoned John, my steward, "John, is there any news from the Empress?"

"No, lord. Had there been I would have sent word."

I would have to wait to see what William of Kingston had to tell me. Impatient for news I went to my quay to await him. He looked surprised to see me as he sprang ashore, "My lord? I had not expected to see you here."

My heart sank, "Why not?"

"I was in Bristol a month since and one of the Empress' men wondered why you had not responded to her summons for help."

"I received no summons. What help did she need?"

"The Earl Of Gloucester left for Normandy almost three months ago now and King Stephen began to attack the castles surrounding Oxford. He captured Cirencester and cut the road from Gloucester to Oxford. The Empress is cut off."

"Treachery!"

"What, my lord?"

"Not you, William, but the messengers she has sent have been intercepted. It is that damned renegade and turncoat Ranulf of Chester who is treacherous. The land between here and the Empress is now not safe. Thank you for your warning. I pray I am in time."

"Would you wish me to sail there with you, Lord?"

I shook my head, "I need to be there quickly. I will leave this night. A voyage would take many days."

My squires and Dick were in my hall and I rushed through the gates. It was two hundred and fifty miles to Oxford. If we used spare horses then we might make it in four days perhaps even three but there were perilously few places for us to stay. Even as I entered my hall I had made a decision.

"Sir Dick, we leave for Oxford this night. I want you and the best six men you have. I want to travel quickly and to be hidden."

Dick had served with me long enough not to be surprised by such a request. He nodded. Harold, Tristan and John were there and heard my words.

"Lord, that is madness. You will be travelling the length of the country just about and it is filled with your enemies."

"I know but the Empress needs me. She is surrounded by Stephen's forces. They are closing in. Time is of the essence. Her brother left for Normandy three months since. I would dearly love to take all of my knights and men but that is what the Scots want."

Dick turned and said, "If we take four sumpters and remounts for us we can carry the mail on the sumpters and travel quickly. There are places we can stay. You are right, lord, with just eleven of us we can stay hidden and the places we can stay will be smaller. I will arrange this. Come, Gilles, bring the squires and we will teach young Henry how to pack light."

"We will not need the standard, Henry."

"Aye, lord."

I waved over John, my steward. "I will be leaving for Oxford. I know not when I will return. Sir Edward commands in my absence. Harold, you will tell him."

"Aye, lord."

"I need him to keep a close watch on the borders and be ready to repulse the Scots if they dare to venture south. Alice, we may be away some time. Have you winter cloaks?"

"We have, lord, but I have not had time to dye them with your colours. They are plain white."

"They will have to do. How many are there?"

"I have ten."

Then pack those and as many furs as we can carry on our sumpters."

"Which servants will you take, lord?"

"None, we travel light."

"You are a great lord! You should have servants and slaves to wait on you."

I laughed, "When I am old and in my dotage, I shall do so."

As she left I heard her muttering, "If you live to old age."

She cared for us and I forgave her insolence but she was right. One day I would take a risk too many or a younger version of me would come along and I would fall.

Chapter 12

Dick led us south along the Great North Road. It was a risk but we could move quickly and once we had passed York then we could disappear. Dick was taking us to the tiny hamlet of Cadeby a few miles from Doncaster. We were some miles along the road and passing Osmotherley when I asked him why.

"When I was an outlaw the priest there was kind to us. We can take shelter in his church and, as it is a grange, he has a barn. It is close to the forest in case we are pursued."

"It is many years since you lived there. He may be dead."

"He may but he was young. He was my age."

Henry had heard his words and said, "You put a lot of faith in this priest, Sir Richard. He may have changed."

"He is my cousin. I trust him."

It was almost eighty miles to our destination. Had we not had to watch for enemies we could have travelled quicker but each time Rafe signalled that there were travellers ahead we took shelter. It was dark by the time we left the Great North Road and headed west and south to the small hamlet hidden by the eaves of the forest.

Dick halted us by the forest. "If you stay here, lord, then I will go first. I do not want him frightened by mailed men. To those who live in the forest mailed men are oft time enemies."

After he had gone Henry asked, "Was he truly an outlaw?"

"He was and the archers who are with us were too. Sir Harold was an outlaw before he became my squire."

"And can you trust them?"

I heard a snort from Long Tom behind us. "You have fought with these men and seen them fight for me, your mother and you. What do you think?"

His head dropped, "I think that I should learn to think before I speak." He turned to Long Tom, "I am sorry if I offended you. I am young."

Long Tom grinned and said, "No offence taken, young sir."

Dick returned, "Come, my cousin, Robert lives still. I will show you his barn."

With the horses unsaddled, fed, watered and hidden, we went into the rude hut which lay close to the church. The church was substantial and made of stone. We learned from Robert that Roger the Poitevin had built it.

I could see similarities with Dick but while Dick was broad and powerful the priest was thin and looked as though a good meal was needed. He tried to press food upon us but we had brought ham, cheese and bread. We shared it with him. We might have to go on short rations soon but the shelter was worth the sacrifice.

Dick said, "How goes it here now, Robert? Is life as hard?"

"It is more unpredictable. It was hard and then the Scots were given the Honour of Clitheroe and the taxes have not been collected these four years. We have no protection but it is free to live here. The Bishop of Lincoln sometimes sends for his tithes but they are fearful of the outlaws."

"I thought they had all gone."

"They disappeared for a while and then when the Civil War began men sought refuge here. I do what I can for them and I minister to their needs." He peered over to Henry. "And this is the boy who will be king."

I think Henry bridled at the term boy but he remembered his disparaging comments to Long Tom and he merely nodded.

"He will be a good king."

The priest looked at me, "How do you know, Earl?"

This time it was Gilles and Richard who took offence at his tone. I shook my head at them. "He has served with us. He is brave but not reckless. He is thoughtful and yet decisive and he has lived amongst us. That is how we know."

The priest smiled and crossed himself, "Then thank the lord for that! The sooner he becomes King and ends this anarchy the better. I would not mind paying taxes for some peace and safety."

The next day we headed south. The Great North Road was no longer our route and we had other roads to use. They were narrow and rarely straight. They passed through smaller places but there were far more of them. It would be a tortuous journey. Every clutch of huts and hamlets could house enemies or alert our enemies to our presence deep in their land.

We had been travelling for a short time when Henry said, "I have a great responsibility do I not, Warlord?"

"You do indeed."

"That tiny hamlet where we stayed is so small and yet a decision from me could either make their lives a misery or joyful beyond belief."

I said nothing for this was how I knew he would be a good king. He was learning.

Dick asked, "Do we try to ride until we reach Oxford, lord? It is a long way and our horses may suffer overmuch."

"No, for I would do the last part with fresh horses. We know not where Stephen and his forces are. We may have to fight our way through their lines."

"Then I know of no other place we could stay." We would have to sleep in the woods and hedgerows.

"Bedworth, lord."

I turned to Richard. My squire rarely volunteered information unless he was confident and he sounded as confident, "Bedworth?"

"When I was a squire we stayed in the inn there. It is on the main road and visitors use it. The landlord seemed like a fair man and it is far from a castle."

Dick said, "That is dangerous."

"Perhaps, Sir Richard, but even if we are betrayed it is but fifty miles to Oxford. I offer the suggestion only. It is not perfect I know."

"We will try it. Who knows, it may prove to be the best decision we have made."

Bedworth had no manor. Rafe reported that when he returned to us after scouting it out. We had arrived before dusk. We had ridden a long way but we had not pushed our horses. The hardest day could be the next. "It looks quiet, lord, and I saw no warriors of any description." He grinned, "The inn looked inviting and it had a large stable."

"Then let us cast the die and see what befalls us."

The village had a green on which animals were grazing. It was not on the Great North Road, we had left that soon after our last halt and it lay off the cobbled road which led to Northampton, along a greenway. There were few people about as we rode through save one old man who was watching the animals. He knuckled his forehead as we passed and then stared at me. The inn was the largest building in the village and had two floors. We reined in and I handed my reins to Gilles. "Be ready for a swift departure." I wondered if the herder had recognised me. "Come, Dick, let us see what sort of welcome we have."

The entrance was low and we had to stoop to enter. It was dark and the interior was lit by smoky tallow candles. There were half a dozen men inside. The owner, or at least, I assumed he was the owner, strode over to me. "My lord, what can we do for you?"

I was not certain if he recognised me but my spurs marked us as knights. "We have another nine men with us and twenty odd horses. We seek beds and stables for the night. Can you accommodate us? We have the money."

He looked dubious. I had no doubt that there were many who would stay and try to leave without paying. A lack of gold was the least of our worries. I took out my purse and picked out an Imperial gold piece. It was a large coin and would pay for the inn never mind the rooms.

His eyes lit up, "Aye lord and we have the finest food between London and York here." He frowned, "I only have four rooms here in the inn but there is a stall above the stable."

"That will be fine. For that I want the horses grooming and feeding grain."

"Of course, my lord."

I nodded to Dick who left to fetch my men. I was weary. My shoulder and my knee ached. I sat, acutely aware that every eye was on me. My cloak covered my surcoat and they would wonder who I was. I doubted that many here would know my wolf emblem.

"Wine or beer, lord?"

I knew that any wine he could have would be like vinegar and I saw that the locals all had foaming ale. "Your beer will be acceptable." I smiled when I saw the relief on his face. He would have had to apologise for the wine. Dick and my squires walked in. I knew that, for Henry, this would be the first time in such a place. He had been cosseted. He stayed in castles and fine halls, not inns with wildlife racing through the roof. "Fetch beer for us all."

They sat down and Henry peered around, nervously. Gilles said, "It will be fine Henry. These are just ordinary folk. The fare will be plain but wholesome and we will sleep in a bed this night."

I smiled, "The three of you will share a room. It may just be straw on the floor."

The ale arrived along with my six men. They sat at an adjacent table. The five of us on my table looked like nobles. The six archers looked like a bunch of cutthroats. Men who might have ventured a comment suddenly found their beer more interesting.

We ordered food and I began to relax. Suddenly the door opened and the man who had been tending the animals stood there. The landlord said, "Tom Lame Leg, what are you doing here? You cannot afford even a horn of ale."

He said, "I just came to speak with the lord."

"Leave them be. They are important men and do not wish to be bothered by the likes of you."

He began to turn and I said, "Stay. Do you know me?"

148

"Aye lord. You are Alfraed, Earl of Cleveland and I served you and your father in Norton when the Scots came. I was there when he was killed. He was a fine man."

I stared at him desperate to bring a name to mind. He looked ancient. Then again it had been more than twenty years since my father had died. It suddenly came to me. "Tom, it is Tom, son of Garth! What happened to you?" He shuffled towards me. "Here, Gilles, make room for an old comrade. Sit, old friend. Landlord, ale for this warrior and food too."

"Thank you, lord, but I do not wish to be a bother."

"This is no bother. We fought together and that makes us brothers. What happened to you?"

"When you went to the east to our father's home in the city of the Emperor I had cross words with some of those in the manor. My wife had died of the fever and I drank too much. I was argumentative in those days. The lame leg didn't help. I left."

"Had you stayed, there would have been a home for you."

"I know, lord, but you were away a good six months and... well we all make mistakes. I went on the road and I had some hard times. I never took to the hood though. I was never an outlaw. Now I look after the animals. They let me sleep in their pens."

The ale and food had arrived. Tom looked up at me, "Do not wait for an invite. Eat and eat heartily. I do not forget an old comrade." I ate too. The food was well cooked but it was hard to digest for I thought how many other Toms had left my service. I had been so concerned about the Empress that I had forgotten so many. I could almost hear my father and Wulfstan chiding me. I saw my squires looking at the emaciated skeleton that was now Tom Lame Leg. I knew that they were wondering how he had been a warrior.

I finished my food and told them. "Old Tom here was a mighty warrior. When the Scots came and slew my father Tom was one of the few left defending his battered body. They were outnumbered but they fought as heroes. They had no mail like you, young Richard. They had a leather

149

hauberk, an old helmet, a sword and a round shield but we sent the Scots packing."

There was pride in Tom's eyes and his voice as he said, "Aye, we did that, lord."

The food had been served, not on dishes but bread platters and Tom was about to devour the platter. "Landlord, more food and ale for Tom. He is my guest this night."

Dick understood Tom more than my squires. I could see Henry frowning as he struggled to understand why I was making such a fuss of this smelly old man. I began to become annoyed and then realised it was not their fault. All three had spent the time not with the poor, nor even the men at arms but knights and their equals. I reached into my purse and took our four gold coins and ten silver ones.

"We have rooms here and in the stables this night, Tom. I would have you share with us. The archers will make you more than welcome."

Dick nodded his assent, "Aye they will, old friend."

"And this small pile of gold and silver is for you. I would urge you to take one of our horses and head north. Return to Stockton. There we shall find you a home. But if not then use it for yourself."

"I cannot take this, lord! It is too much."

"I never released you from my service, Tom. You are owed this for your time since I left. Obey my command."

I saw relief flood his face. "Aye lord, I will go home. I will go back to Stockton. I do not need a horse, I can walk."

"We have a spare horse and you hurt your leg in my service. The day we forget our old warriors is the day we lose." I looked over to Dick who nodded.

We left early but we made sure that Tom was safely on his way. Rafe gave him a spare sword and the moment he strapped it on he became a little younger and his back was straighter.

"It is some years since I had a sword, lord. Memories come flooding back to me. I will wait for you after your journey."

We rode with him to the Great North Road. With the coins in his purse, he was a tempting target but he had a weapon and he could defend himself. As we turned south Dick said, "I feel happier for that encounter, lord. I know not what put the thought in your head, Master Richard but it was a good one. I wonder how many more of our former comrades who were wounded are in such straits."

"I know not but when we return home I will ask John to draw up a list of those old warriors who live in our manors. It would be a useful list to have. They could be a reserve in times of danger."

With happier thoughts than we had had we set off for Oxford. We would be leaving the Great North Road soon for Oxford had not existed before the time of the Saxons. The road was not as straight and there would, in all likelihood, be more enemies before us.

"Lord, how do we get through their lines?"

"I have thought of that. They will have the town surrounded and will be suspicious of all riders but more so from the west. We will approach from the northeast, Bicester, and we will wrap ourselves in our cloaks to hide our surcoats. If we meet any we try to trick our way past them."

Dick nodded, "Then we need Maud, Countess of Chester, she could trick her way into heaven, pick the Devil's pocket and be out before he knew it." It sounded insulting but he was right. Maud, the Earl of Gloucester's daughter, had more spirit and courage than most men. She had won and held Lincoln for us.

"Then we say that we are from York and I am Sir Roger de Lacy."

Henry said, "He is a supporter of Stephen is he not?"

"He is and we captured his brother at the battle of Lincoln. His brother died before he could be ransomed."

"Suppose he fights at the siege already, lord?"

"Then the ruse is up and we fight our way in."

We were approaching Banbury when we had some luck. Rafe rode back to us. He had been a mile ahead. "Lord, there is a wagon broken down ahead. There are merchants and they have guards."

Dick said, "Should we find a way around them, lord?"

"No, we are twenty miles from Oxford let us try our disguise and hope that the merchants do not know de Lacy. His lands are far to the north. He did not fight at Lincoln. We gamble."

Dick was dubious, "Lord, it is one thing to gamble with our lives but Henry here is the future king. It is the country with which you gamble."

He had spoken quietly but Henry had sharp ears. "Do not worry, Sir Richard, my family has a history of gambling. If they had not then my great grandfather would never have risked crossing the sea to capture a whole country."

"There. We have the approval of our next monarch!"

As we approached the guards around the broken wagon became wary. I held up my hands, "We are no danger to honest travellers. Can we help?"

"I am Ralph of Northampton. We are transporting goods to Bicester for the King and the wagon broke." He glared at the carters. "These fools charge me a fortune for inferior wagons."

"It is the metal we carry, my lord. It is too heavy for our wagons."

I pointed to the spare cart horses they had. "Then pack some heavy goods on the spare horses. You will have to travel more slowly but that will still be faster than this will it not?"

Both the carter and the merchant smiled. The merchant snapped, "Get on with it then. Load the horses and get the spare wheel fitted." He turned to me. "I am indebted to you....?"

"Roger de Lacy of Fulford. It is near to York."

"I know of Fulford. I have sent goods there before. Would you do us the honour of travelling with us, lord? These are parlous times and I would be grateful for your protection. I will pay for food on the way."

"We are heading for the King's camp at Oxford and we should be there as soon as possible."

"Bicester is but a little out of your way and the King needs what I carry." He leaned over to me. "I transport a trebuchet. The King intends to assault the walls before winter."

I had heard of the trebuchet. It was more powerful than a mangonel. The Emperor had some. I knew that they were more complicated to make than a simple engine to hurl rocks. I nodded, as though reluctant, "Very well as you serve the cause of King Stephen then I will escort you."

"Besides Bicester is where he has a vast camp. You may find yourselves quartered there."

With my advice heeded, we were soon on our way. I did not need to tell my men to watch their tongues. They played the part of dour northerners. If the guards thought them miserable and unfriendly it would not hurt our cause.

I rode with Ralph of Northampton and I spoke to him. "I had thought the siege and the war might be over. I heard that the Earl of Gloucester is in Normandy. With just the Empress to capture the war could soon be over."

"It is not the Earl of Gloucester who should worry you. I would have thought that living close to York you would have feared the Wolf of the North more; the fiendish Earl of Cleveland! I just thank God he is fighting the barbaric Scots. Let them both slaughter each other and keep us safe."

"He does not venture down to York overmuch."

"And for that, you should be grateful. The mention of his names makes honest men lock their doors and double their guards."

"So the siege will soon be over?"

He shook his head, "The town has strong walls and the castle is protected by the river from the town. But by Christmas, the King will dine in Oxford. Nothing gets in and nothing gets out of the town. They will starve soon."

We halted halfway to Bicester. The merchant knew the road and there was an inn. We ate well and rested the horses. I could tell that Dick fretted about the delay. His eyes flickered at every new arrival. I believed it helped us. As we left an autumn squall struck us. It followed us intermittently all the way to Bicester. We had our cloaks pulled tightly around our heads to afford some protection and conversation was, perforce, limited.

There were guards on the road into Bicester and we were halted at the town gates. "State your business!"

"I am Ralph of Northampton and I have materials ordered by the King."

I peered from under the hood of my cloak. There was a sergeant at arms and four men. We could slay them but that would do us no good.

"And who are you?"

"I am Roger of Fulford and I bring men to serve the King."

He seemed satisfied. "The wagons can be left on the south side of the town but you, sir knight, must travel to Temple Cowley, it is just a couple of miles from Oxford. The King has his main camp there. He will be pleased to see more men, no matter how few in number. His sergeant at arms will give you the passes you will need to travel. We are wary here. There are rumours of a rebel force in the east."

"Thank you."

And with that, we were allowed through the gates of Bicester. The merchant's company helped us out of the gates and to the huge camp of wagons and supplies which were gathered there. Stephen was preparing for an attack and from the number of wagons and carts, it was imminent. We could not get to Oxford soon enough. We bade the merchant farewell and spurred our horses. I had planned on reaching Oxford before dark but the merchant had delayed us. It had been a fortuitous meeting for we were closer to Oxford than we would have been otherwise. We rode tightly together and we rode hard. The leisurely journey had saved our horses and with Oxford just ten miles ahead we could afford to gallop.

Rafe and Long Tom rode ahead of Dick and I. Henry, Gille and Richard were riding tight behind us with the four archers and the spare horses bringing up the rear. We found the enemy or rather the enemy found us, just half a mile from the walls of Oxford.

"Halt!" Eight men had a brazier at the side of the road. They wore leather armour and looked to be men of Northampton for I recognised the livery.

This time we could not afford to halt for we would be discovered. We had no passes and we were so close that we had to force the road. I drew my sword, "At them!"

Rafe and Long Tom had been ready with their weapons and they leaned forward to slash at the two men before them. Dick and I burst between them. The Sergeant at Arms thrust his pike at Dick who flicked it away and I brought my sword across the side of his head. Gilles and Richard slashed at and wounded two surprised looking guards and the other three fled. Their voices, however, had raised the alarm. There were others camped nearby. The dusk had hidden them from us but now I heard the alarm being repeated down the lines. We had our chance and I seized it.

"Gilles, lead the horses and the squires towards the castle. Henry, you must gain us entry."

As they galloped past us I threw off my hood. I needed a disguise no longer. I grabbed my shield and we rode after our companions. I heard men rushing from our left and right. In the darkening gloom, it was hard to make them out. We kept a hundred paces behind the last of the sumpters. We wore no mail. That was on our pack horses. It meant we could ride quicker. I heard hooves behind us. Glancing over my shoulder I saw four riders. One wore mail. Ahead I saw the walls of Oxford looming up and I could hear an alarm bell ringing within the town. In the time it took to look at the town walls and gatehouse, then back the riders were less than thirty paces from us.

"Dick, Rafe! Turn!"

I turned first and my move took the four riders by surprise. I brought my sword across the chest of the mailed man. The edge bit into his mail and the force of my blow allied to his speed threw him from his horse. I wheeled Rolf around and slashed at the back of a second man. I hacked through to his spine. Dick, Rafe and Long Tom took care of the other two. We slapped their horses on their rumps and they galloped down the Banbury Road with us.

The gates were still firmly closed when we reached them. Behind us, I could hear the thunder of hooves as we were pursued. Henry's voice sounded shrill but he showed that one day he would command, "I demand you open the gate! I am Henry Fitz Empress!"

I shouted as I reached the bridge, "And I am the Earl of Cleveland!"

There was a pause and then the gates creaked open. Above us, I heard the crack of crossbow bolts as the defenders saw our pursuers. Dick and I were the last ones through the gates. We had made Oxford but now we would be trapped inside. We were besieged in the castle of Richard D'Oyly! But we had reached the side of the Empress. No matter how black things looked we had achieved the first part of my plan. I now had to work out a way to extricate her from the town and castle of Oxford.

Chapter 13

We hurried through the narrow streets of Oxford towards the castle. Word had spread of our arrival. I heard my name and that of Henry whispered and murmured as we rode through knots of people summoned by the sound of the alarm bell. As more came out they grew into shouts.

"Warlord, is your army following?"

"Praise God we are saved! The hero of Lincoln has come!"

"Have you come to defeat Stephen again?"

"We have Henry and the Warlord, what cannot we do?"

Those were the words I heard but there were others. I did not have the heart to say that the eleven of us were all the relief force that could be mustered. The Empress with Robert D'Oyly and her two ladies awaited us. I allowed Henry to dismount first and greet his mother. I followed and handed my reins to Gilles, "Sir Robert, are there stables enough for our horses?"

He nodded, "There are stables enough but we lack grain and I fear that we shall be eating the horses soon unless the siege is lifted."

I spoke quietly as the Empress was hugging her son and I did not want to spoil the moment for them."I fear that there will be no relief. Stephen has war machines arriving. Soon he will begin to batter your walls."

The knight nodded, "Then we shall have to defend our castle. As you know the moat surrounds the castle and it will not be easy for him to break us down."

"But the town walls are vulnerable. I saw that as I rode in. I would bring in as much food as you can to the castle. Winter comes and that might be our best ally."

The Empress turned to me and said, as she put her hands on my shoulders, "You have done the impossible again and brought my son to me. Henry has told me that my messengers did not reach you. If it was not for your ship and his captain then we would be trapped here. Now that you have arrived we have hope once more."

I nodded not daring to break the bad news to her. "Your son has done well. He has been a good and faithful squire. I shall be sorry to lose him."

Henry looked up at me, "Lose me? But I am your squire!"

"No, for that office ends now. You are with your mother, the Empress. The two of you are the future of England. While your mother was free then we could indulge our belief that you and I could be knight and squire. Now is time for reality, Henry Fitz Empress. You will make a fine knight, is that not so Gilles?"

"Aye lord, he has learned well. He will easily earn his spurs."

"High praise indeed from a hard taskmaster. Now you must learn to be king. Your mother can begin to instruct you and then you must return to your father for if I hear aright then Normandy will soon be yours. You will be Duke of Normandy. That is a higher rank than is mine."

"But you are Warlord!"

I laughed, "And I answer to no one. If you are Duke then you have the King of France as a liege lord as well as the Pope. I have no such masters."

Maud put her arm around him, "Come we will get food and warmth." She smiled at Dick and the archers, "And I owe you seven a debt of gratitude too. Thank you for bringing my son safely home."

As we headed towards the mighty keep I wondered just how safe this castle really was. My squires and archers took the horses to the stables. I looked around at the walls: with a keep, a strong barbican and five towers I knew that we could hold the enemy at bay. Hunger and disease were different enemies. The Great Hall, in the heart of the Keep, was well lit and warm. The Empress had been about to dine and we ate well. While she caught up with her son I spoke with Robert D'Oyly about the defences.

"The city wall is not as high as the castle walls but up until now, Stephen has not tried too hard to take them. We are lucky for the gates have good strong towers. If he attacks there he will struggle and would bleed his army away."

"So as long as we can hold the walls of the town then we are secure?"

"Until the food runs out."

I looked at the plate of food before me. "Then, in that case, I would suggest we go on rations now. This will be the last feast until we are relieved."

"And where will the relief come from?"

"Unless Sir Miles or Sir Brian takes command no one until the Earl of Gloucester returns. I am assuming that he has been told of the danger?"

"We sent word by ship. Help should come." Sir Richard did not sound confident.

"However it might take longer than we thought. We may have two or three months to sit out the siege. Is that not so?" He nodded glumly.

After we had eaten I was shown my quarters. I was lucky enough to have a small chamber for myself. It was close to the Empress' and when there was a knock at my door I knew who it would be. Margaret and the Empress stood there. I admitted the Empress and Margaret nodded as she closed the door. She was loyal and discreet, she would watch the corridor.

Maud threw her arms around me and kissed me, "I have missed you and your strong arms."

"And I you but we both know these are fleeting moments."

"I know. Hold me tightly and I will keep the memory longer." We stood in silence and she sighed. It was a sigh of contentment. Eventually, she pulled back and said, "Henry has told me all. The young are honest. Excommunication?"

159

"It was a threat. They could not have carried it out and even if they did it would not upset me o'er much."

"There you are wrong for the people would have had difficulty in following you had such a writ been issued. The ordinary people believe what the priests and bishops say."

"I think your son might disagree there. He seems to have a sceptical attitude towards the clergy."

She laughed, "That is your bad influence, my lord. You are making our son into a rebel!"

"Why did the Earl travel to Normandy? It seemed out of character."

"That was your doing. You had such success at Mortain that he wished to emulate you. Here he could only win small battles. There he can gain glory and treasure. All spoke of the chests of coins and treasure you brought back."

"I hate to say it but we need him and his men here now."

"It is that bad?"

"Food will run out in less than two months." I had given her the stark truth and it hit home. Her eyes widened and I nodded. "I have told Robert that we now begin rationing. All of us must cut down what we eat and eke it out."

"I know you are giving me the worst but I believe with you here that we have a chance."

"I hope so but at the moment I cannot see how we can get out of this trap. With Stephen surrounding the town and but one way in and out we need a miracle."

The next day I walked the walls and saw for myself that Stephen had decided to begin the assault. War machines were being constructed beyond arrow range. He had men moving huge shields into place to protect those who would work the machines. They would also provide cover for his archers and his bowmen. As I walked the walls with Sir Robert, Dick and my squires it became obvious to us all that we could not defend all the walls. Luckily we only had the four main gates but even there our paltry numbers of archers and crossbows would not be as effective as they might.

I shook my head, "When I think of the archers we have at home, Dick. Every farmer and burgher can pull a bow."

Sir Robert said, "I am afraid that the people of Oxford are a prosperous folk. They think that pulling a bow is beneath them. The garrison is all that we can depend upon."

"Then when Stephen takes all their goods and wealth from them they might reconsider."

The three of us made our plans. The castle did not need defenders. It could neither be overlooked nor assaulted. Therein lay a problem for if the town fell then there was no escape. The stream which led to the Thames and the moat around us had no bridges. We would be trapped. The barbican was well made as was the bridge across two moats to the castle. It was a castle within a castle. We placed our archers and crossbows in the gatehouses. I could not risk an attack at night and so they slept there, watching in shifts. The knights and men at arms were allocated a section of the town walls. Sir Robert forced the burgers to take up arms and watch the walls too. Their reluctance was in direct contrast to the attitude of my people when the Scots had besieged us.

Three days after we had arrived the Empress, Henry, the Constable and myself were summoned to the town gates. Stephen had arrived for a truce. He had taken off his helmet and was flanked by William of Ypres and William Martel his two most experienced commanders. I stood next to the Empress and Henry.

As soon as he saw me he nodded, "It was you who sneaked into the castle. I thought it would be. You cannot stay away from the side of my cousin overlong and young Henry too. We are well met eh? Although perhaps the circumstances suit me a little better this time than the last time in Bristol."

The Empress asked, "What are your terms, Stephen? We are quite comfortable here."

"They are simple. Quit the castle and return to Normandy. Your brother and husband appear to be as successful there as we are here. I fear I have lost Normandy but then you have lost England too."

Henry began to become irritated and I said, quietly, "Be a squire again and listen. Do not rise to his jibes." He nodded. I said loudly, "I think England is too big a mouthful for you,

Usurper. This castle is strong and even if it were to fall I have yet to see a foe who could take my valley from me. So long as I hold the valley then England shall never be defeated."

"Brave words from someone who has but a handful of his men with him. I know how many men you brought and a handful of Sherwood archers will make little difference to the outcome of this battle. If that is your decision then prepare for battle. When I capture you, cuz, you shall enjoy the hospitality of the Tower. It is less pestilential than Bristol. And as for you Earl, I fear this may be your last stand. You have not your knights and archers about you."

Dick said, quietly, "Let me send an arrow his way, lord! We can end this now!" I knew that Stephen's jibes had got to him.

"No, Dick, there is a truce and it is not honourable." I turned back to Stephen, "I have enough. First, catch me before you think to display my head!"

He nodded and turned away.

"They will come soon. He has a plan and he did not expect us to surrender. He just wanted to be seen to be doing the right thing. Henry, take your mother back to the Keep. You will need your new mail and helmet before too long."

Dick said, "I shall have my archers here, lord, at this gate."

"I will be here too. Sir Robert, you know your knights and people best."

"Aye, I will keep about the walls. I will have pig fat and water ready. We will give them a hot reception."

The only bridges over the Isis were protected by three strong gates. The one upon which we stood had two small towers and Dick and his archers took their place in them. It afforded them a good view and a greater range for their war bows.

The enemy approached behind a wall of shields. They did not have many horses. There was no point. Stephen and his household knights were the exception. They were gathered on a small piece of high ground just to the north of us and safely out of bow range. I wondered if he posed a threat on his horses but there was a river before him. Perhaps he wished to intimidate us by showing how many men he had at his disposal. The enemy dragged the mangonel into position. As they began to adjust the tension Dick and his archers let loose with their arrows. The men working the machines fell to the deadly rain of arrows. William of Ypres quickly ordered shields to be raised to protect them. It was an illusion for as soon as they prepared to send their rocks at the walls my archers slew the men working the machine when the shields were removed. Even so, they managed to hit the walls with a dozen or so rocks. The damage was clear but they would still have to risk the bridges and there we had the pig fat and boiling water. It would take weeks to destroy the walls.

Gradually they worked their way closer to the walls using the huge shields and the shields of the men at arms to draw closer. Our archers took a terrible toll but Stephen's men moved relentlessly towards the river and the bridge. It was during the middle of the afternoon when they tried their first direct assault. We had the pig fat ready for them should they try the ram we saw approaching but Stephen was clever. Forty men ran forward carrying four ladders and protected by their shields. Their archers and crossbows sent a shower of missiles towards us and we sheltered beneath our shields. Had it not been for my magnificent seven archers then more would have crossed the bridge but only two ladders made it and were pressed against the walls.

I turned to my squires and the ten men at arms Sir Robert had left with me. "Now we shall see their mettle! Stop them before they reach the top!"

"Aye Warlord!"

We had rocks ready for this situation. The men at arms were strong and the rocks were big. My archers kept loosing at others who tried to cross the bridge but, inevitably some made it. I joined the men at arms who were hurling the stones at the knights and men at arms who were ascending. One was pitched from the ladder and fell with a crunch on the bridge. Others, however, had done this before and they angled their shields so that the stones slid off the shields. I had my sword ready. Gilles and Richard watched one ladder while I watched the other. Thanks to Dick and his archers these were their only way in.

"Keep hurling stones at those who ascend. If you hit them from the side then their shields are less useful."

"Aye Warlord."

I saw the blue and white shield of the first knight as he closed with me. I did not strike his shield but I waited. His left hand held his shield and his right hand held his sword and the ladder. He must have thought there were no defenders for no one struck at him. As his face appeared above the crenulations he realised his mistake when I drove my sword through his open mouth and out of the back of his skull. As I withdrew my sword he tumbled from the ladder taking two climbers with him. Gilles and Richard had not done as I did and the knight had a foot on the walls before a man at arms swung his axe and bit into the side of the knight. He flew from the ladder and landed with a splash in the river.

There was a hiatus as the men below reorganised themselves. "Gilles, Richard, wait until you see a face and then stab. They have to hold onto the ladder with their right hand."

"Aye lord. Sorry!"

"You are doing well!"

I heard shouts from below. I risked peering over the top and saw men at arms preparing to ascend. The first four each carried a war hammer with a spike on the top. They could use that against us as they were climbing. I turned, "Fetch pitching forks!" I cursed myself for not having them on the walls. Had this been Stockton then John of Craven would already have seen to that. A pitching fork, pushed by three or four men, could force the ladder from the wall. Until they were brought I would have to use my sword.

The men at arms had thrown the largest rocks. The ones which remained were smaller and thrown to dislodge the climbers. They were less effective. I put down my shield. As the first man at arms drew near me I grabbed the edge of his shield. He tried to jab up with the spike on the war hammer

164

but my left hand was on the opposite side of where he thrust. I pushed his shield and he began to overbalance. I punched him in the face with the hilt of my sword and he tumbled backwards, his arms flailing. His fall took him away from the ones who were climbing. I leaned over and saw that Gilles and Richard were working as a team and their ladder was half empty. The men at arms were falling onto those climbing.

I saw that the next man at arms who climbed was using both hands to hold onto the ladder. As soon as he was in sword's length of me I slashed across his hands. The tip of my sword hacked through the mail and took his fingers. The spurting blood made the rung slippery and he could not retain his grip. He fell.

"My lord! Pitching forks!"

I grabbed one of the forks and jammed the prongs onto the top rung of the ladder. I tried to push but the weight of men on the ladder was too great. "You men, help me!"

With four of us pushing the ladder began to move. I wondered if it would break but soon, I saw that it was moving away from the wall. "One three, push! One two three! We all pushed together and the fork was in fresh air for the ladder was crashing back, falling on those who had been waiting to cross the bridge. There was a cheer as Gilles and Richard, along with their men at arms repeated our feat. I was about to congratulate my men when Dick shouted, "My lord!" He pointed to my left. I saw that Stephen and his men had swum their horses across the moat and were already scaling ladders. They would soon be over the stones. The town wall had been breached!

"Back to the castle! Now!" Gilles and Richard looked at me as though I had gone mad. "The wall is breached. We cannot hold."

At the bottom of the gate, I waited for Dick and his archers. They had further to descend from the two towers. Already the men at arms attacking the gatehouse had put the ladders in place and were ascending.

"Gille, Richard, at my side. We will back down the road. We have to buy time for the others to reach the castle." Dick and his archers tumbled out of the gatehouse. "Get to the barbican. We shall need your arrows! Warn them that we have lost the town!"

Dick and his archers ran beyond us. The men at arms who had been on the walls with us stood behind us as we walked backwards down the street.

"Fill the street and make it hard for any to pass us." The men at arms took their places next to Gilles and Richard. We were within six hundred paces when the first of the enemy men at arms descended the ladder. I could hear fighting to our left where Stephen and his men had scaled the walls but until they opened the gates we would have time. The first enemy began to unbar the gate. We had four hundred paces to go. I was aware of men joining us from our left and our right. The ones from the left showed that they had been fighting. They were wounded.

"Get the wounded inside the castle. The rest of you behind us."

As soon as the gates opened the enemy flooded in. We were less than two hundred paces from safety but there were still men who still survived trying to reach us from the walls. We would need every sword we could gather if we were to survive a siege. Five enemy warriors outran the rest and hurled themselves at us. I had no doubt they saw our livery and sought to gain some glory. The leader was a young knight and he leapt at me, swinging his sword wildly. I held my shield up and let the blade slide down. I stepped forwards on my right leg and stabbed as I did so. He impaled himself on my sword. I pulled it out sideways and his body fell in front of the man trying to get at Richard. He tripped and Richard brought his sword down on the man's spine. I heard it crack. The other three were butchered by Gilles and the men at arms who punished them for their reckless attitude.

I glanced over my shoulder and saw that we were less than fifty paces from the bridge and the barbican.

"Everyone, across the bridge!"

For the briefest of moments, there were just the three of us there. I was daring another to risk my wrath. I heard William Martel shout, "Form shields!"

We stepped back and I felt the wood beneath my feet. As the shields came towards us arrows began to strike any flesh which was shown. Two men at arms fell. Suddenly from our left, Robert D'Oyly and four men managed to make the bridge. All of them were wounded and had lost shields. I waited until they were on the bridge and then continued under the barbican.

A voice behind said, "Hurry Warlord! Let us raise it!"

I knew there would be men still trying to reach the castle but it was too late for them. As I stepped beneath the gatehouse the bridge began to rise. I stepped into the barbican and the gates were slammed shut. We were now truly trapped.

Chapter 14

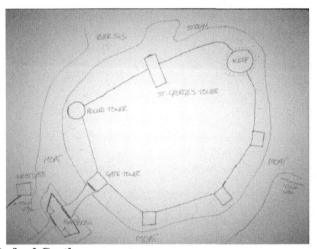

Oxford Castle

We had lost fewer men than we might have expected by the sudden attack of Stephen. He was my enemy but I admired his action. He had struck where we had the least men. The Constable was wounded but the healers assured me that it was not life-threatening. We were lucky; the castle had a physician and he was tending to the Constable. Had not my archers been alert then we would have lost even more men but their skill saved lives.

The Empress and Henry looked distraught. I smiled. Despair was the last thing we needed. "That means we have fewer mouths to feed! Stephen will have to find food for the townspeople."

Henry asked, "How did they get through our defences so quickly, Warlord?"

"Not enough men and walls that were too low. This castle has much stronger and higher walls than the town. He will struggle to break our defences." I reassured Henry but I could see the doubt in the Empress' eyes. "Henry, go and find Gilles, tell him that his lord is thirsty and hungry. Killing gives me an appetite!"

When he had gone we were alone and the Empress shook her head, "Lying to our son! The last thing you want after combat is food. I know that of you. We are in dire straits are we not?"

"We are. The food will run out and we have no avenue of escape save through the town for the moat and the stream bar our way."

She nodded, "You and your men could swim the stream and escape." I nodded. "But you will not leave us."

"No."

She shook her head and held my hand in hers, "So chivalrous and so foolish. What you are saying is that we will die here together or face a future in captivity?"

"I do not foretell the future but I do know that I will not give up hope. Until they prise my sword from my dead fingers there is a chance. I did lie to Henry but it was a white lie for I do not want him to be consumed by despair."

Had I been in Stockton I would have called a meeting of my knights to discuss the situation and to plan what to do. However here I had only Dick. Sir Robert and his knights were brave but this was a new experience for them. I would be Warlord and I would make the decisions. After returning the Empress to her ladies and Henry I sought out Dick. "I put you in command of the archers. The barbican is the only way in or out of the castle. You and the archers must keep them as far away as you can."

"We will run out of arrows unless we are relieved."

I would not lie to my men. "We will not be relieved. Either they give up the siege or we are captured."

"Or die."

"Or die but let us hope it does not come to that. We have much to do in our valley eh, Dick?"

He nodded, "Besides when I die I want it to be in the open and not in a stone tomb. I will find the archers first." He hesitated, "I have the authority?"

"You do, but just to clarify the situation I will see the Constable."

The Constable was in the healing hall. The priests and the physician were tending to the wounded. Some looked serious and I wondered how they had dragged their bodies back into the castle. The cold part of me realised they were another mouth to feed but they had fallen in battle and deserved our care. The Constable was lying on a pallet of straw. He lay on his back and his eyes were closed.

I stood over him and looked at his bandages. His right arm and leg were heavily bandaged. He would not fight for some time. I was about to turn away when he opened his eyes, "Earl. This is a pretty pass. I am sorry we could not hold them. We did our best."

"Do not berate yourself. It was a clever ruse and no one could have foreseen it. We are secure now. The physician said you will recover but until then I will take command."

"Of course. But there will be no help coming to us!"

"Keep that to yourself, Robert. We hold on for as long as possible. Who knows the Earl may return. The last I heard was that Normandy was almost ours. Even Stephen admitted as much in his talk. The Count of Anjou will not leave his wife here. Miles of Gloucester and the other leaders may well try to raise an army and relieve us."

"You do not believe that."

"No, but I hope for that."

"You will command?"

"I have given orders already."

"Good." He tried to rise but he could not. "Take my seal. I cannot even rise. It gives you added authority."

I did not need the seal but I nodded and took it. "You know the state of the castle better than I do. What supplies do we have?"

His voice was flat as he replied, "We will run out by January."

I left him and went out in to the inner bailey. The walls were high and protected by a moat and a stream. A ram would not work. He would need to build a bridge and use siege engines to reduce the barbican. My squires and Henry found me as I looked around at the defences.

"Gilles and Richard, come with me. Henry, ask the Empress to meet me at the castle gate tower."

As we walked I said, "You two will need to act as knights until we escape. We have few enough of those. I will need you to command men."

"But lord, am I ready?"

"We will discover that, Richard, but I have faith in you. You have learned well and your defence of the town gate was heroic. Besides we have little option."

I led them up the stairs of the gate which lay behind the moat and the barbican. There were just four men at arms there. "Who commands here?"

The oldest said, "Me, my lord, Thomas of Abingdon."

"Do you have bows?"

"No lord. We have two crossbows."

"Sir Richard will command the barbican and he has archers. I will be there with my squires and the men at arms. If we have to concede the barbican then you four will have to enable us to reach the castle. Get yourself two bows." I pointed to the narrow bridge which led from the barbican to the gate below. "If we have to cross we will be followed closely. Our lives will be in your hands."

"We will not let you down, lord."

The Empress ascended with Judith and Margaret. Henry followed. The men at arms bowed. I led the Empress to the wall, "My lady, that is where the battle will be decided." I pointed to the barbican. "Our best men will be there but if it falls then we withdraw to here." She nodded. "If we hold the barbican then we hold the castle. I would have you and your ladies take charge of the supplies and the rations. I will need every man on the walls."

"The Constable?"

"He is wounded and will not fight for some time. I have his seal."

She laughed, "You need no seal to command."

"No, but it is good to have one." I brought her closer to me so that I could speak quietly. "Do you want Henry with you?"

"I do but he would hate it. He resents the fact that you seem to have discarded him. I know that you did it to keep him safe and I thank you for that but he is part of this. He can stand a watch."

I nodded, "Henry, I shall need you by my side." His face lit up. "It may only be as a messenger but that may be the most important job in this siege."

"I care not. I get to wear my hauberk and helmet and my sword is sharp."

"Good. Then we will go to the barbican and see what the enemy does."

The light was fading as we walked through the gate and across the moat to the barbican. Sir Robert's father had built a good castle. The barbican was like a small castle in the moat. The diversion of the stream had been a masterstroke. The bridge across which we walked could be destroyed if the barbican fell. We ascended the ladder to the fighting platform and towers atop the barbican. In contrast with the gatehouse, this was crowded. Dick had collected many archers and they were in the towers and on the ramparts. He had men at arms guarding the bridge mechanism.

"How goes it, Sir Richard?"

"They are busy moving men into the town. They will not attack today."

"Good. I will be here with you tomorrow. I will let you organize the sentries. We will need to rest while we can. Food will be served in shifts. Gilles and Richard can stand a watch too."

Dick nodded, "Aye, they can command. They have grown."

"Then we will return to the hall. I will relieve you Dick and take the watch until midnight. Gilles, you will command the night watch."

172

"Aye lord."

"Come, let us walk the walls."

We returned to the gate tower and we walked the ramparts. The five towers all had four men in each of them. They would have little to do and I decided that I would rotate them with the men in the barbican. The round tower and St. George's Tower were the strongest after the Keep. When we reached St. George's Tower I descended to the sally gate. When I had it opened I saw that it was wide enough for a horse. It was like the one at Durham. We walked outside. The Isis lay on one side of a tiny spit of land and the stream leading to the Thames on the other. The ground was soft and spongy. It had flooded at some time and the ground was heavy.

"This is somewhere the enemy might attack. They could swim the river as they did by the walls."

Gilles looked at the walls. "The walls are high here. They could not scale them as easily but the gate is vulnerable."

"It is. Richard, I will put you in command here. You will sleep and eat here. I will send another couple of men. You will need to keep a good watch. I want you to go to the blacksmith and have him make caltrops. They will give you a warning of an attack in the dark of night."

"Aye lord. The nights will be getting longer."

Henry said, "If you put two torches here and kept them burning you would see any approach to the sally port."

Richard nodded, "A good idea."

After instructing the men in the tower to obey Richard we left and walked first to the Keep and then around the southern towers and wall. The points where we could be attacked were the sally port and the barbican. It made life simpler for me. Night had fallen and we walked back to the hall for our first frugal meal.

The nights were getting colder and, as I stood my watch on the walls of the barbican I pulled my cloak tighter about me. Alice's new white cloaks were still to be used. They were woollen and they were warm. I would appreciate them more when winter began to bite. The men at arms had a brazier.

"Do not look into the fire. Let it warm your backs and keep your eyes searching the dark."

The four of them nodded. "Aye Warlord." I leaned over the battlements and stared into the moat below. It would have to be a brave and desperate man who would swim that water at night and then clamber up the walls but it could be done. I pointed to two of them. "Go to the kitchens and bring a pot of pig fat."

"Heated, lord?"

"No, for I wish to make the walls slippery in case any try to climb them."

When they had gone the elder of the two who remained asked, "Would they try such a thing, lord?"

"If I was in their position then I might try something like this." I smiled. "I have, in the past and when I was younger, done such foolish things."

"Men say you cannot be beaten, lord."

"Men say many things but it does not make them true. The fact that no one has defeated me yet does not guarantee that they will not one day."

They nodded. I did not know them. I knew not how they would stand up to death. That was a measure of a man. If he faced death and emerged alive then he would be stronger for it. Even my squires had done that but these two might have served as sentries and never fought an enemy. Should I have brought more men?

When Gilles relieved me I could see that he was nervous. Dick had helped my squire by giving him two of his archers as part of his four-man watch. They would ensure he had an easy watch. I virtually collapsed in my bed. It had been a long day. What would the morrow bring?

Dick and the larger daylight watch were in the barbican when I arrived after a few hours sleep. Henry had been waiting outside my chamber for me. While he fetched my sword Judith, who was passing, told me he had awoken and dressed at dawn. He was learning habits that would stand him in good stead. "Have you eaten yet, squire?"

"No lord."

"Old soldiers eat the first chance they can. That is how they become old soldiers. You go and find us something to eat and I will meet you at the smithy."

When I reached the smithy I gave my sword to the blacksmith. "Put a good edge on that would you?"

"Aye lord." As he began to oil the blade he gestured with his head to a pile of metal to the side. "One of your young squires asked for caltrops. Was that right, lord?"

"It was. Thank you for making them. It may save us being surprised."

"It is many years since I made them." His boy began to turn the grindstone wheel and the edge was sharpened. "This is a fine sword, lord. I never thought to be sharpening the sword of such a famous warrior."

I nodded. Henry ran up with some oaten bread and some cheese. He said, "I found some apples, lord. I have four."

"Then that will have to be our ration for the day." I split the bread and gave him half. He began to tear great chunks from it. "Hold. We will not eat again until this night. Take small bites and chew until it disappears. Fool your stomach into thinking you have feasted."

The smith nodded, "Wise words, Warlord. You heed them, young master. There is no one bringing us more food. Soon we will be eating horses and boiling their bones for soup."

Henry looked appalled, "Truly?"

"I am afraid so. Our warhorses will be the last to go but those sumpters and rounceys we brought with us will not see December."

We headed through the gate tower towards the barbican. I knew that I would grow weary of ascending the steps to the fighting platform. Already my left leg was aching. I was not used to climbing such steep stairs.

Dick pointed, "Good morning Warlord. You have come at the right time. They are preparing something. I think they will attack soon."

"No war machines?"

"They would have to demolish houses. I think that they will test our defences. I have spoken with the archers. We will husband our arrows."

"How will they cross the moat?"

Henry's question was pure curiosity. Dick shrugged. "They could make a bridge easily enough. They have the gate from the town they could use but they will struggle to break down this gate. They could easily make one. It would only have to bear the weight of men. If they were close to the gate we would find it hard to loose arrows at them. I think the Warlord is right. They will have to resort to war machines and that will give us time."

I was not as sure as my archer. Stephen was clever and he was aided by two very able commanders.

It was not knights who advanced towards the gates but men at arms. They advanced behind a wall of shields. Dick's voice boomed out, "No one is to release an arrow without my command."

The buildings in the town came all the way to the edge of the moat and the men who advanced were forced to use the narrow streets. When they reached the edge of the moat men began to release arrows from behind them. Others poked crossbows through the gaps. The arrows from the archers clattered against the roof of the gatehouse. The crossbows were more dangerous here for they could be aimed horizontally.

"Use your shields. Let them waste their missiles."

It did not take them long to realise the futility of their attack. Perhaps they thought we had nothing to send in reply or they grew careless. Dick spied a gap in the shields and he sent an arrow to pierce the chest of the crossbowman who was exposed. He chuckled; archers hated those who used the crossbow.

Henry said, "What is that?"

I looked in the direction he pointed. They had done as Dick had suggested. They had removed one of the gates from the town walls. Stephen must have been desperate. "It is the gate, or one of them, from the town wall. They can protect them with their shields until they reach the moat. When they try to bridge the moat they will be vulnerable."

Dick said, "Stockton archers, let us show them the range of our bows and the skill of our archers."

The gate was a hundred and fifty paces away. Men carried shields to protect those who were carrying the huge wooden bridge. However, their legs could not be covered and these men were not encased in mail. Their legs were unprotected. Rafe, Long Tom and the others chose their targets carefully. Three of my archers loosed and three men were hit in the leg. They were forced to drop the gate and in the confusion, other men were revealed. Dick and our other three archers chose their moment well and arrows plunged into their bodies. Confusion reigned. The other archers joined in as more gaps appeared. The enemy struggled on for another thirty paces and then a knight shouted something. They dropped their improvised bridge and the whole of the attacking force retreated to the safety of the houses.

The men at arms on the barbican cheered the archers as though we had won a victory. It was not. We had delayed them, that was all. The wooden gate lay there surrounded by the dead and dying who had carried it. The wounded had been dragged to safety.

At noon we heard the sound of hammering and tearing. A building disappeared in a cloud of dust. "They are up to something, Warlord."

When smoke began to rise and smoke filled the air I had an idea what they were doing. "It looks like they are building a counter castle for their war machines."

"Counter castle, lord?"

"Aye Henry, a small castle. They will make a motte such as the one the Keep stands upon and they will put a palisade around. Then they will begin to lob stones at us. They will make it so that it is as high as our walls. That way they can cause the maximum damage."

"That will take some time."

"It could take a week, maybe even more."

"Then they will not attack again?"

"Oh they will attack and it will be tonight. They will send men under cover of darkness and try to bridge the moat then."

"How do you know, Warlord?"

"Because it is what I would do. I do not underestimate your cousin, Henry. He is a clever man. I have fought alongside him and against him, since first I met your mother. I know how his mind works. He has sacrificed a handful of men and seen the skill of our archers. He will wait until dark when we cannot see as clearly. Come, we can leave a skeleton watch and have some rest. I fear that you will be on duty this night, Sir Richard."

"Better to be doing something than waiting for it."

When we reached the Keep and the Great Hall I sent Gilles to relieve the watch. I then went to Robert D'Oyly. He would need to know what was happening. He did not look well. In fact, he was more listless than he had been the previous day. His physician must have been wrong. I told him what had happened and he lay back. "I am pleased that you command. My castle is in safe hands."

"Soon you will be able to see for yourself."

He shook his head, "The wound does not ail me but I feel so tired that I can barely keep open my eyes."

I went to the priest, "What ails the Constable? I was told that his wounds were not life-threatening."

"It has the doctor confused. The others all recover but not so the Constable."

"Where is the doctor?"

"He is preparing a potion to try upon the Constable. He spends longer with him than any other patient."

"We are lucky to have a doctor."

"Aye, he only arrived in the town two days since. He was on his way to Wallingford. God smiled upon us when they guided his steps here."

I nodded, "Let me know if the Constable's condition worsens."

"I will."

"And I will speak with the doctor when time allows. Tonight I shall be busy but tomorrow I will find the time to discuss the Constable's condition with him." I was no doctor, not even a healer but I had seen enough wounds and doctors over the years to have a better understanding than most. A talk with the physician would put my mind at rest.

The Empress was equally concerned about the Constable. "My ladies and I have nothing to do. We will visit with the sick and see if we can minister to their needs. They earned their wounds in our cause. It is the least we can do."

"I think there will be an attack across the moat tonight."

"Should we be worried? You seem unconcerned but that is your way."

"The attack tonight will fail but when they have built their counter castle then we will be in more danger. However, so long as we hold the barbican and the moat we are safe enough."

Knowing that we would be busy that night I went to my chamber and lay down. Henry asked, "What should I do, lord?"

"I would say rest but I know that you will not. Go and see how Richard fares in his new command. Then you can speak with Gilles. As for me I shall rest my body for tonight will be an attack and I will have to fight."

I lay down and he closed the door. No matter how positive I might be I could not see a way out of this dilemma that did not involve captivity. I could avoid death and injury to most within the castle but unless we were relieved then Stephen would win and we would be captured. When we ran out of food it would all be over. Exhaustion must have taken over for I fell asleep.

Chapter 15

I was awoken by Dick and Henry.

"It is dark, lord. I thought you would wish to join us."

"Aye, Dick." I went to the bowl of water and splashed it on my face.

"There is food, lord." I looked up. There was a bowl with some stew. "One of the horses which we brought in when they attacked went lame."

I nodded, "It is God's will."

The food was hot and it was filling. The dead horse would feed the garrison for two days. We would boil its bones and add the vegetables which were going off to make a soup. That would be how we would live from now on. We would measure our lives in meals. We would yearn for a stomach that did not ache from hunger. And each week another horse would die. Before the end came, my men and I would ride out and die with glory. Rolf would not be butchered. I would take my chances.

"I have visited with the Constable." The Empress' voice behind me reminded me that I would not take the glory road while she was in the castle. I had to protect her and Henry.

"How is he?"

"It is strange he does not appear to have a wound which threatens his life and yet he grows weaker. We will go to the chapel and pray for him." She noticed my sword strapped to my side and the helmet which Henry carried. "There will be violence this night?"

"They will attack. They may make the barbican. If they do then we will have to fend them off." Her eyes flickered towards her son. "Do not worry, he will be safe. You have my word."

It was dark when we reached the walls. I relieved Gilles. "Shall I stay, lord?"

"This will be a long siege, Gilles. You need your rest."

He nodded, "I will see Richard before I retire. He is the captain of St. George's Tower now!"

Dick was already there when I arrived at the fighting platform. "I heard movement, lord."

It was pitch black in the town. We could see nothing but the sound of metal on metal was unmistakable. Men were moving around.

I hissed, "Stand to!"

The hiss of swords being drawn from scabbards was followed by the sound of my archers sliding an arrow from their precious horde. We would have little use for the swords until they closed with the walls but it was as well to be prepared. Dick walked to the battlements and peered over. He pulled up his bow and released an arrow into the dark. There was a cry and then a flurry of bolts and arrows clattered against the walls and the roof.

"A fine hit!"

"I saw a movement and thought it worth risking an arrow." His head whipped around, "But if any of you risk such an arrow you will have to face my wrath."

"They will be picking up the gate and moving it towards the moat. We should be able to see it then. They will have to allow the moat to support its weight or risk men in the moat and I do not think they will do that."

"I think you are right, lord."

"Then use your archers to kill those holding it when it is close. If they lose control the gate itself may do our job for us."

I had examined the gate after they had withdrawn. It looked to me to be as wide as the moat, just. That meant they would need to place it precisely with both ends touching the ground. If we could make them drop it prematurely so that it was skewed then they would not be able to cross on it. They had to have a flat surface; especially if they intended to use a ram.

"Men at arms, put your shields in the gaps in the walls. The archers will tell you when to lower them."

As soon as the shields were placed in position arrows and bolts thudded into them. It was like hailstones on a tiled roof. They clattered and clanged. After a while, they stopped wasting valuable arrows. Dick nodded to the Sergeant at Arms and he moved his shield a little to allow Dick a view of the moat.

"Archers, ready! On my command slay those at the front of the gate." You could have cut the tension with a knife. "Shields! Down!"

As one the men at arms lowered their shields and then the twelve archers sent arrows across the moat. The distance was less than forty paces but it was dark. The seven archers I had brought would not miss. I hoped the other five would have learned from them. There were cries and splashes as men fell into the moat.

I heard a voice shout, "Hold on to it! Keep it close!" Then the voice screamed as Dick's arrow found him.

There was a much bigger splash and I risked looking over. The gate had slipped into the moat and lay at an unnatural angle. Although made of wood it had metal studs buried in it and a metal knocker. The weight of the metal dragged it below the black waters of the moat. Even as I watched I saw more men struck by arrows as our archers slew those trying to rescue their bridge. They failed.

"Well done, Dick! They cannot use that one."

"No, but they now have protection close to the moat." He pointed and I saw that one corner of the gate stuck up affording some protection to them.

"It cannot be helped. We have beaten off one attack at least."

"They will bring the other gate."

"I know and this time they will strip the metal from it and extend it but that takes time. We celebrate small victories here."

Dick nodded, "Aye. Bring me the shields. We will see if we can reclaim any of these arrows. Henry, see if there are any lying on the ground."

Long Tom stood on the battlements and, holding on to the roof, reached up and began to pull out the arrows which had stuck in the wood. The blacksmith could make new heads by melting down damaged arrowheads but we had no way to fletch. The arrows we collected could save lives. We stayed on watch until long past midnight. Henry fell asleep. I sat with Dick.

"These are minor victories, lord but I cannot see how this will end well."

"Nor can I but I will take them. Each day we are here make it more likely that the Earl will return and come to rescue his sister and nephew."

"It seems strange to me that he left for Normandy when he did."

I could trust Dick. "Aye and me too. Perhaps I see plots everywhere. Why I even worried that someone was trying to poison the Constable."

"What?"

"His wounds are healing but he is not. Tomorrow I shall speak with this doctor. He must know the cause of the ailment."

I carried Henry back to his bed. It seemed but a moment that my eyes were closed and I was woken. It was daylight. Gilles stood there, "Sorry to disturb you, lord but Dick sent me. They are building a second counter castle."

I wearily rose and splashed water on my face. "Thank you, Gilles. Other than that is all well?"

"Aye, lord. I visited with Richard. He has grown in the last few days. He commands now and the men in the tower are much taken with him."

"Good."

He laughed, "That doctor is a strange one."

"You met with him?"

"Aye, he asked Richard if he could go out of the sally port and collect flowers!"

I felt a cold shiver down my spine. "Has he done this much?"

"Richard said every day, and always after dark."

"Go and find him. Just watch him until I get there but do not let him near the Constable. Stop him with force if you have to!" Gilles nodded, "Tell me what flowers did he collect?"

"Blue ones; they looked a little like the flowers which grow in the woods by the Tees!"

"Did they resemble a blue hood?"

"Aye lord, how did you know?"

"I was taught about such things in the east. Be careful of this doctor. He is not what he seems."

That decided me. I knew that the flower was called monkshood. It was an aconite and was distilled to make a potion. I had been given just such a draught. In mild doses, it helped sleep but in larger ones, it could be lethal. I now knew why the Constable was not recovering. I ran to the tower.

Dick pointed, "There, lord, they have begun to clear another area. We saw the smoke and we heard the noise of destruction." He swivelled and pointed to the east. "They have begun to build the platform for the siege engines."

"We can do little about this." I glanced at the moat. The dead bodies had been removed but I could see that the gate had partially blocked the river and made a small weir. Stephen would find it even harder to bridge it a second time but we would find it equally hard to lower the drawbridge. I had planned a sortie to destroy the platforms. That could not happen now. We had been trapped before but at least we had had a way out of the castle. Now we did not. "I have some treachery to deal with. Send for me if danger threatens."

I was angry as I strode towards the house of healing. As I drew close I heard a commotion. Gilles was being restrained by four of the Empress' guards. She stood looking angry.

"What is going on?"

"Your squire was trying to restrain the doctor. He has lost his mind."

184

"No, Empress, he was obeying orders; my orders. Let him go!" They looked at Matilda. I shouted, "Let him go! Now!"

They did so.

"Now bind the physician."

"I protest, my lord! What have I done save to heal the sick?"

"Have you lost your senses, lord?"

I whipped my head around, "How is the Constable?"

Father Abelard said, "He worsens, lord. He has lost consciousness."

I strode over to the doctor and took his leather pouch from over his shoulder. "They are my medicines! You know not what they are!"

I took out some blue flowers. "But I know what these are! I too have read the books in the great libraries of the east." As soon as his shoulders sagged then I knew that I had it right. "This is monkshood or leopard's bane and is a poison." I turned to the Empress and the priest. My eyes and my voice were bleak. "It makes a patient sleepy. The doctor was not curing the Constable. He was killing him."

Father Abelard nodded and said, "I have seen this flower. The Warlord is right and there is no cure for the poison."

"Feed him ground up charcoal and water. It will make him vomit. Mayhap we might yet save him."

As the priests left I took out my dagger and held it to the doctor's throat. "Who sent you? What were you doing here?"

His resignation had become calm. "You cannot make me talk and you will not kill me. You are too honourable. When the castle falls I will return to my master."

I lowered my dagger to his groin and I smiled what people had called the smile of the wolf, "Who says I will not kill you? I have killed in cold blood before now or I could order your execution. You have tried to murder the Constable." I was aware that Henry was watching, fearfully. He was as afraid of me now as was the doctor whose eyes showed that he believed I would hurt him.

The doctor said, "Then kill me and you will learn nothing."

My right hand suddenly flicked up as I slashed into his upper leg. Blood spurted and he screamed. "Take him to the dungeon and chain him. I will talk to him when I have finished my investigation There is more to this than just the murder of the Constable."

"But the Constable might live!"

I faced the Empress, "He might but I doubt it. This man was placed here before the enemy began the siege. His attempt on the Constable was an opportunist. He had another purpose. I will discover it."

I wiped the blood from my dagger. I had nicked his leg but the wound would serve to make him fear me. "Come, Henry, Gilles. I need your young eyes."

"Would you kill him?"

"Of course, Henry. I would not enjoy it but if it was necessary then I would. There are other ways to get what you want. I will let him stew for a while. When you are King remember that there will be many who wish to hurt you. Be on your guard."

When we reached the tower Richard was sleeping. I woke him. "Sorry, lord, I had not slept for half a day and I was tired...."

"I am not here to criticise you. Let us go out of the gate."

One of his men unbarred the gate and we stepped out. I saw the swampy ground was covered in blue flowers. The doctor was an opportunist. "Where did you put the caltrops?"

Richard waved his hand around. "All over there." He looked down. "They are gone! What has happened to them?"

"I fear the doctor has thrown them in the river. We will lay more. Come with me. I want the three of you to look for anything which looks unnatural."

"Like what?"

"If I knew that, Gilles, then I would tell you."

We walked down to the stream. The ground was swampy. Richard sank up to his knees at one point. "This is hopeless, lord. We know not what we look for."

"You should have looked over here. The ground is much firmer. These stones are like stepping stones and they are all white." I pointed to the ground on which I stood.

Gilles saw it as soon as I did. We raced over to Henry. There was a path that had been laid from the water directly to the gate. It was not straight but curved around. "This is what the doctor was doing. He was laying a path. They will try to do as Stephen did at the river. They will cross here but at night and attack the gate. Your tower will be attacked. Richard have your men move the stones and put them where we can use them on the men who will attack you. Henry, go and get more caltrops from the smith. We have found this treachery just in time!"

It took some time to clear the stones and to lay the caltrops. We were filthy when we had finished. "Gilles, I want you and four extra men here with Richard."

"Will the enemy come here?"

"The stepping stones suggest that they might. However, they may have watched this spit of land and they will have seen us clear them. That might deter them. The doctor did not know about your caltrops until he went out seeking the flowers and laying the stones. I suspect he found them the hard way. It explains why he went out at night. The white stones would stand out more in the dark and he could see them easier after he had laid them. Get yourselves cleaned up. Henry, I will meet you by the smithy."

I went to the stables and washed off the worst of the mud from my boots. Returning to the house of healing I saw a huddle of bodies around the Constable. I went to them and they parted as I arrived. There was a pool of white flecked black vomit in a large bowl and the Constable was awake. The Empress said, "He has not spoken yet but his eyes are open and he breathes. Father Abelard gave him a watered beer."

I took her arm, "Come with me, we must talk." I led her outside where I explained what I had found.

"So the doctor is a spy."

"You doubted it?"

"He is a doctor."

"Had you lived in the east then you would know that the two are not incompatible. I will let him rot for a couple of days before I question him. Although I think I know who sent him?"

"Who? Stephen?"

I shook my head, "Stephen is many things but a murderer is not one. The doctor is Flemish. I think he came at the behest of William of Ypres. The Queen is also Flemish. It makes sense. I have the ground near the tower watched. If they do attack there then it will be at night. I am hoping that those outside await a signal from the doctor. However, my fear is that he has accomplices. I would have one of your ladies tend the Constable and trust no one, except for your ladies."

"Is the crown worth this?"

"Your father thought so and your grandfather went to great lengths to secure it. I would say, aye."

I found Henry at the blacksmith's workshop. "We need arrowheads making. Young Henry here will bring you the broken heads and bolts. You can use those to melt down and re-use."

"They will not be as good as freshly forged ones."

"We have to use what we have."

Dick and his archers had sorted the arrows out. There was a pile of broken and damaged ones. Henry collected them and took them away. I told Dick what we had discovered. He pointed to the two counter castles. "I think this work is to distract us. Should I go to the Tower and wait there?"

"No. I have given Gilles and four more men at arms that responsibility. With two of them to command they can keep a good watch. If they do come then they must swim the moat. The ground is boggy and it will take them time to cross to the wall. They cannot be hidden. The castle is not so big that you cannot be summoned quickly. We watch."

Three days later and the attack had still to materialize. However, I was urgently summoned to the house of healing. Margaret sat with the Constable's head cradled in her hands. She gave the slightest shake of her head as I knelt. The Constable opened red-rimmed eyes. He gave me a wan smile, "It seems all your efforts to save me, lord, were in vain. Father Abelard has heard my confession and I am ready to meet my maker. Will it be purgatory or heaven do you think?"

"You have been a good man and the Empress has prayed for you. You will go to heaven. But have hope you might live. You speak and your eyes are open. Where there is life there is hope."

He shook his head. "There was blood in my water and I can feel life leaving me. Already my feet grow cold. I had to speak to you." His fingers grasped my hand. "I have lived in this castle for most of my life. Things look black but when there is white there is hope. Watch for the ice!" His fingers released their grip and his eyes glazed over. He was dead. I had never seen anyone die as suddenly. It was as though he had clung on to life to give me the message but I did not understand it.

Margaret folded his hands across his chest and made the sign of the cross. We rose. "What did he mean, lord, *'where there is white there is hope'*? I did not understand it."

"Nor did I but I will think on it. Mention it to no one. He told us when there was just we two there."

"The Empress?"

"No one. I want no false hope. And now I need to have a word with a murderer."

She grasped my hand in hers and her eyes pleaded with me, "Lord, do not blacken your hands with his murder. He is not worth it."

"I know he is not but he will be punished. Ask the Empress to join me in his cell." I smiled, "I will not murder him."

I went to the kitchens and found a stale loaf and a jug of small beer. The prisoner had been fed only water and he was weak. I went to the dungeon. One of the two guards said, "He stirs little."

"Then perhaps he is ready to speak."

I entered and the doctor opened his eyes. "My wound is infected!"

"But it stopped bleeding."

He nodded, "You have skill with a knife. I had thought you intended to take my manhood but the dagger just opened my flesh. You are clever but I will not speak. You cannot make me!"

"I did not ask you to. Here is the bread and also beer."

He took them greedily. He broke a piece of bread off and soaked it in the beer. I watched him savour each mouthful. He clung to life. He was trapped with no chance of escape and yet he did not choose death.

He had finished half of it when the door behind me opened and the Empress, her two ladies and Henry appeared.

The doctor drank some beer, "So what is this? Are you here to gloat."

The Empress said coldly, "The Constable is dead. You are a murderer!"

He shrugged, "And that is supposed to make me talk? I will say nothing. Kill me if you must but I will not talk."

It was my turn to smile. "No, Doctor, I do not want you to talk. I want you to listen. You were sent here by William of Ypres." I just came out with the words and took him by surprise yet I saw in his eyes that it was true. Then he hid his thoughts again and his eyes became cold, hard stones. "Your task was not to murder the Constable. You saw an opportunity and took it. That is why you had to collect the flowers to make the poison. You did not bring it with you. Your task was to prepare a path for the men who will attack across the boggy ground close to the stream. Your use of white stones collected from inside the castle was clever. It began when first you arrived. Then you saw the caltrops my men had laid and you removed them."

His face tried to remain neutral but I saw that I had hit home. Hatred filled them.

"The only thing I do not know is the signal you will give that you have succeeded. There may be none. It matters not. We know the plan and we will be ready."

"You know nothing. There is no help coming and your food will run out soon. It will soon be November and the cold will kill as the hunger bites. When your vigilance drops then the castle will fall and you, Warlord of the North, will die! You are an enemy of the Church. There will be no ransom for you. There will be a trial and then you will be executed. The Champion of the Empress will die like a criminal!"

The three women and Henry were more shocked than I was. This was not Stephen's doing but Queen Matilda and William of Ypres. I saw now the complicated plot which had been hatched. The Church, the Queen and Prince Henry of Scotland had all been complicit. It actually made me feel better that I had the truth of it.

"Then your trial is here and now, Doctor. Do you confess that you murdered the Constable?" He hesitated. "Would you die unshriven?"

He saw his predicament, "I confess I murdered the Constable."

"Then I sentence you to death. These six people are witnesses to the confession and the trial." I turned and the two guards along with the Empress and her women all nodded. Henry just stared. "Have a priest come to hear his confession and I will send word."

"Aye lord."

As we walked into the light the Empress said, "What did he mean, *'enemy of the church'*?"

"Henry of Blois conspired with the Queen and Prince Henry to have me excommunicated for attacking Carlisle. It did not worry me and I am happy now that I know all."

Henry said, "But how do you know all? He told us nothing."

"I put the pieces together and his last words confirmed it. Now we send a message to William of Ypres. Perhaps it may forestall an attack on the Tower."

The Empress nodded, "We will see to the Constable's body. He should be buried with honour."

"Aye for he deserved that. He was loyal."

We buried the Constable at dusk. I slept in St. George's Tower but no attack came that night. The doctor was shriven in his cell and the next morning I had him brought to the barbican. With his hands tied behind him, he had to be helped up the steps. He was still weak. Dick had a rope already suspended from the roof.

The doctor looked at the rope and nodded, "I had thought you would have hung, drawn and quartered me. This is a kindly death."

"The kindness is an accident." I pointed to the two platforms which were being built some way away. The enemy beavered like ants. "I wish your master to know that you are dead. I want him to know that his plot has failed."

I waited until Gilles arrived. He had a trumpet with him. As soon as he arrived I nodded and Dick put the noose around his neck. Rafe and Long Tom helped him to the battlements and secured him there. I would order his death. He would not take it himself.

"Gilles, sound the trumpet."

Gilles gave three sharp blasts on the instrument. They were strident and not in tune but they had the desired effect. Those working on the platforms stopped and looked. I allowed them to see the doctor and then I shouted loudly across the space, "So die all murderers!"

My men pushed him. The rope was just long enough to break his neck and yet not tear his head from his body. We all heard the snap. Then his body swung back and forth. I stepped onto the battlements. I took out my sword and shouted, "I will be looking for you, William of Ypres! This is not over!"

My words would not reach him but those close by would hear and repeat them. As I stepped back a flurry of bolts clattered into the battlements. They missed and the body swung as a symbol of my wrath.

Chapter 16

It was November by the time the counter castles were finished. It took a week for them to assemble and build the stone throwers. Watching and waiting proved wearier than fighting. Inside the castle, the hunger and the tension were taking their toll on those not walking the walls. It seemed that the castle was inhabited with skeletons waiting to die. We awaited an attack on the sally port which did not come. We waited for stones to shower our walls and they did not fall. Waiting is an insidious disease. The new Constable, whom the Empress had appointed, was Roger de Villiers. He was an older knight and he held lands in Banbury. As Stephen now held Banbury he was happy to have the chance to fight back.

He came to see me one morning, "Lord, we have had some minor fights in the warrior hall. One of the men was badly cut."

I nodded, "They want to fight and there is no enemy for them. We must begin to spread the men around and vary their duties. Have some sent to replace those in St. George's Tower and the barbican. I have my men in those two strongholds and they can contain such dissension. Use my name as a threat to the others."

He nodded, "Lord, the food is running out. I have spoken with the steward. Even with rationing, we have but three or four weeks supplies left."

"I know. If you look for an easy answer, Roger, I cannot give one. I know no more than you. There is no relief column coming. The enemy outnumber us and when they begin to hurl their stones then the castle will be slowly destroyed."

"That is bleak."

"That is the truth and I will not hide it from any."

"We will not surrender?"

"It may come to that but things will have to be desperate for that to happen. If we surrender then Stephen has won for he will have the Empress and her son. We will have lost England and for you, there will be no Banbury to return to. We fight and we do not surrender for there is no alternative."

Revelation filled his face, "And that is why we hang on. The future of England lies within these walls."

"And we do not give that up easily."

The first stones struck the walls that afternoon. They were stones sent to find the range. They hurled the first ones at the wall between the two square towers to the east of the gate tower. It was dark by the time they stopped and they had done little, apparent damage. I had the Constable dismantle some of the buildings inside the castle and have the timbers ready to shore up the walls. "Tomorrow they will use more stones and they will also attack from the second position. This is just the start."

That night I dined with the Empress, her ladies and Henry. I say dined but the soup made from horses bones and offal did not sustain. "From tomorrow the assault will begin. If they had not made obstruction in the moat then I would have sallied forth with my men and destroyed the war machines. That cannot be and we will have to endure the stones and the hunger."

"Will not my father and my uncle come?"

"Your father is still winning Normandy for you and your uncle... I have no answer for that." I looked over to Maud and saw that she too was disturbed by the lack of support from the Earl of Gloucester.

"It may be that it is winter, my son."

Dick was a realist, "Winter has barely started. We have had rain and wind; that is all. There has been frost yet. If they wanted to relieve us then last month would have been the time to do so. No one is coming. When winter freezes men's bones then warriors will start to die."

I shook my head, "Dick is a little blunt but he is right. However, our fighting ability has not been diminished and the walls stand. There is hope."

The next day the assault on the wall continued and the second group of stone throwers threw their stones at the barbican. They hit the walls and the roof but the barbican was strongly made. The greatest danger appeared to be from flying splinters when stones struck wood. Walter of Crewe had his cheek laid open by one such splinter.

"Have the men take cover. There is nothing to be gained from watching the stones as they fly. When the machines stop we assess and repair any damage. We both know, Dick, that it takes time to reduce walls unless you can mine beneath the walls. Here they cannot do that."

The first attack on the walls stopped just after noon. I suspected that the machines needed repair or they had run out of stones. The damage to the walls and the barbican was not great. One section of the wall to the east of us needed shoring with timbers. Had we had mortar we would have repaired them. I retired exhausted.

I was woken by Henry. "Lord, it is a messenger from Gilles. The Tower is under attack!"

"Fetch Dick."

I donned my helm and grabbed my sword. I followed the man at arms to the tower. "It was just a short time ago we thought we heard a splash. Master Gilles sent me as soon as he heard it. It may be nothing."

"My squire does not make foolish decisions. There will be something." We raced up the steps to the fighting platform. Gilles and Richard were armed and ready. Gilles pointed to the stream. "I saw shadows moving, lord. I am certain that there are men there."

"You may be right. There are many small streams and rivers in Flanders. I have heard that many of the warriors from there can swim. We will watch from here. If they come close I will lead a sortie."

We peered into the dark and I saw a brief flash of white. It was a face. I heard a grunt in the dark and a whispered curse. They had found the caltrops. A movement behind me made me turn. It was Dick and my six archers. I pointed into the dark. He nodded and they prepared their bows. I could see why they had chosen this night. It was a cloudy sky with no moon. It was warmer than it had been and they would think we were preoccupied with the attack of their siege engines.

Dick hissed, "Now!" and seven bowstrings twanged. We heard cries and bodies fell.

"At them!" A surprisingly large number of Flemish warriors rose like wraiths from the ground. They were dripping and wet but there were many of them. We could not allow them to get to the gate and damage it.

"Gilles, Richard, fetch your men at arms. Dick, continue up here. Kill as many as you can" We descended and I said, "Open the gate. Hit them and hit them hard." There were no caltrops close to the door. We had a thirty paces piece of ground to defend. The twelve of us would have to do the job unaided.

I was the first out and, drawing my dagger and sword I ran at the first Flemish warrior. As I had expected they wore no mail. The first two were carrying a ladder. Their hands were full. I hacked one in the neck with my sword and gutted the second with my dagger. I plunged into the dark. Four men with axes loomed up. They had round shields and I recognised them as Frisians. They were hard men to kill. This was not the time for caution. These were the ones who would batter and break my gate and I ran into the heart of them. Even as I slashed my sword at head height one fell transfixed by an arrow. My sword bit into the neck of a second. An axe came towards me and I just managed to deflect it with my dagger. The fourth raised his axe triumphantly and Gilles launched himself like a spear. His sword went through the Frisian and came out of his back.

I did not want to go beyond Dick's view. My archers would decide this. We had to form a human barrier between them and the gate. "A wall! On me!" I saw Henry with his

sword. "Stand behind me, Henry!" I picked up one of the
Frisian shields. It was heavier than mine but it would block a
blow better than my dagger.

Numbers were hard to estimate. More men were landing
each moment.

"No one gets beyond us. We do not move and we are like
a rock!"

The next wave rushed towards us. Arrows plucked some
from their feet but inevitably some got through. "Go for their
heads! They have no helmets."

As I blocked a spear with my shield I brought the edge of
my sword around to take the top of the warrior's head.
Pieces of bone and blood-spattered those to his left and right.
As I scythed backhand it hacked into the shoulder of the man
to his left. When the warrior's shield lowered Richard
stabbed up into his chest. A Frisian with a war axe smashed
down onto Gilles' shield. It was a powerful blow and my
squire was knocked to his knees. I lunged into the side of the
Frisian with my sword. It rasped off his ribs. Just then a
sword appeared behind me to stab into the stomach of the
warrior who thought he had my back. As I helped Gilles to
his feet I said, "Thank you, Henry." I saw that our line was
shorter. There were six of us and more warriors emerged like
creatures from the depths to try to take the gate. Suddenly
there was a roar and Dick led my six archers to sortie from
the gate. They were all good swordsmen. The extra mailed
men made all the difference. With renewed energy, we
hacked and chopped our way into them. The Flemish did not
ask for quarter and we gave them none. When there was no
movement and just the moans of the dying we halted. I
waved my line forward. We reached the stream and saw that
none remained alive.

"Take their weapons, we can use them. Put the bodies
into the stream, the current will take them to the Thames and
Stephen and William will realise that their plot has failed."

The Sergeant at Arms had a wounded leg but he lived. He
pointed to his dead men. "And what of these, lord?"

"They are your men. Would you have them burned or
buried?"

"Let us bury them, lord, here where they fell. This will be a place where we can remember them."

Dick said, "I will collect our arrows. We will have further need of them."

It was dawn when we finished clearing the field. A priest came to join the Empress and her ladies as we bade farewell to those who had fallen defending the gate. We used the ladders to make crude crosses. When this was all over the Empress promised a carved stone with their names on it.

The stones did not fall upon our walls that day and overnight it began to rain. It was not a slight downpour but a storm of Biblical proportions. The icy rain found gaps in clothes and was relentless. The ropes they used on the war machines would be useless. God had come to our aid. The wind which drove the rain towards us made the corpse of the murderous doctor spin as though alive. It terrified our men and, I had no doubt, the enemy. The rain lasted for four days. When it stopped the skies cleared and became cloudless and at night the ground froze. We woke to bright blue skies and hard frosty ground. Winter had come. It meant we were saved from war machines but we froze in our castle. The enemy stopped his assault. They had another weapon; winter. We had limited wood and we were forced to burn the dried horse droppings. The castle was filled with an acrid smell but, when we were close to the fires, we were warm. On the walls, men wrapped themselves in as many layers as they could. We had no luxuries such as braziers. Those on watch came back inside blue with the cold.

As December arrived Stephen and William of Ypres approached under a flag of truce to our gate. The Empress joined me on the barbican. It was a sad day for us. Two of the castle servants had died of hunger or perhaps they were sick with something else and the lack of food hastened their demise. Whatever the reason the Empress and I were sad. The first deaths would be just that, the first, and others would follow.

"Cousin, it pains me to see you still trapped within your walls. Take my offer. You and your men can march out and we will escort you to Bristol where you will take ship for Anjou. I am being fair."

She pointed to the rope which still hung from the gate. The winds, torrential rains and the animals had long since shaken the skeleton free and it had sunk into the moat but the ropeways a reminder nonetheless. "And was the murder of the Constable fair? The traitor sent by your dog of war there!"

Stephen flashed his head around to glare at his lieutenant, "I knew nothing of murder and I only learned of the spy when I saw his corpse. I am sorry, cousin. It was not on my doing."

"Perhaps it was your wife then but either way it was William of Ypres, Count of Flanders, who hatched the plot." The Empress' voice was as hard as I ever heard.

She looked at me and I spoke, "William of Ypres, are you a man of honour? If so I will come forth and we will have a trial by combat." He was silent. "Surely you are not afraid of one man!"

When he spoke it was thickly accented, "I will not fight you for I have no need. You are going nowhere and soon hunger and winter will bite. The plague will come and we will be able to walk in."

"Then we have no more to say." I turned to Dick. I spoke loudly so that all could hear, "Put an arrow in the heart of that mercenary!"

The Count had quick reactions and he whipped his horse's head around. Dick's arrow hit his horse's rump and the animal threw the Count to the ground. He scrambled to safety. Stephen shook his head and laughed, "You can never predict what you will do, Alfraed. It is a shame you never joined my side. I wish, cousin, that I had such loyalty from my earls." He turned his horse's head and walked back into the town.

"Sorry, my lord, he was quicker than I expected."

"His pride was hurt. That will have to suffice."

The next day the snow came. Blizzards blew and two more servants died. The horses had been grazed upon the motte and the bits of grass which were in the bailey but now it was covered in snow and we had to slaughter more of them. Soon we would have barely twenty left. The day we killed them would be the day we lost. The days grew colder and colder. Outside the world was a blanket of white. You could not see any features for they were covered with snow. Even the siege machines had disappeared. We were forced to take up the crosses of the dead and burn them for firewood. One morning it was so cold that we struggled to open the gates. A man at arms had frozen to death on the walls.

That night as we ate our frugal meal I wondered if this was the end. We were down to the last jug of wine and perhaps that set my mind and my tongue working. "The Constable is well out of this. We thought his death was slow but this is death by inches. Each day we grow weaker. Our future is as black as ever."

Dick said, "I confess I have looked for hope and I see none. All I see is a sea of white."

A voice came to me and I said, "Say that again."

"What lord? All I see is a sea of white?"

"That is it. Do you not remember what the Constable said right at the very end? I thought he was rambling but in those last moments, before he died, he was lucid. He said, ' *but when there is white there is hope. Watch for the ice.* ' It is white and the ice is here."

"What?"

I could see they were confused but I had the clarity of thought at that moment. I understood what the Constable had been saying. "Gilles, Dick, come with me." I raced out and went to St. George's Tower. "Richard, get your cloak." Henry was with us but I would not risk him. "Open the sally port and follow me." I know they thought me mad but I was not. Once we were outside I led them to the stream. The snow was deep but it had frozen and there was a crust upon it. I stepped onto it and it held. "Richard, walk across the stream to the other shore. If you feel or hear the ice crack then return as quickly as you can."

"Aye lord."

It was nerve-wracking watching him and listening for the crack which would announce his death. He returned, grinning. "It is solid, lord."

"Henry, go to your mother and tell her we leave with her ladies. Richard, go to our chests and find those white cloaks Alice gave us. They will disguise us in the night. Gilles, find the Constable and then go and saddle the horses for us, the ladies and our archers."

"Aye lord."

"And Dick, we will see if it will bear our combined weight." We were both wearing mail and were big men. Watching to the west and the town walls, we edged across. There was not a sound. Our breath froze before us but the ice held. We reached the other bank and I saw no sentries. Without a word, we headed back. The ice felt solid. The stream was shallow. I doubted that either the moat or the river would have frozen as hard as this. The Constable knew his castle and land. We went directly to the Keep. There the Empress and her ladies looked at me as though I was mad. Roger de Villiers was there too.

"We have little time. The castle cannot be held much longer. Would you agree with my assessment, Constable?"

"I would. Men are dying of the cold and we have no fuel."

"Then tomorrow morning I want you to surrender the castle."

The Empress said, "But we will be captured! We will be prisoners."

"No, we will not. Richard, the cloaks." He handed out the white cloaks. "Wrap these around your own cloaks. The stream is frozen and will bear our weight. We leave now. I will take my archers and our squires. We have enough horses for them. If we leave a large gap between us then we can cross the ice and mount on the other bank."

The Empress nodded, "It seems impossible but you have never let me down. We will trust your judgement. Come, ladies. Let us see if we can disappear."

I clasped the Constable's hand, "Stephen is a fair man. Delay your surrender as long as you can. I do not think there will be many guards out on a night like this."

"Good luck, Earl, but I think that you make your own luck."

I led a gaunt Rolf through the sally port and across the hard frozen snow. I pointed to the rear and to Dick. He nodded. I took a deep breath and stepped onto the ice. I had done it once but would the weight of my horse cause it to crack? The ice was so thick that it took our weight. Would it survive the passage of another thirteen horses? When I reached the other side I mounted. I could barely see the others. It was their horses which I could see. This might just work and I thanked Alice. She had not planned this but she had given us our escape; the white woollen cloaks had kept us hidden. We blended in with the snow.

As they crossed successfully, one by one, I worked out our strategy. It had to be to go to Wallingford and Sir Brian Fitz Count. It was as strong as Oxford and was prepared for a siege. Disaster struck when Rafe and Dick were almost across. There was a loud crack and the ice began to break. Rafe ran and he and his horse made it across the icy stream. Dick and his mount sank into the water. It only came up to the horse's withers but the crack had alarmed some of the enemy sentries close by the west gate of the town.

Gilles helped Dick to pull his horse from the water and we mounted. "We ride to Wallingford. Richard, stay by Henry. Gilles, watch the Empress. Walter of Crewe, look after the two ladies."

"We need no help, my lord!"

"Nonetheless you shall have it. Dick, you and Rafe, watch our rear. Long Tom, with me!"

I would have to gamble again. There was a bridge across the Thames close to Oxford but I guessed that would be guarded. We would head to Abingdon. It would mean we would have to cross the Thames twice but there might be fewer enemies that far away. The frozen ground was hard for horses that had been on short rations and were carrying mailed men. I dared not ride either as hard or as fast as I might have liked. The air was so cold that it actually hurt. The breath from our horses and from our mouths formed a thin fog before us but we had escaped the trap. A week ago I had spied no hope and now there was a glimmer of a chance.

Abingdon had been held by forces loyal to the Empress but we had been in Oxford so long that I could not guarantee that it was still so. It was but a few miles to the bridge and as we closed I said, "Long Tom, draw your weapon. We may have to fight our way across."

I heard his sword as he drew it. My archers had trained with Wulfric and Dick so that they could fight from the back of a horse. They were the most valuable and valued soldiers. As we neared the bridge I saw the light of a brazier. It was guarded. The hard and frozen ground meant that a stealthy approach was impossible.

As we neared I saw some figures. One turned and shouted, "Who goes there?"

I decided on the truth, "We are for the Empress!"

"Traitors and renegades all!"

I spurred Rolf and he responded. They were still drawing their weapons as I brought my sword down on the captain of the watch. Years of pulling a war bow had given Long Tom an arm like an oak branch. His sword split the watch's head in two. Our horses bundled the other two over the side into the icy river. Once on the other side, we reined in to watch for more enemies but there were none. When Dick and Rafe crossed we returned to the van and continued on.

We had travelled no more than four miles when Dick shouted, "Lord, horses. We are being followed."

As we had passed Abingdon there should be no more enemies before Wallingford but our horses were weak and they would catch us. "Gilles, Richard, escort the ladies to Wallingford. We will guard the rear."

"Aye lord."

As she passed the Empress said, "Take care, Earl! We are so close. Let us make Wallingford I beg of you."

"That is out of my hands, my lady. Watch your mother, Henry. I am relying on you."

They rode into the night and their white cloaks made them disappear almost instantly in the snow-covered country.

"How far behind, Dick?"

"A mile. They are catching us."

"Then let us meet them." We rode down the road until we came through a tiny hamlet. There were three huts. I stopped. "I will wait in the middle. Use your arrows when they come to me." I wheeled Rolf around and drew my sword.

"Aye, Lord, Rafe, Tom, Walter, you go yonder."

I could not hear the hooves as the riders hurried after us. I pulled my shield closer to me. It felt more reassuring than the Frisian one I had last used. My cloak was still around me and I would be hard to see. They, on the other hand, were easier to see for they stood out against the snow. As they neared I reared Rolf and shouted, "Go back or die!"

They had not seen me and they stopped. That was my intention. My archers let fly and struck men and horses. I galloped towards them. I was one man but they could not all hit me for fear of striking each other. My archers would not hit me and I wished to make them fall back. They were Flemish. They were not the best of riders. I slashed my sword and punched with my shield as I burst into the heart of them. I felt blows landing on my shield. One struck my helmet. One hit my hauberk on the right but while my sword was bloody my body was whole. I wheeled Rolf around as horses tried to move out of our way and riders flailed at me with weapons. My archers were the ones who saved me. Four arrows plucked the nearest four riders from their saddles and Dick shouted, "Now, lord! Ride!"

I needed no urging and I spurred my weary mount. I did not glance over my shoulder. My archers watched over me. I heard their hooves and then Dick was beside me. "They are not following, lord. We dropped six of them and you slew three. They have had enough." He spat. "Mercenaries!"

There was no longer the need for speed and I wished to save our horses. We rode slowly down a silent road until I saw the glow from a brazier on the walls of Wallingford castle. The smell of wood smoke was most welcome. The hoof prints in the snow showed that Gilles and Richard had managed to reach the castle. This was no Oxford. Brian Fitz Count was well used to a siege. I could not see Stephen travelling through winter to begin siege again. We had won. As we clattered through the gates I felt like cheering and then I saw the face of the Earl of Gloucester.

Chapter 17

My spirits sank as we entered the castle. He had been this close and yet had made no attempt to relieve the siege. As I dismounted Henry ran to me, "Are you hurt, Warlord?"

"Thanks to my archers I am safe. Is your mother well?"

He nodded, "My uncle sent her and her ladies to the fire in the Great Hall. They were cold."

"Good."

The Earl approached me with his hand held out, "Thank God you escaped! I was worried."

"Not worried enough to relieve the siege though. We have lost Oxford castle!"

He ignored my words. "But Normandy is almost ours. Come to the fire. You are cold and you are weary. Men do not think straight under those conditions." He turned to a groom, "Come, take the Earl's horses. They too look exhausted." He strode towards the inviting door to the Great Hall.

Dick said quietly, in my ear, "Now is not the time, lord." I turned and saw his face. He shook his head, "We need no angry words this night. We have escaped and we live to fight another day. You have told me before to choose my battles. I urge you to do the same."

"You are right."

We followed the Earl into Sir Brian's castle. The others were already in the hall and servants were bringing in hot food and mulled ale. The Empress' eyes lit up when we entered. "You are safe We were worried!."

"They were easily discouraged for they were mercenaries and my archers' aim was true. God was on our side."

The Empress' face was a book which I could read. I saw a worried expression. She feared I would say something which might put our alliance in danger. "My brother explained that he was gathering an army to come to our aid."

I said nothing and used the proffered goblet of ale as an excuse not to speak. Sir Brian entered the room, "It is good to see you, Earl. My men kept a close watch on the siege but we could do nothing about it. We had too few men. It was only when the Earl here arrived last month that we could begin to think of relief."

Lives could have been saved had the Earl come a month back. I sipped the piping hot ale and felt it warm me within.

"Sister, your husband and I have captured all of the Peninsula save for Cherbourg and that will surely fall in Spring. Then there is just Rouen which stands in our way. Stephen has now lost the support of all his earls."

"And yet he still controls large parts of the land."

"We have sent for Sir Miles and the Empress' men in Gloucester. Time is on our side."

I knew it was not but I was too tired to argue. The Earl had his own plan. I could not fathom it but he was right in one thing. If Normandy fell then we had more men we could use in England.

"Perhaps you are right. Does my son prosper?"

"Young William is a rock. The Count relies on him more and more. When he is Duke of Normandy he will heap more titles upon him."

I looked across to Matilda. She gave a slight shake of her head. "Duke of Normandy? Surely the Empress should be Duchess."

"But she will be. Geoffrey is her husband. It is right that he will become the Duke."

I knew then that an arrangement had been made in Normandy. What was the price? Had the Earl been given something? I should not have been surprised. My son had told me as much already. I saw plots everywhere.

"We will talk more in the morning when you are refreshed."

He was right and I was about to go when Sir Brian said, "Surely, my lord, you should tell him of his knights. That is serious news." Sir Brian was the most honest knight I had ever met. He had once told me that he wished to be a priest and that goodness showed through in his words.

"My knights?"

Sir Brian looked at the Earl who shrugged, "I was going to leave the news for the morrow. He can do little about it now but speak. You know as much as I do."

Sir Brian began. "Three weeks ago a rider arrived from Sir Edward at Thornaby. He said his name was Rafe of Barwick. He told us that Waleran de Beaumont, the brother of the Earl of Leicester, had launched a surprise attack and taken Helmsley Castle. Sir Wulfric is besieged in Pickering. Sir Richard of Yarm is besieged in his home. Sir Edward asked for help."

I looked at the Earl who said. "We could do nothing, Alfraed. You and the Empress were our priority. We would have come weeks ago but for the weather. As soon as the snow goes then we will begin our operation to bring Stephen to battle."

"Sir Brian, our horses are almost dead on their feet. I beg of you thirteen horses to take me north to my home."

The Empress started, "My lord! You are tired. You have not eaten well for months. You cannot travel the length of this land and fight a battle."

"My lady, we waited for relief in Oxford. How do think you Wulfric feels in Pickering? The only thing which would stop me would be my death."

"My sister is right and your death may come if you ride in the depths of winter. A few weeks cannot hurt."

"Ask your sister of the deaths which came daily in Oxford, my lord. Each hour we dally means someone will die. Sir Brian?"

"Of course and I will have some of my men escort you to the Great North Road. We have food we can give you."

"Thank you and now I will retire. I intend to be home within two days."

As we were led to the room we would all share Dick said, "Wulfric is made out of granite, lord. He will hold."

"I know but I cannot understand why Edward has not relieved the siege. I left him in command."

"There will be a reason. He sent a message here. Perhaps William of Kingston had news he gave to Sir Edward which we are not aware of."

"Perhaps. Once again I have been away too long."

"You were needed here, lord. Had you not been then the Empress and her son would now be in Stephen's hands."

Weariness took over and I fell into a deep sleep. My body, however, woke me while it was still dark. I rose and awoke my men."Come, we have friends to save."

The kitchens were awake and I sent Gilles to them for food. We were eating when Sir Brian arrived. "Like me you an early riser, lord."

I nodded and swallowed the bread. "Once again I thank you for your help, Sir Brian. You are a true friend and I pray that you will continue to watch over the Empress and her son until Sir Miles arrives."

"The Earl is here surely he will watch over them."

"Perhaps but I would be happier if you gave me your word."

"And you have it."

Henry burst in. "You cannot go without me! I am your squire!"

"And you did a good job while you were. Now you have a greater responsibility. You must learn to be a leader. It may be some time until you are King of England but soon you will be heir to Normandy. I have no doubt that your father will send for you. Besides this task I have set myself is a hard one. You know how hard it was to get south in the summer. How much more difficult will it be in winter?"

The Empress, wrapped in a fur came in with her ladies. "I told him, my lord, but he would not listen."

I knelt and put my hands on his shoulders. "I have shown you how a knight behaves. You have fought alongside your people. This is preparation for when you are king. You must be king! Too many good men have given their lives to your cause! Do not waste those lives. You have a greater responsibility than Gilles and Richard here. If they fall in battle it will be sad and a tragedy. If you do before you are a king then it would be a disaster. Ask your mother to tell you of the death of her brother on the White Ship. I do not ask you to do this. I command you. It will be my last order as your knight. If you are a squire then you will obey. You will become King and you will be a great king."

I saw him thinking over my words. He was my son and he was clever. He nodded. "I will obey but you are to be my champion when I am king,"

"And I will fulfil that role with pleasure. And now we must leave. We have many leagues to go this day."

There were too many people in the outer bailey for me to have the farewell with the Empress which I wished but our eyes spoke for us. We galloped through the gates and headed over the frozen land heading northeast. We were going home.

I rode next to Dick so that we could talk. Sir Brian had given us strong and well fed horses. They ate up the miles. With his men before us, we had the luxury of not having to watch for danger.

"Do we head for Pickering, lord?"

"No, we head for Piercebridge and Sir Philip. I need to rouse my valley and then relieve the siege of Yarm. I know this delays our arrival but there are but ten of us."

Dick nodded. "We would be throwing our lives away and for no good reason."

"We will head for Lincoln."

"Lincoln, lord, but the Earl of Chester has changed sides and supports Stephen!"

"The Earl is a treacherous snake but his wife is not. The fact that he changes sides so often means his heart is in neither camp. He looks after himself. I will gamble. Besides we cannot sleep out of doors. We need shelter. I trust Maud."

"And we trust you, lord but I fear your trust may be misplaced where the Earl is concerned."

The escort left us at Leicester as darkness fell and we hurried up the Great North Road. Surprisingly we were admitted easily into the town of Lincoln and we rode, wearily, to the castle gates.

"Who goes there?"

"The Earl of Cleveland. We seek shelter for the night."

There was silence and then a voice said, "Wait there while we seek the approval of the Earl."

Dick chuckled, "I am waiting for a bolt from the battlements. We seem ever drawn here."

"Aye, we do."

The face reappeared remarkably quickly, "Open the gates. You are admitted, lord."

As we rode through I saw, silhouetted against the light from the Great Hall two figures. One I recognised immediately as Maud and so I deduced that the other was Ranulf Earl of Chester. We dismounted and I handed my reins to Richard.

The Earl of Chester extended his hand, "It must be serious business to bring you out on the road on such a night as this."

I nodded, "We are anxious to get home."

Maud took my hand and pulled me inside, "Then why do you make our guest wait in the cold! You have not the sense of a flea!" I smiled. She never changed and I liked that in a world of such uncertainties.

As we went inside where the warmth hit us like a blanket the Earl said, "The last we heard you were with the Empress and besieged in Oxford Castle. Did Stephen let you go when it fell?"

I spoke not to him but to the Countess. "He did not let us go for he never had us. The Empress and her ladies escaped over a frozen stream. She is at Wallingford with your father."

She roared with laughter, "I told you they would not cage the wolf for long! Well done, Alfraed! Come you shall tell us all over hot food. You look like you need fattening up!"

I nodded, "My men?"

"They will be cared for, fear not."

Dick, my squires and I were the centre of attention. The assembled lords hung on every word. I did not tell them all but I did speak of the death of the Constable and the attack of the Frisians. Then I turned to Ranulf, "And you, lord, whose side are you on now?" I knew it was blunt but I would not dance around with subtle words.

Maud laughed, "The same side he has always been on, his own!"

"I am a practical man, Alfraed. You are far too noble and inflexible. Sometimes you need to bend like the willow."

"But your people in the north suffer great privations from the Scots. I have many refugees from the Honour of Clitheroe and Lancashire. They come to me with tales which would chill your blood."

The Countess said, "And you are no willow, Alfraed, you are an oak."

The Earl shook his head, "The war will end soon. I am afraid that the Empress cannot hold on much longer."

I suddenly realised he had not heard the news from Normandy. "Not even when Normandy falls next year? And it will fall, Earl. The enemy holds two castles: Cherbourg and Rouen. I have been there and there is little support for Stephen. Those two will fall and then what will happen to Stephen's Norman revenues? Will he be able to be as generous as he was when first he came?" I knew I could not sway him to our side but I could put doubts in his mind. I saw his face as he took in my words.

He frowned and sipped his wine. Maud waved a hand as though to dispel the words, "Enough of politics. How is my father?"

"He is well. His successes in Normandy appear to have put him in better humour."

"And the Empress and her son? I have suffered a siege and it is hard. It must be doubly so in winter."

"She and her ladies survived remarkably well. They are all, like you, lady, resilient. As for Henry; he will be a great knight and a good leader. He is fearless in battle. Is that not so, Gilles?"

"Aye lord; Richard and I had to restrain him else he would have taken on men three times his size."

"My grandfather would have approved. He liked strong men. That was why he so admired you, Alfraed. You stood up for your beliefs even if you were the sole voice."

We both knew that she criticised her husband but he was still thinking of his future. "And now, lady, we must retire. I have to reach home by the morrow."

"That is a hard ride."

"I have two castles under siege and I must relieve them. I cannot let my people suffer."

Ranulf roused himself, "Forgive me for my inattention, Alfraed. Your words disturbed me. I wish I had your strength of conviction. You still believe that the Empress and her son will win."

"If more men believed that then she would have won already."

Leaving that barb in the air I retired. I was about to undress when there was a knock on the door. It was Maud. She slipped inside and closing the door said, "Do not think too harshly of my husband. He will not betray you and I think your words will sway him. He needs time. I will let you take my personal guards. There are but six of them. You will need them more than I."

"Thank you, lady. I will not spurn any offer of help."

"Return them when you no longer need them." She paused, "Or if they are dead."

We left before dawn. The air was still icy but the skies were clear. We had a long way to go and this time we would be passing enemies all along the road. The Countess' men were led by Robert of Lincoln. I had fought with him at the battle of Lincoln. He was a warrior in the mould of Wulfric.

"Thank you for your service, Robert."

"You fight for the true ruler and that is what I believe too. Besides garrison duty is dull. Life with you will be anything but dull!"

We halted close to Osmotherley. We needed sharp wits on the last twenty miles. We were familiar with the old castle and always used it when we were on the road. There was a well and we drew water. Richard went to make water and he suddenly shouted, "Lord!"

Drawing our weapons Gilles, Dick and I ran to him. He stood over the corpse and head of Rafe of Barwick. The messenger had not returned to Thornaby. They would know nothing. Dick knelt next to him. "He suffered many wounds before he died. They must have ambushed him close by and he fled here." He pointed down the slope, "Look there is his dead horse. We shall bury brave Rafe."

After we had put him beneath the ground we left in a sombre mood. The ones who had ambushed him could be waiting for us. I took a decision soon after we reached the road. "We will head cross country to reach Piercebridge. There will be less chance of ambush."

We were lucky. We saw no one. They had had less snow here and it was a frozen crust. We travelled faster than I might have hoped. It was close to dusk when we spied the river ahead. I sent Long Tom to scout the crossing. He was not away long. "There are twenty men there watching the bridge, lord."

I nodded.

Dick said, "We could ford the river."

"It is icy and that will take time. They know not that we have the seven finest archers in England and six of the best men at arms. We avenge Rafe of Barwick!"

We left the horses with Gilles and Richard. My archers had their bows and I held my sword. The white cloaks helped us stay hidden in this white wilderness. The would be ambushers were camped above the bridge. They were far enough away to be hidden from Sir Philip's men and yet close enough to fall upon any who approached the bridge. Three men were on guard. The rest lay around a fire. I picked my way through the snow placing each foot carefully. I was less than twenty paces from the edge when the first six arrows flew and the three sentries fell.

The rest were disorientated. All that they saw was the three men fall. They did not know where the arrows had been released. I leapt amongst them. I hacked one across the middle as I stepped towards the firelight. More men fell to

214

arrows and confusion reigned. All that I saw would be
enemies. They did not know where the rest were. I held my
dagger in my left hand and I plunged it into the eye of a man
who came at my left side. I lunged with my sword and
impaled one who wielded an axe. All the time my archers
were causing wounds and death as they released their
missiles from the shadows. I could not totally avoid the spear
which was thrust at me but, by turning slightly, it just scored
a line along my mail. I brought my sword across the neck of
a man at arms and took his head in one blow. Robert of
Lincoln and the Countess' men were magnificent. Soon it
was over.

Those in the castle had heard the noise and I saw lights
approaching the bridge. "Gilles, horses!" I turned to Walter
of Crewe, "Collect the weapons and anything which might
identify them."

I mounted my borrowed horse and we rode down to the
bridge. I knew the men would be nervous and I shouted,
"Stockton!"

"Halt so that we may see!"

Two of Sir Philip's archers had their bows levelled at us
while a man at arms approached with a torch. They
recognised me. "Can it be you, lord? We heard you were
dead or captured."

"It is me. Go and help my archers collect the weapons
from the dead. I will see Sir Philip."

The gate was open but guarded. They parted when they
recognised me and my squires. Sir Philip walked from his
hall. "My lord! We heard noises. I did not know it was you."

I pointed across the bridge. "There were twenty enemy
warriors waiting to ambush any who left your castle or
attempted to reach it." I could not keep the criticism from my
voice and I hit the mark.

He dropped his head. "I am sorry, Warlord. When
Wulfric and Sir Richard were under siege we prepared to be
attacked too."

"But you were not. I want your men ready to ride with me
tomorrow. You will skulk in your castle no more. Tomorrow
we go to war."

Chapter 18

As we walked into his castle he asked, "Why did you say skulk, lord? Have I let you down?"

"Not just you, all of my knights but when I find an enemy camped close to one of my castles then I must question that lord of the manor. If you cannot control the land within a hundred paces of your castle what can you control?"

"You were not here, lord. We kept watch on our walls and the bridge."

"I will not waste time arguing with you, Sir Philip. There will be time for recriminations when I have brought security to my land once more."

Dick and the archers entered. "They are the men of De Brus, lord. I am not certain which De Brus but I recognise the livery. They had coins about them; silver coins."

"We ride with Sir Philip's men for Stockton on the morrow. I want a garrison strong enough to hold the walls but I need all of your archers."

I retired early. I knew that I had been harsh with Sir Philip but I was angry with all of my knights. Unless they had attempted to lift the sieges they had let me down. Sir Edward was the most culpable. I had left him in command.

We left before dawn. We knew these roads. I sent Long Tom to Sir Hugh telling him that I needed twenty of his men. There were no armed men at either Elton or Hartburn. I had not expected there to be any. I expected them at Stockton. I rode through the gates with a heart and a face as black as thunder. I strode to my hall shouting, "I want my knights before me now!"

John of Craven, Sir John, Sir Tristan and Sir Harold rushed in as though there was a fire. John my Steward followed them. I threw my cloak to the floor and rounded on them. "I had thought there must be a plague or you had died fighting yet here you stand before me."

"My lord?" Sir Tristan looked bewildered.

"I cannot believe that you left your father besieged in his castle at Yarm! I thought at the very least you would have relieved that siege."

Sir Tristan looked distraught and Sir Harold said, "Sir Richard and his good lady are both dead, lord. The castle was overrun before we could relieve the siege. We rode as soon as Sir Richard sent word. When we arrived his head was on a spear. The castle is in the hands of Sir Rufus Leverhulme. They had destroyed the middle spans of the bridge. There was nothing that we could do."

I had been hasty and I relented immediately. "I am sorry for your loss and sorry that I spoke as I did." Sir Tristan nodded.

Sir Harold said, "They partly destroyed the bridge. The only way across the river now is by the ferry."

"And Sir Edward?"

"Sir Edward's son John died not long after you left. His mother was in such turmoil and despair that she threw herself in the Tees and Sir Edward has not been himself."

"But the messenger, Rafe of Barwick, who sent him?"

"I did, lord. I visited with Sir Edward and made sure that he was being cared for. I did not know the messenger had got through."

"He did but he died on the way back. I thank you for what you did but why did you not go to the aid of Wulfric?"

"Sir Edward received word of a Scottish war band to the north of Norton. They came just days after news of the attacks on our castles. You were not here, lord and we knew not what else to do. If we had left to go south then Norton and perhaps even Stockton might have fallen. We did not want to risk losing the valley."

I sank into my chair. Fate had intervened. The knight I had left in command had not done as I had asked. I could not blame the others. "Sir Harold, ride to Norton. I want everyone brought here. Even man woman, warriors, every child cow, pig, everyone and every animal!"

Dick asked, quietly, "What will you do, lord?"

"As soon as Sir Hugh arrives we cross the river and we take back Yarm. It will be your castle, Sir Tristan. Then we march to Pickering and relieve the siege."

"And Sir Edward?"

"I will deal with Sir Edward. John of Craven, I want your Frisians and your men mounted. You come with us. Erre and his men can guard Stockton. With the combined fyrd of two manors that should be enough to deter a warband and when we have relieved Pickering, we scour the land and hang every Scot that we find." They nodded. "Gilles, come with me. Richard, prepare our horses."

As I strode towards the ferry Harold ran to keep up with me. "I am sorry we let you down, lord but we did not know what to do for the best. We heard that you were captured or dead. We did not wish to lose the valley."

"This is not your fault. It is mine. I left and I should not have done so. I will not do so again. My place is here. I have learned that I can do nothing in the south and the west. The Earl of Gloucester will do as he chooses. I am used as a pawn in a game of thrones. I berated Sir Philip and I should not have done so. I should have taught him better."

"Be gentle with Sir Edward, lord, he has lost much."

I smiled, "I will be careful in my choice of words." We had reached the ferry, "Have we enough food in store?"

"We have, lord. The river only froze just around Christmas and thawed again last week. The *'Adela'* has kept us supplied."

"Good. Tell the others... never mind, I shall tell them myself when all of this is over."

There was a film of ice on the river but the stout ferry soon cleared it. I said nothing on my journey across. I understood Sir Edward's grief. I had endured it myself. Perhaps I had been wrong to ennoble him. Had he still been a man at arms this tragedy might not have happened. The walk to the castle helped to focus my mind. "When we go in the castle, Gilles, I want you to find out how many men we have available to fight from the garrison."

"Aye lord. Things look black do they not?"

"They do but not as black as Oxford eh? I must stop feeling sorry for myself. We have lost one castle, Yarm, and that we shall recover. Pickering I held, along with Helmsley, to spite Stephen. It was pride and arrogance I can see that now. When the siege is relieved I will destroy Pickering."

We were admitted straight away. Ralph, who was the Steward, approached and bowed. "Where is the lord of the manor, Ralph?"

"His is in the Great Hall, lord." He hesitated, "He has been drinking."

I nodded, "Go with Gilles. He will tell you what I need. I want the castle emptied. All must cross the river to Stockton. It is for their own good. There may be other bands of men and I need every warrior to retake what we have lost.

As soon as I entered the hall I could smell the ale. It was like an ale wife's house. Sir Edward stared into the fire. He looked like an old man and was hunched over. This was not the knight I had known for over twenty years. He barely noticed my entrance. "Edward."

Even though I spoke quietly he started and knocked over his ale. It spread like a bloody puddle on the stone floor He dropped to his knees and began to mop it up. I took his arm firmly and raised him. "This will not do, Edward. It is unseemly and not like you."

"Did they not tell you, lord, John died and my wife...? I will never see her in heaven for she took her own life."

That was a hard burden to bear. At least when I died, if God permitted, I would go to heaven and there see my wife, Adela. Sir Edward would not. "When I lost my wife and daughter you told me to be strong. I tell you to do the same. Ale will not bring them back."

"But how can I go on?"

I was becoming angry and I forced myself to remain calm. "You have a daughter and you have a son. Your daughter is of an age to marry. She will have grandchildren. Your son will be a warrior."

"No! He will not die too."

"He will for we all die. It is the manner in which we die that makes us men. You are the lord of the manor. I left you in command and you did nothing when they took Yarm."

"You were not here! I was told you were dead! I did not want to throw more lives away."

"Wulfric was your oldest friend. Would you let him and his men rot away in a siege?"

"I cannot leave my people here undefended."

"And you will not! Even now they are gathering what they own and I will look after them in my castle. Norton comes too. We have stores of food and we can laugh away a siege. But I need you to lead your men! I need you at my side. I need a warrior and not a drunk. Which will it be?"

In answer, he took the jug he had been holding and threw it into the fire. "I am a warrior and I will fight at your side again... if you will have me."

"You too are a knight of the Empress. Come we have much to do."

We left Gilles and Ralph to organise the transportation of those who lived in the castle. The horses were already aboard the ferry. When we reached the north shore Ethelred was there. "Do you have the old ferry yet or was it broken up?"

"No, lord, I have it still. If this one is damaged then I can use it."

"It floats and is serviceable?"

"Of course but why? Is there anything wrong with this one?"

"Tomorrow I will use it to transport warriors down to Yarm."

"But how will we get it back?"

"I know not how but it does not matter. Until the bridge at Yarm is repaired we need a way to cross the river there. You do this for the valley, Ethelred. If we do not then you lose all!"

He nodded, "I just hate waste, lord, that is all!"

"It will not be wasted for it will regain us Yarm."

As I strode into my bailey I felt like a weight had been lifted. I was going to take action. I was no longer reacting to others. I had a plan and I would make it succeed.

John my steward greeted me in the hall. "Where will we put all these people from Norton, lord?"

I smiled, "And the people of Thornaby. I know not yet but you and Alf can devise something. I have a war to make. This task is appointed to you."

He must have realised my mood for he said, "Aye lord. We will work something out."

"You can use the warrior hall for the women, children and old. Most of the warriors will be with me."

The day went in a blur. I spoke with my knights and my men at arms. I checked what weapons we had and how many horses would be fit. By the time dark arrived most of the two manors were dispersed and all that we awaited was Sir Hugh and his men. Alice had been the calmest person in the castle. She was pleased to see the return of me and my squires but she, above all, understood Sir Edward's pain and she was determined to make my castle as normal as possible. She created a feast worthy of a king. All of my knights and their families were there as well as my constables, sergeants and captains at arms. It would be a council of war as much as a feast.

I stood when the platters had been cleared and silence fell upon my hall. "These are perilous times in which we live. Our world is changing. We have lost fathers and we have lost wives. Sons have died." The words hung in the air making the warm room seem colder. "I was absent when I should have been here. For that I am sorry. I have blamed others for what were my errors. For that, I apologise." I saw some of my knights trying to speak but I silenced them with my hand. "That is the past; it is another country. Once more we are alone and we begin to claw back the gains which the enemy has made. I fought the Empress' war; now we fight the Warlord's war. This is our valley and we will fight to defend it!"

I knew I had said what they wished to hear when they began banging their daggers' hilts on my table.

"Our enemy thinks that this is winter and we will wait until spring. We attack tomorrow. This castle is strong and can withstand an attack from raiders. Tomorrow I will take my men on the old ferry and we will sail down to Yarm. It will take most of the day. I will take John of Craven and the men from my castle, Sir Edward and the men at arms from Thornaby. Sir Richard will lead all the rest to surround Yarm. I want it cut off. When we arrive with the ferry we will attack the walls. Our Frisian warriors will make matchwood of the palisade."

I paused to take a drink. "I sent Aiden and his scouts to spy out the castle. From what he could see no one who lived in the castle is now alive. The enemy slew them all. It makes it easy. All that we find will be the enemy." I paused. "Slay them. Everyone!"

We had forty warriors on the ferry and every one of them held a long pole to move us up the Tees. The icy river was sluggish but what current there was flowed against us. The mist on the water made it look as though we sailed in a cloud. We grounded once but our progress was steady. It was not a long journey. Had it been summer I would have feared watchers but this was winter and this Leverhulme did not know my land. With the middle of the bridge destroyed he would feel secure from the north and the south was held by Waleran and his men from York. If my men thought I was still in Oxford then so would the enemy. The indecision of my knights would actually aid us. If we had not stirred yet then it was unlikely we do so now.

As we turned the last bend towards the bridge my only worry was Sir Edward. It had been some time since he had been himself. How would he fare in battle? He looked resolute enough but I could no longer see into his heart.

The castle lay five hundred paces from the river on a low natural bluff. The motte had been made from the ditch which surrounded it. I knew that my horsemen would have reached the York road and closed it so that the enemy was trapped. Their attention would be on Dick and my men. His archers would already be stringing their bows. When we landed we would have to race as quickly as we could up the slope and

222

get across the ditch. We carried the poles for they would be our bridge across the obstruction which was the ditch.

I saw that they had just destroyed the central span of the bridge. It could be repaired. The bank was covered in virgin snow. No one had been down to the river. I stepped ashore with Richard and Gilles. We did not bother to tie up the ferry. It would drift down the river. If it grounded I would send Ethelred to free it. We had to run. The snow was not soft. It had fallen some time ago and had a hard, frozen crust. The going was far easier than I had expected. Behind me, I heard the crunch of feet on snow. My men and those of Sir Edward carried the poles. The only ones who did not were the four of us.

We were spotted with just two hundred paces to go. The four of us stood out from the rest for we led them and we became the target for their stones and their arrows. We made another hundred paces before the first missiles hit our shields. We reached the ditch and made a shield wall. John of Craven led his Frisians and they hurled their poles across the ditch. Then they joined our shield wall and the enemy wasted arrows. It did not take long to make an improvised bridge. We moved carefully over and the four of us held our shields above us as my Frisians began to chop their way through the wooden walls. Thankfully it was just stones that were dropped upon us. They had neither oil nor water prepared. As more men crossed there were more men cutting holes in the walls.

Günter of Bruges was a huge warrior and it was he who made the final breakthrough. His axe hacked through a timber, dislodging the two on either side. He said, "Stand aside, my lord!" He put his shoulder down and used his body and shield as a human battering ram. He burst through the remaining wood.

"In!"

I was the first through after Günter. A man at arms was lunging with his spear at Günter's side. The reckless Frisian did not have his shield held as high as he should and invited the strike. I brought my sword over to smash the haft in two. I twisted the blade and stabbed upwards under his chin. The

223

blow was so hard his helmet was knocked from his head and I tore the weapon out through his face.

"Stockton, to the gate! Sir Edward, secure the keep."

"Aye Warlord!"

Yarm had but one way in and out. Sir Richard and his men had defended it well for, as we ran towards it I saw that it had been hastily repaired. Had it not been built of stone Dick and the others could have forced it themselves. The Frisians are frightening looking warriors. The men at the gate fled at the sight of them. While John of Craven and his men opened the damaged gate I turned towards the wooden keep. We ran up the slope and passed the stables and the bakery. The Frisians were busy clearing a path for me. The men of Thornaby had done as I asked and gone straight to the keep. Sir Richard had made this more secure and the bottom floor was made of stone. The ladder leading to the door had been raised and, when I reached it, Sir Edward and his men had it surrounded.

He turned to me and I saw a spark of the old Edward. His surcoat was spattered with blood and his blade was bloody. He was grinning. Laughing he took off his helmet. "God but it is hot! We have them now, my lord."

"Aye, we do." Behind me, I heard those who had not made the safety of the keep being slaughtered. My plan had been to kill them all but I now knew that it would cost me men and I was now short of warriors. "I will speak with this knight." I turned to Gilles, "Come with me but keep your shield up. I want no more deaths!" They could not escape now and we had them surrounded and outnumbered. It was over.

"Aye lord."

I turned, Dick and the rest of my knights had joined Edward. I saw that they had taken off their helmets and were laughing at something Dick had said. They were old comrades. "Have the archers ready. I will go and see if they wish to surrender. It will save us losing men in an attack."

"Aye lord, but be careful. Beware treachery"!"

Holding our shields before us we approached the keep. I lowered the ventail on my coif so that I could speak. "Sir Rufus Leverhulme! I would speak with you!"

I looked over the edge of my shield towards the fighting platform. A young face looked over. Every knight I faced now seemed younger than my son. "Is that you? The Earl of Cleveland?"

"It is and I ask you to save slaughter and surrender."

"I thought you dead."

"You were misinformed."

"It matters not. Your castles will be taken one by one. You have no machines of war. You cannot take us!" I saw him nod and crossbows appeared and let fly a volley. Gilles and I barely had time to raise our shields before the bolts thudded into them.

I heard Dick shout, "Loose!" and a black cloud of arrows appeared above us.

Sir Harold shouted, "Run, Warlord!"

Holding my shield behind my head I joined Gilles to run back to the safety of my archers. I was so busy watching my footing that it was not until I reached them that I saw the body of Sir Edward. A bolt had pierced his forehead. He had joined his family and I was now the last Knight of the Empress.

Anger burned within me. I had gone to speak and my oldest friend had paid the price. I looked at Dick, "Fetch fire! We will burn the keep down! We have lost one man and that is one man too many!"

Chapter 19

With improvised fire arrows and kindling thrown around the stone base of the keep the flames soon took hold. The damp wood and the cold slowed down the fire. I had lost one warrior and I would lose no more. The screams from inside told us that the fire was catching hold. We just watched as the flames crept higher. When they reached the door they joined with the flames from the fire arrows in the wooden walls. A sudden draft sucked the flames and they leapt up the inside of the castle keep. Men threw themselves from the fighting platform, preferring a sudden crash to a long and painful death.

As it burned I walked to Sir Hugh and Sir Tristan. "This was your father's home and it was yours. I would have you as lord of the manor of Yarm. What say you?"

Sir Tristan was watching the home in which he had grown up burning. His mother and father's bodies would lie within the ashes when they ceased to burn. He nodded. "Aye lord and I will make it stronger. It will be a memorial to my parents."

"And you, Sir Hugh, will have to break the news to your wife that her parents are dead."

"She knew already, lord. A messenger was sent from Sir Harold and I could not keep that from my wife. She knows."

Even while the last of the enemy died I set John of Craven to use the poles to repair the bridge temporarily. We needed our horses. As soon as they had made a rough repair I sent men back to my castle for horses. We would strike south as soon as we could.

We buried Sir Edward and the warriors of Sir Richard who had fallen defending their castle by the small stone chapel which Sir Richard had built. Of the lord and his lady, there was no sign. Aiden told us that he had seen the head of Sir Richard on a pike. We could not find it. Sir Edward and the others were laid in the ground by the small stone chapel which lay inside the wooden walls of Yarm.

I stood over Sir Edward's grave. "You were the first of my men at arms and you served me loyally. I had hoped your son would follow in your footsteps but it was not meant to be. Your name and that of your son will live on and we will honour you each winter when we remember the sacrifice you made. Know that I will care for your children as though they were my own. Farewell, old friend."

We walked back to the camp in a sombre, reflective mood. Sir Edward's death somehow made ours seem a little bit closer.

The horses were brought to us after the burial and while we were eating. My men had brought me my mount, Copper. He was a fine horse but I had not ridden him for over a year. As they were placed in the stables I wandered over. I stroked his mane as I spoke to him. "Tomorrow we ride to war. I hope you remember that you are the Warlord's horse. All eyes will be upon us. The old warriors are fewer now!"

He nuzzled me. Horses never forgot and he would be as reliable as Rolf.

As I sat amongst my knights it struck me that there was only Wulfric left of my old guard. All the others were young and most had been squires. Dick was the only one who was of an age with me. I had outlived all of my peers save the Earl of Gloucester. There was irony. I was aware that all eyes were upon me.

I smiled, "You wonder how we retake Wulfric's castle?"

Dick nodded, "It had crossed our minds, lord. If they have enough men to besiege it then they outnumber us."

"That they do. We have however two advantages. One, they know not that I am alive and roused!" They laughed. "Second, we are all mounted. My experience at Oxford has told me that they will have built a counter castle. With our excellent archers, we can make the counter castle untenable and use our mounted men to sweep them away."

"But what if they outnumber us?"

"They may well, John of Craven, but our secret weapon is Wulfric. When we attack he will sortie forth and I cannot imagine that it sat well with him to be under siege and unable to fight back. Besides, I have lost one old friend in Sir Edward. I will not lose a second."

The journey was but forty miles and there was no need to rush. If Wulfric had held out this long then he could hold out a little longer. I intended to arrive in the late afternoon before dusk. They would have had a day assaulting the castle or working the machines and they would be tired. More importantly, they would be unprepared. As the enemy held Helmsley we would have to go over the moors and use the small road by Chop Gate. I had no doubt that the road might either be blocked or hard to negotiate for it was still winter. I wanted time to do that. It was good to ride with my own scouts out once more. We would not be surprised. My squires and I had retained our white cloaks. It was not just that they helped in the snow, they felt lucky.

The hardest part was the greenway known as Clay Bank. It was hard going for the horses. The bank was north facing and lay in the lee of the hills. We had to dismount and walk our horses up its frozen surface. We rested at the top. It was while we were resting that Aiden, Edgar and Edward appeared.

"The castle still holds, lord. They have a camp to the north of the counter castle. It sprawls over a large area. I would estimate a hundred horsemen and two hundred men on foot. It was hard to be accurate. I counted fires."

"Do they have a ditch around the camp or palisade?"

"No lord. They seem confident. Their horse lines are even further north."

"Then I see an opportunity to increase our stock of horses while destroying their camp. Aiden, take the squires. I want you close to their horses. I will attack with my horse and we will charge their camp. When we do so then capture the horses or as many as we can. Dick, you and Sir Philip have your archers slaughter the men working the war machines and then destroy the machines."

They all nodded. "Gilles, you command the squires. Aiden, you will instruct the squires in how to be hidden." I pointed to my scout. "Listen to him!"

"Aye lord."

"May God be with you."

The ten of them mounted and then galloped off. I did not worry. Aiden would get them close and they would succeed. "John of Craven, when we attack you and your men will support the archers. Your Frisians can use their axes to help the archers destroy the war machines."

Dick said, "But lord, that will only leave you seventy men to charge the camp. Will it be enough?"

"It will have to be."

The road flattened out. It was cold and the wind whistled from the east but the going was easier. We had two valleys to cross and we had to dismount to ascend the roads out of them. We reached Cropton and halted. It was a small village a couple of miles from the counter castle. There we prepared for battle. We tightened girths and checked straps. We watered and fed our horses. Some men knelt and prayed. Others did so silently.

Dick said, "We are ready, lord."

I nodded, "Get into position. We have no horn but you will know when we attack."

"We will see you at the castle, lord!"

And then they disappeared into the woods which went all the way to Aislaby. They would appear like ghosts. Dick would ensure that they were not seen until he chose the moment. Tristan and Harold flanked me with Sir John and Sir Hugh behind me. Sir Tristan's lust for revenge had not been satiated. He would ride on my left. We rode in a column of three for we could make quicker time that way and be harder to see. Behind my men at arms rode the Countess' six men at arms. I might not have many men at arms but the ones I had were the best.

We knew roughly where the camp was and that there was a road that bisected it. I would give the order to spread into line once we were through it. I spied the smoke from their campfires. I drew my sword. Soon someone would see us. I kept a steady pace. My shield was held lower than normal for we would be fighting men on foot. The blows would strike lower than fighting men on horses. Most of my men had spears but I used my sword.

We were three hundred paces from the camp when we were seen. We had passed through some trees and into an open area. I kicked harder. I could see the men inside the camp as they ran to get weapons. Horns sounded the alarm. That was good for it would signal both Aiden and Dick that we were attacking. The majority of the warriors were at the siege machines or attacking the castle. We burst into the camp. I leaned to my right to slice through the neck of a fleeing sentry. Tristan was laying about him to the left and to the right. He did not miss one man. I hoped that Aiden and the squires had heard our attack and taken the horses.

My scout had been right. It was a haphazard camp. There was no organisation that I could see. I stood in my stirrups, raised my sword and shouted, "Into line!" While I was standing up I could see that Dick, Sir Philip and John of Craven were in the counter castle. Their arrows fell like rain. Half of the defenders fought John of Craven's men while the rest were hurrying back, with their knights to defend the camp. They were too late. The survivors from the camp hid or fled. We moved towards the mound that was the counter castle.

Someone tried to form a shield wall. We were too spread out to hit it with any great force but it is hard for a man on foot to face horses unless he is many ranks deep. They were two ranks in depth. Nor did they have the ideal weapon to face horses. They had neither spears nor pikes. The danger was not to us but our horses. Sir Tristan was so keen to get to grips with the enemy that he sped ahead of me. An axe was buried in the chest of his mount. Sir Tristan's sword took the warrior's head but he was thrown from his horse. As he tumbled from the saddle I pulled back on Copper's reins and to the right. His mighty hooves reared up and smashed into the shield and helmet of the knight before me. As he fell there was a gap and I spurred him through it, striking out with my sword as I did so.

I could not look to see if Tristan survived. We had momentum with us and victory was in sight. I wheeled to the left into the gap vacated by Sir Tristan. My archers were effectively driving the men from the counter castle towards us. I rode towards them, swinging my sword from behind me. I sliced across the face of a man at arms who fell screaming. A crossbowman knelt to take aim at me and he fell face forward with two arrows in his back.

Then I heard Sir Harold shout, "Warlord, there is a knight rallying the men ahead of us."

I saw that there was a piece of high ground and a handful of knights had their standards waved to draw men to them. We had killed many but they still outnumbered us. I reined in, "Form line on me!"

Sir Hugh, Sir John and Sir Harold answered the call along with Wilfred and my oldest men at arms along with the Countess' men. We had a line twenty-one men long. It would have to do.

Behind me, I heard the sound of axes and splintering wood as the war machines were destroyed. "We break these and we have won. Keep the line steady! For God and the Empress!"

We trotted forward. This time the knights had formed their men so that they were six men deep and eight men wide. It was a solid block. As we rode I shouted to Alain of Auxerre, who was on the extreme left, "Alain, go to their right and we will follow!

"Aye lord."

I regretted not having a spear for using my sword brought me and Copper in range of their swords too. Alain wheeled his horse and jabbed with his spear. I struck a man at arms in the shoulder, just above his shield but he kept his place in the shield wall. Raymond of Le Mans was more accurate. His spear went through the ventail and into the mouth of a knight. As he pulled it sideways the knight's mouth and cheek erupted in blood. By the time I reached the two men had been wounded and one was dying. As I brought my sword down on a helmet and shield a sword jabbed blindly out and hacked against my leg. My hauberk held. As Alain reached the end of the line he wheeled right and here the men had to suddenly turn to make a square. I had read of Roman legionaries doing just this.

Sometimes accidents happen. Wulfstan had called such happenings *wyrd*.

Pierre Le Grand had just clattered his sword off the helmet of a man at arms when another brought his axe around to hack into the chest of his horse. Pierre turned his horse as it was struck. At the same time, a spear was thrust from behind and it struck him in the chest. Horse and rider fell into the serried ranks of our enemy. A mailed man and a horse are heavy and they are big. Alan son of Alan of Osmotherley saw his chance and he wheeled his horse into the centre of their square through the gap made by the dying warrior and his horse. Before him were backs and he stood in his stirrups to hack left and right. Sir Hugh followed him and Oswald. The three of them carved a path through the heart of the enemy formation.

I saw a gap beginning to appear and I kicked Copper towards it. An axe clattered against my shield. I stabbed down and found the gap between the man at arms' coif and his hauberk. As I pulled it out I slashed blindly to my right and felt it clang off metal. I looked and saw that I had hit a knight's helmet. As he stumbled Sir Harold skewered him. With more men joining my twenty the enemy were slaughtered. None asked for quarter. I would have given it but they fought like madmen slaying three horses.

Darkness had fallen and I wondered how we would see when there was the sound of a horn and Wulfric and his men rode forth carrying torches. They galloped to the counter castle and soon we had enough light to see for they set fire to the war machines. It was a grim end to the battle as we fought in the fire lit dark. The archers had put away their bows and drawn their swords. The slaughter was only ended when the survivors fled in the dark. We would hunt them but not yet.

I rode back to where Tristan had fallen. He was being tended to by the priest from the castle. I dreaded a wound such as John of Thornaby had suffered but I saw that all he had was a badly cut leg. He shook his head, "I was too reckless, lord! My blood was hot and vengeance was in my heart."

"I understand. We won and that is all that really matters."

Wulfric looked a little thinner as he dismounted but his grip was as strong as ever. "It does my heart good to see you, lord. I am sorry we lost Helmsley."

"It matters not. I was wrong to try to hold on to them without support. It has cost us dear."

Wulfric looked around my knights. "Where is Sir Edward?"

"He died when we avenged Sir Richard of Yarm."

It was as though someone had punched Wulfric. He turned to Sir Gilles and dropped to one knee on the ground. He held his sword before him and closed his eyes in prayer. Sir Gilles had been Sir Edward's squire for many years and he looked ashen too. It had been Sir Edward who suggested he be knighted. Gilles said, "He died well?"

"He died well."

"I will tell his wife, lord. I knew her well."

Harold looked at John and then said, "His wife and son died before. There is none left now."

Wulfric looked up and stood. He took his axe from his cantle and smashed through an enemy shield. He screamed in rage as he did so. The shield was smashed in two. "And I thought we had won! I thought that all was well."

He jumped on his horse and galloped off. I understood his anger and upset. He had lost one close friend, Roger of Lincoln and it had been a dark time for him. It had been Sir Edward who had got him through that.

"We will collect the treasure on the morrow. Ralph of Wales, go and find Aiden and the squires. They should have the enemy horses. As for the rest, we will see if there are any prisoners to be taken. We stay here tonight."

I sought Sir Gilles out. "Tell me of the loss of Helmsley and the siege."

"We were tricked, lord. It is as simple as that. A messenger rode to us and said that Normanby was under attack. We left a small garrison at Helmsley and we prepared to ride. Sir Wulfric sent his scouts to Normanby to discover the enemy numbers and when we were halfway there we discovered the truth. I was sent back to Pickering with half of the men. I was told to send a messenger to Sir Edward and Sir Wulfric rode to Helmsley. He was too late. It had fallen and the garrison's heads adorned the walls. Sir Wulfric was chased back by the army you defeated. Sir Wulfric barely made it within the walls. He lost half his men in the pursuit. He was not happy."

"Come, let us find him. We have much to say."

We found him in his castle in the small chapel by the east wall. He was weeping. In all the years I had known him I had never known him to weep. While we waited I asked Sir Gilles, "Why did it take you so long to sortie the castle?"

He smiled, "Sir Wulfric had had the gates nailed shut and it took time to open them. In the end, he took an axe himself and chopped them apart. It will take some time to repair them."

"We will not repair. We will destroy."

"Destroy?"

"I will explain when Sir Wulfric is present."

He stood, "I am ready now, lord. I am sorry that I fled. It is not seemly."

I turned to face the bear of a man who had seemed so vulnerable just a moment ago. "It matters not. I have much to tell you both." As we walked into the warmth of his hall I told them of the siege of Oxford and the manner of our escape. I spoke of the Earl of Chester and then the threat from warbands. "So I have decided that we give up Helmsley and Pickering. We have not the men to man them. Tomorrow we burn this castle before we leave. I would do the same for Helmsley but I am worried about the Scots. Wulfric, you shall be the new lord of Thornaby."

"Lord of Thornaby?"

"Sir Gilles here can be lord of Normanby can he not?"

"Of course but Thornaby..."

I smiled, "Who do you think Sir Edward would wish as his successor?" He nodded. "Besides I need that side of the river in strong hands. We are on our own. I will not be going south again. My war is here in the north. I will support the Empress and Henry but I cannot abandon the people."

"Then I accept."

We turned and looked to the gate as Aiden and my squires led the captured horses inside the castle. Wulfric said, "And at least we shall be well mounted!"

We had great quantities of treasure but no prisoners. The knights had either been killed or escaped. They would probably be in Helmsley. While Sir Hugh led most of my knights and the captured horses, weapons, mail and treasure back to Stockton, I stayed with my squires, Sir Wulfric and Sir Gilles. We destroyed the castle. A castle is difficult to hurt from the outside. The walls protect the most vulnerable parts. His men dug beneath the walls of the keep and the gatehouse and lit fires. They burned every wooden building and the wooden roofs. As we headed north a black pall of smoke rose from Pickering. It could be rebuilt and repaired but the task would take at least a year. We had lost three castles but we lived to fight again.

Aiden and my scouts said that the survivors of the battle had headed northeast. They would take shelter, I had no doubt, in the remote moors. They could wait there until the weather improved and I would hunt them down. My bigger priority was the threat from the Scots to the north. I had to rid my land of them first.

Chapter 20

The weather changed on our journey home. The hard ground became softer as the snow started to melt. Within a day of our arrival back in Stockton, only the cobbled roads were passable. We had to delay our search for the warbands which were reported to the north of us. I left Tristan to rebuild Yarm. He used William the Mason. Wulfric garrisoned Thornaby and I sent Erre back to Norton. Sir Hugh and Sir Philip left for their castles. I wanted a tight ring once more. I had decided to take just my household knights and Sir Gilles with me. We would find any Scots, brigands and bandits who lurked in the forests and hidden places of my land. Perhaps they would have fled already but if not then they would feel my anger. I sent for Sir Edward's daughter, Mary and his young son, James as soon as I arrived back. Mary was almost fourteen and I hoped that she would cope with the news. James was only seven. It would be hard for him. I made sure Alice was close by. I was unused to the task.

Mary had a sad look on her face and her eyes showed that she had been crying. She had either guessed or been told already of her father's death. That did not help me. James looked confused. "Lord, where is my father? Did you appoint him another task?"

"No, James, as your sister has, I think, guessed, he fell in battle. Your father is not coming home. You are now the man of the house."

He threw his arms around his sister. She held him tightly. "There are just the two of us now, Jamie, we will have to be strong for each other."

I saw Alice's face. She was as upset as the two young ones.

"I will take you as my wards. I made your father a knight and the two of you will be brought up here as though you were my own children. Mary, there will be young nobles who seek a wife. Until that time Alice here will continue your education to be a lady. James, you will be brought up a lord. That means you have a choice, will you be a knight or a priest?"

His back stiffened, "I will be a knight, lord."

I nodded. "Then we start to prepare you to be a knight. Sir Harold needs a second squire. When you become a knight I will find you a manor."

"What of Thornaby, lord?"

Mary had thought of their home first but I saw James' face as he took in my words. "That is now the manor of Sir Wulfric."

Mary nodded, "That is good for he and father were great friends." She looked down at James, "Father would like that."

I turned to Alice, "I leave them in your charge, Alice. I still have tasks to complete. The land is not safe yet."

"I will look after them, lord, as though they were my own bairns."

Mary took my hand and kissed it, "Thank you, lord. I know we seem not grateful but, after John and my mother, the news is hard to bear."

"There is no need for gratitude. I have a responsibility for Sir Edward was a friend and he was one of my knights. We do not forget our own. Alice will arrange for your quarters, your clothes and I will see my steward about an allowance and, when the time comes, a dowry for you, Mary." Edward had been rich and I would ensure that all his money was kept safe for his children. Mary's half would be the dowry and James' would go to his new manor. I felt happy with my actions. I slept easier that night.

I decided to send back Robert of Lincoln and the Countess' men. They had fought well. We gave them six spare horses and some of the treasure we had captured. They did not wish it but they had earned it. Robert bowed before mounting his horse. "If ever you need us again, lord, it would be an honour and a privilege to follow you. We have learned much."

"Keeping the Countess safe is all I need. Farewell."

They headed south.

The night before I was due to leave Sir Wulfric arrived unannounced. "Lord, I beg leave to come with you."

"But Thornaby?"

"Sir Edward's men can garrison it. My men and I are keen to avenge Sir Edward."

"But it was not the Scots who killed him."

"They caused his death! Let me do this, lord, I beg of you. I have not slept since we returned home. This will rid my dreams of ghosts."

"Very well."

In truth I was happy for his experience was invaluable. The horses we had captured made up for those we had lost in battle but we had not replaced the men. This time John of Craven and my Frisians would remain in Stockton, Erre would be in Norton and I would just take my depleted men at arms and Dick. The information given to Sir Edward had been that the warband was south of Durham. However, we knew that they had spies who were close to our lands. They had been waiting for us to make a mistake. Our first task was to find the spies and scouts. While Aiden and his scouts headed north we spoke with William of Wulfestun who lived at Thorpe. He had been forced into a life of banditry. Since he had given it up and taken to farming he was our best eyes and ears on the Durham road.

"Have you seen any strangers who might be of danger to us, William?"

"I killed two bandits just before Christmas, lord. Other than that it has been quiet."

"Sir Edward heard rumours of an enemy warband in the north."

He laughed, "Then they must have been hard men, lord, for the winter was cold."

I was perplexed. We continued north and Aiden met us a couple of miles from Thorpe. "Lord, I have seen no signs to the north. I travelled as far as Fissebourne and there was no sign. I spoke with the farmers. They have had a peaceful winter."

"You scouted north of Norton, already, did you not?"

"We did and there were none there."

I waved my knights forward. "I do not have Sir Edward to question. Do either of you know who brought the news of this warband?"

Sir Harold and Sir John both shook their heads. "We only know it was one of his men. He had patrols riding south of the river but he must have sent one north too."

I suddenly turned. "North of the river? Then they must have crossed the ferry. We would have known. Did any of Sir Edward's men cross the river?"

John and Harold looked at each other and shook their heads. Sir Wulfric said, "I can find an answer to this." He had brought ten men at arms with him including two from Sir Edward's retinue. "Thomas and Alan, come here."

Two men at arms detached themselves from the column. "Yes lord."

"Who brought the news of a warband north of Norton?"

They looked at each other then Thomas said, "That would have been John of Eston."

"What was he doing north of the river?"

"I am not certain, lord."

Alan said, "I heard that he visited his sister who married the miller at Norton."

I nodded, "That explains what he was doing north of the river but not how he discovered an enemy. Where is he now? Is he still at Thornaby?"

"We have not seen him since our lord fell at Yarm."

"He died?"

"I did not see his body, lord. We buried six good men that day but he was not with them."

Alan said, "And his horse went too."

Wulfric said, "I like not this, lord. There is no evidence of any Scots. We are being moved around by someone who wishes us harm. I can see that clearly now. The attack on Yarm, the capture of Helmsley. It is all one plot."

"And intended to draw us south and north."

Aiden had been listening, "Excuse me, my lord but that leaves two directions, east and west. You came from the west."

"Aye I did and the men we slew were from the same conroi as attacked Yarm. Sir Hugh saw no sign as he headed east. That leaves the east."

Wulfric's face fell. "Normanby! We have left Sir Gilles there with a handful of men."

"We still have time. Let us turn around and head there. Those knights who fled Pickering did not travel south or west. Their trail led north and east. I should have pursued them immediately! I am guessing that more of their fellows were to the northeast."

"Guisborough!"

"I think you are right. I spied the De Brus livery and that was ever his haunt of old. We have little time to waste."

We turned and rode quickly down the Durham Road. As we went I began to unpick this plot. It had all the hallmarks of a De Brus web. It was overly complicated and devious. The man from Eston was obviously in the pay of Sir Edward. It also explained how they had known of Rafe of Barwick. Had Sir Edward not been consumed by grief for his wife he might have questioned how his man at arms had seen the warband. Whatever the reason it had pinned our forces in the valley allowing De Brus a free hand to retake three castles. If it had not been for the resilience of Wulfric then he might have succeeded. There might, indeed, be no further threat but I thought there was.

I cursed myself for not following the survivors of our battle. There were over a hundred according to Aiden but I had not worried for they had been on foot. I had wondered why they had not gone to Helmsley. Then I remembered that they would have had to pass my army. Guisborough! It had been the De Brus home until I had destroyed it. With

240

fighting in the south, no one from my small castle at Normanby would have been watching there. They could have refortified it. The change in the weather might be just the spur they needed to expand. If they could take Normanby then they would have me encircled.

It took some time to cross the river. Ethelred had still to recover his spare ferry. I sent Dick over first. He had his archers could reach Normanby quickly and allow us to arrive together. With just eighty men we would be outnumbered. Sir Gilles had a small garrison and we could not count on much help from them. I just hoped my youngest and newest knight had his wits about him.

It was mid-afternoon and under grey, rain-filled skies that we finally left Thornaby for the six-mile ride to Normanby. We were met halfway there by Alan of Grange, one of Dick's archers. "Lord, Normanby is under siege." He pointed to the cloud-filled skies. "Sir Richard says the rain will affect our bows. They will not have the range you need. He urges you to hurry."

I waved my arm and we began to canter. Time and the weather were not on our side.

Dick and his archers had not been able to use their bows from a great distance but they had managed to eliminate the sentries and scouts. He met us at the edge of the wood where the land rose to the wooden castle. "They have no siege machines but they have the castle surrounded. "

"Form line!" We emerged from the woods and formed a double line. "Dick, be ready to pursue any who flee."

"Aye lord."

It did not take us long and the gloomy skies helped to hide us for the first hundred paces from those who surrounded the castle. They must have felt the ground vibrate beneath their feet for some turned and then a shout went up. They began to form a shield wall. We had spears and we would use them. Our charge, however, would be slow. We were travelling uphill and across the wet and damp ground. The rain had melted the snow and made it a quagmire.

I saw a De Brus banner. It was the banner of William De Brus. I had last seen that banner at the battle of Lincoln. I veered Copper towards it. With so few knights now my squires had to become warriors who rode in the front rank now. Richard carried my banner on my left and Gilles rode on my right. The shield wall had swords and hand weapons. We had a slight advantage for we would strike with our spears first. I lowered my shield to cover my thigh and side and I pulled back with my spear. At the last moment, De Brus stepped out of the line. I punched into fresh air. Gilles struck the squire who had been to the right of De Brus and he impaled him on his spear. I pulled my arm back and thrust it into the face of the next man at arms.

De Brus' cowardice had let us inside the shield wall. I pulled back on Copper's reins and he reared. His hooves hit the shields of two men who fell to the ground with the force. His hooves landed on one of them. Blood spurted from his mouth. I stabbed down at the other. He grabbed the spear and wrenched it from my hands but it was the act of a dying man. I drew my sword and whirled. The enemy shield wall was now two knots of men. Wulfric was wreaking his own special vengeance and he galloped along the line with his axe slaying all who dared stand before him. Not many did and the enemies before him fled.

I reined in and looked around. Sir Harold and Sir John had a second band in a circle. "Gilles, Wilfred! Follow me. Richard, signal my men."

I charged towards my two knights and their men. They were holding their own. The extra weight I would bring would crush the spirits if not the bodies of the men at arms and knights. I held my sword behind me and, as we approached them, I began to swing it. I jerked Copper's head at the last minute as I brought my sword up and across the knight. It tore through his mail and into his gambeson. I saw blood and I quickly withdrew it and, as I passed, backhanded him across the neck. He crumpled to the ground.

"Quarter! Quarter!" The survivors dropped their swords.

"Those who yield shall live."

Richard shouted, "Lord, De Brus escapes!"

"Dick, fetch your men. Wulfric, take charge of the prisoners and relieve the castle." I looked around to make sure that Gilles and Richard had survived. Their weapons were bloodied and they had cuts to their surcoats, as I did, but they were whole! "Richard, which way?"

He pointed. "They headed to the south and east."

It would be to Guisborough. I spurred Copper. Dick and his archers soon joined me. "If this rain would stop we might do something about them, lord."

"We know where they go. We will catch them. Fear not. I am just pleased that we reached Sir Gilles in time. He had perilously few men in the castle."

I knew that it would be night before we reached Guisborough. We had destroyed the castle over a year ago. Had the enemy rebuilt it? I answered myself for of course they had. Wulfric had been preoccupied in the south and Sir Gilles was getting to know his role as lord of the manor. Inattention had cost us dear. We had no reason to visit that manor save at tax time and that lay a month or more ahead of us. Once more I rued my absence. It had cost me dear. I had lost two lords of the manor and three castles. And for what? The Empress and our son were no closer to the crown than they had been. If anything they were further away for we had lost a third of our army.

"Lord, I see them!"

Richard's sharp eyes had picked out the yellow and gold surcoats in the darkening gloom ahead of us. We were gaining. The sight of them gave us hope that we would catch them and we would end this threat. The horses at the rear of the enemy column were flagging.

As we neared them four men at arms held up their arms. "We yield!"

"Alan son of Alan, take these men prisoner."

As the ground began to rise towards the distant priory I saw the ramparts of a castle. They had rebuilt it. This time it was between the priory and the coast. As we neared it I could see that they would make it before we managed to catch them. However, as I could not see any men on the walls I hoped we could stop them from defending their walls. I spurred Copper and he gave an extra spurt. They had a wooden bridge over the ditch. They managed to gallop over it and slam the gates shut but I arrived with Wilfred and my squires even as I heard the bar being dropped.

"Richard, hold Copper!"

I slipped my feet from the stirrups and stood on the wooden saddle. I reached up and grabbed the top of the wooden palisade. I began to climb. Wilfred did the same. I was about to pull myself over when a man at arms ran at me along the fighting platform with a spear. I could not let go and I could not defend myself. Dick's arrow struck him on the shoulder and threw him to the ground. I scrambled over the top and drew my sword. My shield was still hanging on the cantle of my saddle. I waited until Wilfred had joined me.

"Down the ladder and let us open the gate for the others!"

It sounded easy but spears were suddenly thrown at us as we ran along the fighting platform to the ladder. One struck me in my right arm. I pulled it out and held it in my left hand. It would have to do in lieu of a shield. Once we reached the ladder there were eight men waiting for us at the bottom. If we turned our backs to climb down we would be butchered. I looked at Wilfred, "Have you ever thought of being a bird, Wilfred?"

"Not until this moment, lord but it seems like a good idea." We both stepped back and then had a leap of faith into the air. They were not expecting that. The two of us crashed into them. Their bodies, ironically, broke our fall. Even so, the wind was knocked from me and another man at arms ran at me. A spear flashed over my head and struck him squarely in the chest. I saw Gilles and he was on the fighting platform. I quickly stood and stabbed at one man with my sword while I impaled a second with my spear. Wilfred rose unsteadily. His left arm hung from his side. He slashed his sword as he stamped on the neck of a man at arms lying at our feet. Gilles leapt into the fray and with the three of us wielding weapons we dispatched the last two men.

Ignoring the blood coming from my right arm I helped Wilfred to his feet, "You are hurt, Wilfred. Come, Gilles, let us get the gate open."

We had been left alone as the rest of the men had fled into the wooden keep which was on a mound fifty paces from us. Already arrows were being loosed at us. Wilfred sheathed his sword and grabbed a shield to protect both him and us.

Gilles and I unbarred the gate and opened it. Dick and my men poured in. "To the keep."

We ran towards the keep. The arrows they sent our way were woefully short. The rain had dampened their strings. Dick and his archers, in contrast, had fresh strings they had kept dry. Dick said, "Halt here, lord. They are going nowhere. Archers, string your bows." He turned to me. "We can release ten arrows before the strings become too wet. That will give you time to break into the keep, lord!"

"Good man. Raymond of Le Mans, axes!"

The first five arrows all found flesh and three bodies plummeted from the top of the keep. It allowed us the opportunity to close with the gate. My men began to hack into it. The wood was new and I do not think they had seasoned it. After a short time, we saw the interior. A spear was thrust through the hole we had made. Raymond of Le Mans pulled hard and we heard a crack as the spearman's head hit the door. Two strikes later and the door gave way. We burst in. It was dark and men raced down the stairs to fight us. They chose the wrong men to fight. My men at arms were the best. They cleared the ground floor in a dozen strokes. They were about to ascend the ladder when I said, "No! We waste no more men." I went to the bottom of the ladder and shouted. "We will light a fire and burn you alive unless you surrender."

"You will give quarter?"

"You have my word."

"Then we yield."

The ten men descended and handed over their weapons.

"Where is your, lord?" These were just men at arms.

He pointed to the priory. "He sought refuge with the Prior!"

"Secure these men and then burn this castle down. Gilles, Richard, come with me."

Gilles said, "First, lord, let me bind your arm." He tore a piece of surcoat from a dead man at arms and made a bandage around my arm. "It will stop the bleeding, lord."

"Thank you, Gilles." He was right. I needed to have my wits about me when I spoke with the Prior.

I was angry as I strode to the Priory. The gate was barred. I banged on it. "Open up in the name of the Warlord!"

The Prior himself appeared at the door. "You cannot come in."

I had had enough of priests, "Prior, I do not fear any punishment for entering a church. If I wish to come in I will."

He was not afraid of me and he smiled, "I do not doubt that. You did not fear ex-communication but what of your men? Would they dare desecrate a priory?"

He was right; they would not. "William De Brus is within I would have him."

"He has claimed sanctuary and may not be removed."

"He is a coward who deserted his men."

"He will speak with you but you touch him at the peril of your eternal soul."

I felt Gilles and Richard move backwards. They would face any enemy with me but not risk the wrath of God.

The young knight appeared but I saw that he stayed behind the Prior. "Your men have yielded. Honour demands that you do too."

"I will not yield. I have claimed sanctuary."

I nodded, "Then I will have my archers watch this door and the moment you step forth they will slay you. No matter how long you hide here they will wait."

His face filled with anger. "My uncle told me that you were unyielding! The world is changing, Earl! My uncle, the De Brus is dead as is his son. The family is now allied with King David! King David is an ally of the Empress. Where will you turn now? Who will support you? The hourglass is running swiftly and marks your demise. You have lost your castles and soon you will lose your valley."

I so wanted to reach in and pull the puling rat from behind the priest but I would not. Instead, I said, "Prior, your

246

priests and canons can come and go but this man either surrenders or dies. That is my will."

He nodded, "God be with you!" With that, he closed the door.

We had won the battle but had we lost the war? My world was suddenly much smaller.

Epilogue

Life returned to normal in my valley save that we were even more vigilant. William the Mason worked hard to improve our castles and his sons help to rebuild Yarm. The vast sums we made from ransom we used to pay for more men. The hope we had was that my land prospered. The sacrifices and deaths had kept it safe and after a hard winter was even stronger than ever. The bad news was that William De Brus had escaped my archers. He had escaped in the disguise of a nun. My archers were annoyed with themselves for falling for such a ruse but I knew that it could not be helped. We would meet again.

I sought out Tom Lame Leg. He had reached my valley. He lived between Norton and Stockton. He had a small farm and had three pigs. It was little enough but he was happy. He offered to return the horse and sword but I told him to keep them. My manor was richer for his presence. I gave John my steward the task of finding others like Tom who had served me and been wounded. I would do the same for them. I could do nothing for the dead but I could for the living.

My valley returned to some sort of normality. We had less land but more people. Refugees still flocked to this island of mine. All of my people worked hard to ensure that we were prepared to face any foe who dared to threaten that for which we fought. I had two wards to care for and that gave me a replacement for the grandchildren whom I might never see. The two of them would need all of my care and attention.

When *'Adela'* docked in March she brought supplies, more wealth and, most importantly, news. The Empress was safe and the Earl of Gloucester had Stephen besieged in Wilton Castle. In the east, around Ely, Geoffrey of Mandeville had risen in revolt. Perhaps it was not as black as it had been but my heart was still heavy with regret. My world had changed. We could never go back but what did the future hold? Would Henry ever become King of England? I could not as yet see how but if it was at all within my power then that would happen. I swore a silent oath to myself. I would make it so.

The End

Glossary

Al-Andalus- Spain

Aldeneby - Alston (Cumbria)

Angevin- the people of Anjou, mainly the ruling family

Arthuret -Longtown in Cumbria (This is the Brythionic name)

Battle- a formation in war (a modern battalion)

Booth Castle – Bewcastle north of Hadrian's Wall

Butts- targets for archers

Cadge- the frame upon which hunting birds are carried (by a codger- hence the phrase old codger being the old man who carries the frame)

Cadwaladr ap Gruffudd- Son of Gruffudd ap Cynan

Captain- a leader of archers

Chausses - mail leggings. (They were separate- imagine lady's stockings!)

Conroi- A group of knights fighting together. The smallest unit of the period

Demesne- estate

Destrier- war horse

Doxy- prostitute

Fess- a horizontal line in heraldry

Fissebourne- Fishburn County Durham

Galloglass- Irish mercenaries

Gambeson- a padded tunic worn underneath mail. When worn by an archer they came to the waist. It was more of a quilted jacket but I have used the term freely

Gonfanon- A standard used in Medieval times (Also known as a Gonfalon in Italy)

Gruffudd ap Cynan- King of Gwynedd until 1137

Hartness- the manor which became Hartlepool

Hautwesel- Haltwhistle

Liedeberge- Ledbury

Lusitania- Portugal

Mansio- staging houses along Roman Roads

Maredudd ap Bleddyn- King of Powys
Martinmas- 11th November
Mêlée- a medieval fight between knights
Moravians- the men of Moray
Mormaer- A Scottish lord and leader
Mummer- an actor from a medieval tableau
Musselmen- Muslims
Nithing- A man without honour (Saxon)
Nomismata- a gold coin equivalent to an aureus
Outremer- the kingdoms of the Holy Land
Owain ap Gruffudd- Son of Gruffudd ap Cynan and King of Gwynedd from 1137
Palfrey- a riding horse
Poitevin- the language of Aquitaine
Pyx- a box containing a holy relic (Shakespeare's Pax from Henry V)
Refuge- a safe area for squires and captives (tournaments)
Sauve qui peut – Every man for himself (French)
Sergeant-a leader of a company of men at arms
Serengford- Shellingford Oxfordshire
Surcoat- a tunic worn over mail or armour
Sumpter- packhorse
Ventail – a piece of mail that covered the neck and the lower face.
Wulfestun- Wolviston (Durham)

Maps and Illustrations

Historical note

This is a work of fiction. I have used real events as the backdrop for a story about a fictional character. I have tried to be as accurate as I can but I have made minor changes to dates and amalgamated the actions of some characters into one. I make no apologies for this. I am a storyteller.

The book is set during one of the most turbulent and complicated times in British history. Henry I of England and Normandy's eldest son William died. The king named his daughter, Empress Matilda as his heir. When her husband, the Emperor of the Holy Roman Empire, died she remarried. Her new husband was Geoffrey of Anjou and she had children by him. (The future Henry II of England and Normandy- The Lion in Winter!)

King Stephen did swim the Isis to scale the town walls. He even built two mounds from which he could use his mangonels but he did not use them. Instead, he prepared to starve the garrison to death. The Empress escaped just as the food was about to run out. Robert D'Oyly died before the Empress escaped. I have made up the manner of his death. I just know he died and not the intimate details. The Empress' escape from Oxford castle is well known however a word of caution to any who use Wikipedia for research. The article about Empress Matilda has her escaping in early 1143 or late 1142. I lean to late December 1142 however the Wikipedia article about Oxford castle has her escaping Stephen in December 1141- patently impossible as he was in London being crowned and did not besiege Oxford until the following year. For those interested, I have put the links to three sites so that you can compare them for yourself.

http://www.historic-uk.com/HistoryUK/HistoryofEngland/Empress-Maud/

https://en.wikipedia.org/wiki/Oxford_Castle

https://en.wikipedia.org/wiki/Empress_Matilda

The Earl of Gloucester spent the summer and autumn of 1142 in Normandy helping Geoffrey to recapture more territory from Stephen's supporters. By 1143 the Norman campaign was over.

Counter castles were built close to a castle under siege. A force besieging a castle would build one to mount their own war machines. There would be a palisade around it to prevent a sortie. The two at Oxford were called Jew's Mount and Mount Pelham. For some reason, they were not used. Below is a photograph of Pickering Castle and the counter castle built there. It is the high green area to the left of the castle.

Books used in the research:
The Varangian Guard- 988-1453 Raffael D'Amato
Saxon Viking and Norman- Terence Wise
The Walls of Constantinople AD 324-1453-Stephen Turnbull
Byzantine Armies- 886-1118- Ian Heath
The Age of Charlemagne-David Nicolle
The Normans- David Nicolle
Norman Knight AD 950-1204- Christopher Gravett
The Norman Conquest of the North- William A Kappelle
The Knight in History- Francis Gies
The Norman Achievement- Richard F Cassady
Knights- Constance Brittain Bouchard
Knight Templar 1120-1312 -Helen Nicholson

Griff Hosker
August 2016

Other books by Griff Hosker

If you enjoyed reading this book, then why not read another one by the author?

Ancient History

The Sword of Cartimandua Series
(Germania and Britannia 50 A.D. – 128 A.D.)
Ulpius Felix- Roman Warrior (prequel)
The Sword of Cartimandua
The Horse Warriors
Invasion Caledonia
Roman Retreat
Revolt of the Red Witch
Druid's Gold
Trajan's Hunters
The Last Frontier
Hero of Rome
Roman Hawk
Roman Treachery
Roman Wall
Roman Courage

The Wolf Warrior series
(Britain in the late 6th Century)
Saxon Dawn
Saxon Revenge
Saxon England
Saxon Blood
Saxon Slayer
Saxon Slaughter
Saxon Bane
Saxon Fall: Rise of the Warlord
Saxon Throne
Saxon Sword

Medieval History

The Dragon Heart Series

Viking Slave
Viking Warrior
Viking Jarl
Viking Kingdom
Viking Wolf
Viking War
Viking Sword
Viking Wrath
Viking Raid
Viking Legend
Viking Vengeance
Viking Dragon
Viking Treasure
Viking Enemy
Viking Witch
Viking Blood
Viking Weregeld
Viking Storm
Viking Warband
Viking Shadow
Viking Legacy
Viking Clan
Viking Bravery

The Norman Genesis Series

Hrolf the Viking
Horseman
The Battle for a Home
Revenge of the Franks
The Land of the Northmen
Ragnvald Hrolfsson
Brothers in Blood
Lord of Rouen
Drekar in the Seine
Duke of Normandy

The Duke and the King

Danelaw
(England and Denmark in the 11th Century)
Dragon Sword
Oathsword

New World Series
Blood on the Blade
Across the Seas
The Savage Wilderness
The Bear and the Wolf
Erik The Navigator

The Vengeance Trail

The Reconquista Chronicles
Castilian Knight
El Campeador
The Lord of Valencia

The Aelfraed Series
(Britain and Byzantium 1050 A.D. - 1085 A.D.)
Housecarl
Outlaw
Varangian

**The Anarchy Series England
1120-1180**
English Knight
Knight of the Empress
Northern Knight
Baron of the North
Earl
King Henry's Champion
The King is Dead
Warlord of the North
Enemy at the Gate
The Fallen Crown

Warlord's War
Kingmaker
Henry II
Crusader
The Welsh Marches
Irish War
Poisonous Plots
The Princes' Revolt
Earl Marshal
The Perfect Knight

Border Knight
1182-1300
Sword for Hire
Return of the Knight
Baron's War
Magna Carta
Welsh Wars
Henry III
The Bloody Border
Baron's Crusade
Sentinel of the North
War in the West
Debt of Honour
The Blood of the Warlord (Feb 2022)

Sir John Hawkwood Series
France and Italy 1339- 1387
Crécy: The Age of the Archer
Man At Arms
The White Company

Lord Edward's Archer
Lord Edward's Archer
King in Waiting
An Archer's Crusade
Targets of Treachery
The Great Cause (April 2022)

Struggle for a Crown
1360- 1485
Blood on the Crown
To Murder a King
The Throne
King Henry IV
The Road to Agincourt
St Crispin's Day
The Battle For France
The Last Knight
Queen's Knight

Tales from the Sword I
(Short stories from the Medieval period)

Tudor Warrior series
England and Scotland in the late 145th and early 15th
century
Tudor Warrior

Conquistador
England and America in the 16th Century
Conquistador

Modern History

The Napoleonic Horseman Series
Chasseur à Cheval
Napoleon's Guard
British Light Dragoon
Soldier Spy
1808: The Road to Coruña
Talavera
The Lines of Torres Vedras
Bloody Badajoz
The Road to France
Waterloo

The Lucky Jack American Civil War series

Rebel Raiders
Confederate Rangers
The Road to Gettysburg

The British Ace Series
1914
1915 Fokker Scourge
1916 Angels over the Somme
1917 Eagles Fall
1918 We will remember them
From Arctic Snow to Desert Sand
Wings over Persia

Combined Operations series
1940-1945
Commando
Raider
Behind Enemy Lines
Dieppe
Toehold in Europe
Sword Beach
Breakout
The Battle for Antwerp
King Tiger
Beyond the Rhine
Korea
Korean Winter

Tales from the Sword II
(Short stories from the Modern period)

Other Books
Great Granny's Ghost (Aimed at 9-14-year-old young
people)
For more information on all of the books then please visit the
author's website at www.griffhosker.com where there is a
link to contact him or visit his Facebook page: GriffHosker
at Sword Books